"I WANT YOU, BETH," MICAH MURMURED, HIS hand caressing her shoulder, his mouth close to her ear.

She couldn't breathe, only gaze up at him.

"I want to hold you and kiss you and make love to you until I can't think anymore." His lips brushed her ear, and he didn't know if her shiver was from his words or his touch.

He liked knowing he could make her shiver. "Yes, Beth," he whispered. "I want you because you arouse me faster than any woman I've ever known. But I also want to hold you at night, and I don't know why, because I've never wanted to hold a woman all night through."

His tongue traced the delicate shell of her ear, and she gasped softly.

"I want you, Beth," he said, then gently brought her lips close to his. "I want you for things I've never wanted before, and I don't even know what they are yet." He brushed her mouth with his. "Tell me what you want."

She swallowed, and her sigh was warm on his lips. "I want to believe that what I feel for you is real. . . ."

WHAT ARE *LOVESWEPT* ROMANCES?

They are stories of true romance and touching emotion. We believe those two very important ingredients are constants in our highly sensual and very believable stories in the LOVE-SWEPT line. Our goal is to give you, the reader, stories of consistently high quality that may sometimes make you laugh, sometimes make you cry, but are always fresh and creative and contain many delightful surprises within their pages.

Most romance fans read an enormous number of books. Those they truly love, they keep. Others may be traded with friends and soon forgotten. We hope that each LOVESWEPT romance will be a treasure—a "keeper." We will always try to publish

LOVE STORIES YOU'LL NEVER FORGET
BY AUTHORS YOU'LL ALWAYS REMEMBER

The Editors

Loveswept ® 712

BLACKTHORNE'S WOMAN

VICTORIA LEIGH

BANTAM BOOKS
NEW YORK · TORONTO · LONDON · SYDNEY · AUCKLAND

BLACKTHORNE'S WOMAN
A Bantam Book / October 1994

If you would be interested in receiving protective vinyl covers for your
Loveswept books, please write to this address for information:

Loveswept
Bantam Books
P.O. Box 985
Hicksville, NY 11802

ISBN 0-553-44446-8

Published simultaneously in the United States and Canada

Bantam Books are published by Bantam Books, a division of Bantam Dou-
bleday Dell Publishing Group, Inc. Its trademark, consisting of the words
"Bantam Books" and the portrayal of a rooster, is Registered in U.S.
Patent and Trademark Office and in other countries. Marca Registrada.
Bantam Books, 1540 Broadway, New York, New York 10036.

PRINTED IN THE UNITED STATES OF AMERICA

OPM   0 9 8 7 6 5 4 3 2 1

ONE

The diner filled him with the sense of being a rare and unexpected visitor to civilization's last outpost, in a land too raw and rugged to encourage exploration, much less tolerate settlement. It stood by itself alongside the two-lane highway that pierced the sparsely inhabited wilds of central Colorado. Its neon lights and grimy, gravel-pitted linoleum were a welcome change to the snow-blanketed nothingness Micah Blackthorne had traveled through to reach it.

Not that he had anything against wide-open spaces, but after three days of tracking the woman and kid, he found it a relief to be under the same roof with his quarry—even if it was the middle of the night. He'd caught up with her a few hours earlier at a truck stop, but had been forced to watch as she filled up with gas and bought coffee. The place had been too crowded for what he had to do.

Closing his hand around the ceramic mug, he brought it to his mouth for a swallow of the scalding, burnt-flavored coffee and stole another look across the room.

The woman looked as tired as he felt, but satisfaction, not pity, stirred inside him. Her shoulder-length brown hair looked as though it could use a good brushing, although the way she let the baby grab and pull it, he didn't imagine it would do much good. Dark shadows beneath her eyes accentuated the paleness of her skin, the startling lack of color a convincing mark of her exhaustion. From his seat at the end of the counter, her eyes looked almost black under the delicately arched eyebrows.

He knew they were brown, though. Like everything else he knew about her, that information was in the file he'd been given. The file went beyond physical characteristics and habits, enumerating as well all the facts that had come out in the hearings, and others that hadn't. Bethany Sarah Corbett would have been appalled to discover how few secrets she had from Micah, but the woman's sensibilities didn't concern him.

Bethany. What the hell kind of name was that? Micah silently rolled the syllables over his tongue, then shook his head in disgust. It was a society name, evocative of pampered princesses and snotty debs. The name fit the woman, he mused, although dressed as she was in faded jeans and a sweater that touched her thighs, she didn't look much like a princess.

His gaze eased past her to the baby she was playing with. Set atop the scarred Formica table, the six-month-old boy was reclining in one of those cushioned baskets that doubled as a chair and bed, with restraining straps cinching him around his waist and bottom. From this position of total security, the towheaded baby flailed his chubby arms and legs, gurgling contentedly as the Corbett woman teased him with a small stuffed bear she referred to as "Pookey."

Micah grunted and looked away, not understanding

where she got the energy to entertain the baby. While he'd been following false trails and doubling back to pick up new ones, she'd been laying those same trails, driving hard across roads that were treacherously icy. And taking care of the baby, which included lugging him around in that basket thing that looked sturdy enough to weigh more than the kid. Bethany Corbett wasn't a big woman to start with, under five and a half feet tall and, in Micah's judgment, even lighter now than the hundred and ten pounds she claimed on her driver's license. He could tell by looking at her that three days of running had taken a heavy toll.

He could imagine how she felt, because he was damned tired and all he'd had to do was take care of himself as he tracked her to this diner in the middle of nowhere. The thought of what was to come didn't make him feel any better. Instead of catching a couple hours of sleep like he needed, he had another long night of driving to look forward to if he was going to stay in front of the blizzard that had been tickling his rear bumper for the past several hours.

With his luck, the kid would scream all the way to the airport.

Gulping the rest of his coffee, he set the mug back on the counter and signaled the waitress for more. He didn't worry that the waitress would be able to identify him—if, in fact, Bethany Corbett actually dared to call the cops. Micah doubted she would, but simple caution had required that he tip his Stetson low over his eyes instead of taking it off when he'd entered the restaurant. He hadn't taken off his bulky sheepskin coat either, although he'd had to unbutton it to avoid succumbing to the almost overwhelming heat of the diner. Flexing his shoulders under the heavy coat, he dug some change from his pocket and slid the coins onto the counter. He needed to be ready when she was.

He tensed as Bethany Corbett shoved her half-eaten meal aside, then leaned heavily on her elbow. With her chin cupped in her hand, she continued to play with the baby. Micah thought her hand trembled slightly as she smoothed her fingers over the boy's thatch of white-blond hair, which bristled straight out as though the kid had stuck his finger into a light socket. She'd fed him earlier, patiently spooning tiny portions of something from a jar into his greedy mouth. Now she reached into the bag at her feet and brought out a bottle that was filled with something that appeared to be milk. Un-screwing the cap, she gave the bottle into the baby's grasping hands, then laughed when the nipple landed closer to his eye than his mouth. Her husky laughter trailed off into a sigh as the baby corrected his mistake and began to suckle.

Micah watched the scene in the cracked mirror be-hind the counter. He figured the chances were good she'd leave the kid on the table when she went to the rest room over by the front entrance. Besides the woman and baby, the diner was deserted save for himself and the waitress, who could be diverted with a simple request for something from the kitchen. Given Bethany Corbett's exhaustion, she couldn't be blamed for leaving the child for the short time she needed behind the closed rest-room door. He certainly wouldn't be surprised.

Such willful neglect would be in keeping with what he already knew about her.

As though she'd read his mind, she pushed herself to her feet, shoved a hand through her hair, and sighed again. Just as he thought he had the opening he'd been waiting for, she slung her purse over one shoulder, the diaper bag over the other, then hefted the baby into her arms, basket and all. He thought she winced as she shifted the bulky load, but she turned her back before he could verify that fleeting impression.

He forced himself to relax, waiting with already stretched nerves until the rest-room door opened again and the woman exited. She headed back to the table and parked the kid at its center, then took a short, almost painful breath as she flipped over the bill the waitress had brought in her absence. Leaning over, she dug into her coat pocket for some cash and put it on the table. Micah had decided to wait until she was out the door before making his move. By that time, he judged, not only would the waitress be too far away to render any aid, but the kid would be dressed for the elements and Micah wouldn't have to worry about grabbing any clothes or blankets. Once they were a decent way down the road, he'd take time to pull over and put the kid into the child's car seat he'd borrowed for the job.

Micah nodded in satisfaction at the plan. This was as good a chance as he was likely to get, even if he wasn't sticking precisely to the client's preference for no witnesses.

He again watched their reflections in the mirror, impatience growing inside him as Bethany Corbett took what he thought was an inordinate amount of time stuffing the baby into his snowsuit. When that task was finally accomplished, she tucked the kid's half-empty bottle of milk into the bag at her feet. He realized then that he'd have to take the bag too. His preparations hadn't included food.

When she finally reached for her coat, Micah slid off the stool and began winding his way toward the door. His boots crunched loudly on odd bits of gravel, which were what remained from the passage of dozens of pairs of snow-encrusted boots. He kept his gaze lowered so as

not to look at either the Corbett woman or the waitress
. . . which was why he was able to avoid stepping on
Pookey when the small bear suddenly landed in his path.

Micah hesitated for a second, weighing the risk of
making any sort of contact with Bethany Corbett against
the certainty that the hovering waitress would take more
notice of him if he refused to perform this small cour-
tesy. All in all, it seemed prudent to pick up the damned
bear. Micah bent over and closed his long fingers around
Pookey's little neck.

The bear squealed, startling him so much that he
nearly dropped it. He stared at the bear, which was
smaller than his hand, fervently wishing he'd been just
five seconds faster getting to the door. Now, though, not
only did he have to hand the thing back to the baby's
mom, he'd have to apologize for almost strangling it.

"Jeremy's been trying to do that for weeks."

Strangle it? he asked silently, wondering if her voice
was naturally husky or if that, too, was a sign of exhaustion. Slowly, he turned and handed her the bear, realizing too late that she could easily see his face as she
looked up at him. Too late to do anything but get
through this and get outside.

"Trying to do what?" he asked, reluctantly curious
even though he knew better than to prolong the conversation.

"Get Pookey to make a noise." She smiled and
shoved the bear into her coat pocket. "He's not strong
enough yet to squeeze that hard."

"I didn't squeeze hard." This close, her face looked
even more delicate, her skin almost translucent. Soft
skin, he imagined, to go with the soft life she'd led. He
could understand why Steven Corbett had been attracted to her. The packaging was superb.

She laughed. "You wouldn't have to squeeze hard. What's natural to you is beyond Jeremy's capabilities."

At least she hadn't realized he'd squeezed the little bugger on purpose. Nodding his head at her thanks, Micah turned and moved toward the door, his boots sounding a quick retreat as though the few moments he'd lost talking with her had been important ones. He was just about to push through the frosted-glass door when a man's shape approached from the other side. Finely honed instincts that had saved his butt more than once made him abruptly change direction and shoulder his way into the nearby men's room.

He pushed the door shut, catching it with his boot tip just before it closed as he reached for the revolver holstered at the small of his back. Leaning into the corner, he squinted through the minuscule opening as the man came into the diner. He was a touch smaller than Micah, with light blond hair and pale blue eyes that were bereft of any expression save a trace of victory.

Sutton. *Damn!* How had he caught up with them so quickly? A long string of curses trailed across his mind as he watched the other man saunter past the door where Micah hid and approach the woman. It would be useless to try to sneak up behind Sutton, he knew, recalling the crunch his boots had made on the linoleum. Besides, the woman would see him coming and do something stupid to tip Sutton off. The revolver that was a familiar weight in his hand wasn't much good as a threat from this distance, because Sutton would simply grab Bethany Corbett or the baby for a shield. They'd be in a no-win draw where someone was bound to get hurt. Backshooting Sutton was a temptation, but Micah figured with his luck he'd kill him, and he didn't need the kind of hassle that would bring. He slipped the gun back into place and decided to wait for Sutton to get careless.

Sutton reached the Corbett woman, and Micah didn't have to work too hard at imagining what he was saying to her. The expression of absolute terror on her face said it all. When Sutton grabbed her arm and shoved her backward, Micah dispassionately watched her fall, hoping that he had pushed her hard enough to keep her down. Otherwise, she'd just be in the way when he made his move.

A startled noise from behind the counter made Sutton look sideways; he said something, and the waitress turned and fled into the kitchen. Smart woman, Micah thought, and spared a glance to where Bethany Corbett lay motionless on the floor. She was either stunned or unconscious, he decided when she didn't move, and he eased the door shut and pulled off his boots and coat. Now that the woman was out of the way, he could chance sneaking up on Sutton. He threw his hat on top of the pile on the floor, then cracked the door open again.

Sutton had shouldered the diaper bag and was reaching for the baby when Jeremy let out a startled cry. Micah took advantage of the noise to push open the door. Moving swiftly across the linoleum, he came up behind Sutton and was about to slam the side of his hand on his unprotected neck when Sutton pivoted and raised a blocking arm. Micah's blow landed on Sutton's forearm, doing less damage than he'd intended but still eliciting a groan that was audible even over the baby's now deafening screams. As Micah raised his arm for another hit Sutton swung his other hand and gleaming steel slashed across Micah's bare knuckles.

Blood spurted from the wound, but Micah didn't so much as flinch as he followed through with the blow to Sutton's gut. His opponent bent double, caught off guard by Micah's stubborn disregard of his wound. With deliberate precision, Micah landed three more punches that sent Sutton reeling over a table to crash on the floor. The knife hurtled across the linoleum toward the counter. Micah shoved the table aside and was waiting for Sutton to get to his feet when he saw the woman crawling toward the knife.

Swearing because she could get killed if Sutton got hold of her, Micah circled the man, who was twitching facedown on the linoleum, and stomped on the knife just as Bethany Corbett reached for it. "What do you think you're doing?" he demanded when she jerked her hand back, her eyes huge and frightened as she stared at him.

"Getting the knife out of the way," she said, a dazed note in her voice. "I wanted to help—"

Micah reached down and fisted the hand that wasn't bleeding in her sweater. Keeping an eye on Sutton, he hauled her off the floor and pushed her roughly toward the baby. "Get the hell out of this, lady. The kid needs your help more than I do."

"But—"

He glared furiously at her and shouted, *"Get out, I said!"* That was all he had time for, because Sutton was on his feet again. Micah was quick enough to lure him away from Bethany Corbett, but not quick enough to sidestep the attack. He took a couple of wild punches before getting in a few of his own, then he got fed up with the whole thing and landed a jaw hit that rendered Sutton unconscious. He slumped and fell in a heap on the dirt-streaked linoleum. Micah bent over and relieved him of the snub-nosed revolver Sutton carried under his arm, then reached for the knife that still lay between two stools. A noise from behind caught his attention, and he glanced over his shoulder to see Bethany Corbett's backside disappear through the diner's door.

He swore and dragged a clean handkerchief from his

pocket, wrapping it around his knuckles as he sprinted to the men's room. Blood was dripping freely from the wound as he lifted the toilet lid and dropped Sutton's weapons inside. The knife hadn't inflicted any serious damage, but the blood was a nuisance. Micah had to stop and use his teeth to knot the makeshift bandage before shoving his feet into his boots. He was still swearing fast and furious at the little witch for running out on him when he pulled on his coat and hat and headed after her.

He pushed open the diner's main door to a howling wind that drove icy pellets into his face and an involuntary shiver down his spine. Ignoring the elements with the same single-mindedness as he'd ignored the knife wound, he rounded the building to the parking lot and skidded to a halt. Bethany Corbett was in the backseat of her Ford Explorer, obviously putting the kid into his car seat. She hadn't gotten away. Micah hadn't thought she would; he'd only been a few minutes behind her and he moved a lot faster than she could with all that baby paraphernalia she lugged around like a pack mule.

Micah started toward the Explorer, but drew back against the dark side of the diner as he heard the distinctive roar of a large truck. Glancing up, he saw a snowplow turn off the highway and head straight for the diner. The giant plow came to a halt about twenty feet away. In the purple glow cast by the diner's neon sign, Micah could just make out the shadows of two men in the cab. He was calculating the odds of their keeping their noses out of his business when Bethany Corbett backed out of her truck and slammed the door shut. She didn't look behind her, and Micah knew she wasn't aware she was being watched. It would be so simple to force his way into the truck, now, before she even got the engine started.

He couldn't accomplish anything with an audience,

though. Frustrated and cold and tired, he stood in the shadows of the diner and watched as both doors of the snowplow sprang open. Brilliant spots of color jumped into the white-dark night, and two men in orange jumpsuits trudged across the parking lot as the Explorer came to life with the purr of a well-kept piece of machinery. By the time the two men disappeared inside the diner, Bethany Corbett had maneuvered out of her parking slot and was making slow forward progress across the unplowed lot.

Micah waited until she'd pulled onto the road heading south before leaving the shadows and going to the car he knew was Sutton's. The only other vehicle in the lot besides the plow was a compact pickup parked near the kitchen door, and he figured that belonged to the waitress. Lifting the hood of Sutton's car, he tore out the distributor cap. He threw it into the back of his own car before sliding in behind the wheel. Reversing, he backed away from the cinderblock wall and followed the tracks the Explorer had left in the fresh snow.

Micah decided to give her a few minutes to settle her nerves before he did anything. At least she hadn't doubled back and headed north again, he mused, flexing his injured hand. He hadn't seriously expected her to backtrack into the storm, but then, Bethany Corbett had done a lot of things he hadn't expected over the past few days. He was learning to take nothing for granted where she was concerned.

Reaching out without taking his eyes off the road, he grabbed his cellular phone and punched in the number for his office. His instructions were brief, and he disconnected knowing they'd be relayed to his backup within minutes. With luck, the man would get to the diner before Sutton came to.

In the meantime, it was up to him to find another

way to stop Bethany Corbett. He didn't worry that he couldn't see the Explorer's taillights. There was only one road and she was on it. East and west options were at least thirty miles south. Micah planned to head east eventually, across North La Veta Pass—*if* it was still open to traffic, as the weather station had promised an hour earlier. If not, he'd have to hole up in Alamosa.

Since he intended to have the baby with him by then, he sincerely hoped the pass was still open. None of his plans had even remotely allowed for the possibility of sharing a motel room with a screaming kid.

TWO

Beth drove cautiously through the untamed swirls of snow and ice, worried because she knew this was only the leading edge of what was reported to be a vicious storm. That particular tidbit had been repeated a dozen times over the past half hour, the husky-voiced deejay imparting details of the coming blizzard with what she considered unconscionable glee.

The deejay wasn't out in the middle of "Colorado's worst winter storm in thirty years." He could afford to delight in statistics. Beth wasn't nearly as rapturous about the predicted record-breaking low temperatures and snowfall that had already immobilized most of Idaho and Wyoming. With visibility already erratic and ice thickening beneath the snow, it was all she could do to keep moving ahead. She didn't have a choice, though. The only thing behind her was the diner, and she certainly couldn't go back there.

If she could just manage to keep going, she'd be safe. As would Jeremy. The man Steven had sent after her would be caught by the storm. Beth had seen enough of what the cowboy had done to him to know he'd be unconscious long enough to make a difference.

Cowboy. The description somehow didn't fit the tall, dark stranger who had come to her rescue and been injured in the process. She winced as she remembered his bloody hand, guilt riding her hard despite the knowledge that she'd made an effort to help before running out on him.

She couldn't imagine what had come over her, going for the knife like she had. Keeping Jeremy safe was supposed to be her first and only priority. Everything else—and that included common decency—was a luxury she couldn't afford. She gripped the wheel harder and concentrated. Even at twenty miles per hour, she felt as though she were being hurled forward, with only the random probability that the road was where she needed it.

It occurred to her that only an idiot would be out on such a night. Two idiots, she corrected herself after a glance in the rearview mirror. She dismissed the notion that the blond man had somehow scraped himself off the diner's floor and was following her. The cowboy had taken care of at least that worry, she reassured herself as the headlights grew in the mirror.

Cowboy, or whatever he was. It wasn't that the hat and sheepskin coat didn't suit him, she mused, then wondered why it mattered. She'd never see him again. It was just that there was something in the way his dark gaze had met hers over Pookey's polka dots that made her think he did something other with his days than brand cows and chase strays.

Fighting off rustlers would be his style. *If* he was a cowboy.

She didn't think he was.

The vehicle behind her moved into the next lane to

pass, and she gripped the wheel tighter and fixed her attention on the road ahead. "Idiot," she muttered as the car whooshed past and disappeared over the rise in a cloud of snow. She added, "Show-off," and wished she had the guts to go faster than her present snail's pace.

She didn't, though, and placated her raw nerves with the promise of a respite at the next town . . . if there *was* a next town. As tired as she was, she could almost believe she'd taken a wrong turn upon leaving the diner and that the road she was following led to nowhere. But she hadn't taken a wrong turn, because there hadn't been any choices. Just north or south, and she knew she was headed south because the storm was like a hand reaching out from behind to grab her as she ran.

Shaking her head to clear it of such depressingly vivid images, she checked the panel to reassure herself that the Explorer's four-wheel-drive was engaged, then accelerated to a breathtaking twenty-five miles per hour.

It was a mistake that nearly cost her more than she could afford to pay. From out of nowhere, it seemed, a car appeared on the highway in front of her. Slung partially across the road with its front end pointed into the ditch, the car was an obvious victim of the icy surface.

Beth had exactly two seconds to compute and react. The extra speed she'd put on added to the margin for error, and it was all she could do to hold the truck steady as she swerved around the car, missing it by inches, remembering not to touch the brakes even though every instinct screamed at her to do just that. Not even the four-wheel-drive could keep her from skidding over the snow-covered ice, though, and it was several heart-thumping moments before she was able to steer out of the skid and ease the truck to a stop at the edge of the highway.

Stomping on the emergency brake, she threw the

gearshift into neutral, then half crawled over the seat to check on Jeremy. In the green glow of the dash, she could hardly see past the layers of snowsuit and blankets that enveloped him. But as her gaze focused on his tiny form, her son cuddled Pookey closer to his chest, gave a wide yawn without opening his eyes, and snuggled deeper into his soft, warm bed.

Slumping back in her seat, Beth gave her heart permission to start beating again. Her hands were shaking so badly, though, she had to tuck them under her thighs. The nerves and willpower she'd been existing on for the past three days were suddenly at breaking point.

She couldn't succumb. She knew that even as her mind started to pick up the pieces of what had just happened and put them together again. What evolved from the reconstruction made her heart speed up again. The car she'd nearly hit was the same one that had passed her just minutes ago. Even though she'd only caught a glimpse as it had passed, she knew it was the same one.

Whipping her head around, she looked hard into the night. Nothing. She found the gearshift with a hand that was still far from steady and steered the truck through a tight U-turn, praying the only stupid people on the road were the two she could account for—herself and the guy she'd just missed plowing into.

Driving even slower than before, she retraced her path as her mind opened debate over the advisability of what she was doing.

What if the other driver was a threat to herself or Jeremy?

What if someone was injured?

Didn't everything she'd ever learned discourage a woman from stopping to help a stranger?

What if no one else passed this way? Would the driver survive the night? And his passengers, if there were any?

She could drive back to the diner and send help.

She couldn't do that. The diner was off-limits.

She could keep going and stop at the first house she saw. *If* she saw a house, which she doubted because the storm limited visibility to the bare necessities or less.

They might freeze before then. Or get hit by someone who wasn't as lucky as she'd been.

How could she risk her son's life with an act of kindness that might go horribly wrong?

Even as she considered the worst case Beth was convinced it couldn't happen. The man Steven had sent after her was probably still on the floor of the diner. Besides, she could always drive past without stopping if she was wrong. The Ford's headlights picked out a man's shape as he climbed out of the ditch at the side of the road.

It was the cowboy!

Panic surged through her in the wake of confusing images of the brutal confrontation in the diner. She hit the gas and felt the tires slide sideways before finding a piece of solid road and hanging on to it. The cowboy leaped aside as the Explorer shot forward and away, and it was several seconds before Beth sorted through the panic to the facts. The cowboy had been on her side. He'd taken on the man Steven had sent and allowed her the opportunity to escape.

He'd gotten hurt on her behalf, and now she was running out on him again. For absolutely no reason.

She couldn't do it.

She was sweating by the time she got the truck stopped. After doing another U-turn, she inched the Explorer back to where the car was slewed across the road. Swallowing her trepidation, she eased the truck to a stop several lengths behind the car. The man with the cowboy hat was back on the road, looking straight into her headlights, his hands shoved deep inside the pockets of his sheepskin coat. He waited until she'd set the emergency brake—not all that surprising, she mused—then walked slowly toward the truck. In those last precious moments Beth set the auto lock for all the doors, then slipped her hand inside her purse and wrapped her fingers around the butt of the small handgun she'd been carrying for the past week.

She wasn't a fool.

The man came to the driver's door and waited for her to open the window. She did, but only a crack.

He spoke first. "My car went off the road. Can I get a lift to the next town?"

Maybe. Beth looked into dark eyes that were curiously expressionless. "Why don't I just pull you out?"

"We'll have to do that, too, if only to keep someone from running into it. There's enough room to leave it at the side of the road if we can just straighten it out." A sudden gust of wind kicked ice between the window and the man's face, but he didn't so much as flinch in acknowledgment of the brittle assault. "That car isn't going anywhere on its own. I must have sliced the fuel line on a rock. All the gas leaked out."

She was getting tired of having to strain toward the crack in the window, but not so tired that she was ready to widen it. "Can't you tape it together or something? I'm sure you could siphon enough gas from the truck to get you going."

He shook his head. "No tape, no siphon. Not unless you've got them."

Beth did a mental review of the emergency equipment she had stored in the back and shook her head. He waited without attempting a single argument, his gaze steady on her face as the wind flung more ice on the window between them.

She made the only decision she could live with. "I've never used the tow rope."

"I'll take care of it. It's in back?"

"In the cubby over the left wheel."

His eyes held hers for moment, and a shiver crawled up her spine as satisfaction flickered across his face. She was trying to imagine what he had to be satisfied about when he reached up and pulled the brim of his hat low, masking the expression that gave her second thoughts about having stopped.

"You'll have to unlock the door so I can get to it."

Just in case her unease was anything more than a combination of frazzled nerves and exhaustion, Beth tightened her grip on the gun before punching the unlock button. The thunk of door locks being released was indistinguishable from the heartbeats that thudded in her ears, an internal percussive symphony that measured her escalating panic and fed on it. For what seemed an eternity, she waited for him to make the first move—to prove she'd been wrong to stop, to make her use the gun that radiated a deadly chill in her sweaty hand.

She must have imagined the quick glance he shot toward her hidden hand, because he turned and walked toward the back of the truck before she could begin to think about whether she could actually pull the trigger. Her relief was short-lived, though, because he was pulling open the rear gate and she knew the threat wasn't over.

If there was a threat. Logic told her the only real threat was still back at the diner.

She couldn't afford to gamble, though. In a whirlwind of movement, she wriggled to kneel backward on her seat, keeping the gun in her hand—an awkward task, as it was still inside her purse. With her left hand, she reached for a blanket and tugged it over Jeremy's fuzzy head as the wind drove a frigid taste of the storm into the truck. She shivered, this time from cold, and kept her eyes on the man.

She didn't like the realization that her son was between them, in the line of fire.

Micah looked up at the woman kneeling in the driver's seat and saw the frustration in her expression. For the second time that night, he could relate to what she was feeling, although her frustration was likely related to her anxiety to get on her way while his was due entirely to the gun she held.

He hadn't expected her to be armed.

Grabbing the tow rope, he lowered the rear hatch and headed back to his car. He hadn't needed to see the glint of metal to know she was holding a weapon. It had been enough to notice how she'd kept her hand inside the leather bag the entire time he'd been standing outside her window. His satisfaction at her consent to help —reluctant though it had been—had been usurped by the frustration of realizing it wasn't going to be the easy snatch he'd planned.

He didn't bother thinking about whether she'd actually shoot him. He had to assume she would.

Because of that, he'd have to go through with the charade of pulling his car out of the ditch and moving it off the road. Not that there was anything wrong with it. The "accident" had been nothing more than a ruse to get Bethany Corbett to pull over; its success meant that more dangerous means of stopping her weren't required. He'd even made sure to stage the scene where she'd have enough room to react and maneuver, counting on the fact she'd be driving at the same slow pace as when she'd started out. The risk of anyone else happening on the scene was negligible; he hadn't passed another car since leaving the diner, a circumstance he assumed was due as much to the hour as the storm. Not many people had business on this stretch of highway at two in the morning.

Swearing eloquently to his audience of snow, ice, and wind, he attached the rope to the truck and supervised the operation of pulling the car out and to the side of the road, all the while considering his options. There was really only one. He'd have to ride with her until they reached the next town, then leave her in a gas station or restaurant—someplace where she wouldn't freeze to death. Between now and then, he'd get the gun away from her. Not a difficult task, he judged. She couldn't very well drive a stickshift with a gun in one hand.

He unhooked the tow rope and threw it into the back of the truck along with the duffel bag he'd grabbed out of his car, knowing without looking that her eyes followed his every move. He walked slowly to the passenger door, and was about to open it when the window slid down—not just the crack she'd allowed before, but all the way.

It occurred to him that the open window gave her a clear shot. After a moment spent wondering why she'd bothered to pull his car out of the ditch if she intended to shoot him, Micah shrugged off the ridiculous image of Bethany Corbett gunning him down and bent to peer inside the truck.

He immediately wished he hadn't, because all that was missing from the aforementioned ridiculous image was for her to pull the trigger of the small gun she held aimed between his eyes. A decade of practice at concealing his emotions kept him from laughing outright at the notion that she actually believed the gun gave her any control over the situation. Besides the fact that the weapon was not much bigger than a peashooter, she was making the mistake of aiming for too small a target.

She'd have more luck going for a shoulder or belly hit. He studied her calmly and summed up her expression in a single word: Terrified. Chills raced down his spine, because he knew a frightened woman was more likely to shoot than a calm one. Even with a peashooter, she could do some damage.

He tried to soften the natural harshness in his voice when he spoke. "What did I do?"

She rearranged her fingers around the gun's handle. "Nothing, yet. I can't take any chances."

He'd have to get it away from her before anything stupid happened. Micah nodded toward the gun. "If you seriously think you need that thing, I'm surprised you stopped at all."

"I stopped because I owe you one."

"Then why the gun?"

"I'm cautious, that's all." Her expression was both weary and determined.

"You think that maybe I planned this accident on the off chance you—and only you—would happen by to rescue me?"

"There are reasons—"

He interrupted to keep her from telling him too much. He already knew as much as he wanted to know about her. "Unless you're an escaped murderer—"

"I'm not!" She looked shocked that he'd say such a thing about her.

"Thief?"

She hesitated. "No."

"That man back at the diner wanted something from you."

"Yes."

When she didn't add anything to that, Micah just shrugged and let his gaze wander over the creamy line of her throat before returning to stare down the hollow barrel of the gun. "I suppose I'll just have to imagine you believe there's something extraordinary under that coat and sweater that makes perfect strangers go to such lengths to get near you."

"Don't be ludicrous," she said, a frown of irritation crossing her brow.

"You're the one being ludicrous, lady," he returned. "Even if your body rated a nine on a scale of one to ten—"

"It doesn't," she inserted quickly.

Micah pretended he didn't know better. "Even if it did, I doubt I'd stage an accident in the middle of this godforsaken wasteland just on the off chance you would stop to keep me warm."

She regarded him for a long moment, then sighed. "I admit it's a stretch, but I've learned lately not to to assume everything is as it appears."

No, he didn't imagine she would. The only smile Steven Corbett had cracked during his short interview with Micah had been when he'd recounted his wife's total shock when the court had awarded custody of their six-month-old child to him, not her. Apparently, Bethany had assumed Steven Corbett didn't want the child.

She'd been wrong. Just as her ex-husband had wrongly assumed she'd do nothing to remedy the situation. No, Bethany Corbett had surprised everyone by sneaking into the mansion that had been her home for the brief duration of her marriage, and stealing away her son—a coup of timing and luck that she had brought off a mere twenty-four hours after the hearing.

Micah had to admire someone who would try to thwart a man as powerful as Steven Corbett. Admiration aside, though, he still had a job to do.

She licked her lips, and he followed the delicate movement with an interest that was surprisingly distracting. He had to pry his gaze from her mouth when she cleared her throat to speak again. "If you want a ride to the next town, it's by my rules."

"Which are?" he asked mildly.

"You drive. I hold the gun." Even though the handgun was small compared with most weapons, the weight of it dragged her aim low on his chest. Micah was relieved when she corrected upward.

"What if I don't want to drive?"

"Then you stay here and hope I send someone back for you before you freeze." She flinched as a gust of wind showered the front seat with ice particles.

Micah just nodded. He had no intention of staying behind. "Then I guess I drive. Try not to squeeze the trigger on that thing when you climb into the passenger seat." He straightened from the door and walked around the hood of the truck, taking his time because his nerves were frayed and he didn't want them to show. Out of the corner of his eye, he saw her scramble over the console and settle into the seat with her back to the door, the gun aimed in his general direction.

The matter of who was supposed to have the gun would have to wait, Micah decided. As long as she believed she was in charge, she wouldn't cause any trouble. There wasn't a single reason for this job to be complicated by needless posturing or emotion—although, according to her ex, she didn't have any of the latter. In any case, it didn't matter. Steven Corbett had shown him the papers that endorsed his legal rights regarding the child. Micah's job was to restore those rights.

Had Corbett been so inclined, he could have reported the missing child to the authorities. Once Bethany had been caught, he could sit back and watch his ex-wife swing in the twilight, so to speak. Instead, he'd hired Micah to bring the child back, citing a desire that the matter be handled without fuss or publicity. While Micah personally thought Albuquerque's assistant DA should show more confidence in local law enforcement agencies, he could relate to the man's desire to keep his private life out of the limelight.

The fact that this attempt at privacy was a distinct contradiction to Corbett's behavior during his very public divorce was simply food for thought over the long miles, nothing more.

Micah opened the driver's door with fingers that were raw from working gloveless in the harsh weather. The bandage had disappeared somewhere under his car, but the bleeding on his knuckles had stopped and crusted over, so he didn't bother getting a substitute. Tugging off his Stetson, he moved the seat all the way back, then slid behind the wheel. Once he'd unbuttoned his coat, he turned to look at the woman, the crown of his hat still between his fingers. "Mind if I put this on the backseat?"

She must have minded, because she took the gun in one hand and reached for his hat with the other. "I'll do it."

He shrugged indifferently, but had to grit his teeth when she grabbed it by the brim—a no-no when it comes to Stetsons—then compound the insult by tossing it over her shoulder to land on the floor.

"I was kind of hoping for the seat. It's my favorite hat."

The hint of a smile touched her lips. "I envy someone who has the energy to worry about his hat."

Her soft words were laced with a texture that reminded him of secrets whispered between lovers. His body responded to the notion—a sudden tightening in his groin, a changed rhythm to his heartbeat that should have been familiar, but wasn't. He was aroused, yet knew his response to this woman was different from the sexual encounters that had tantalized and excited him before.

Of all the women he'd known over the years, none had ever seduced him with mere words. He was impressed . . . and a little wary, because he was pretty sure she hadn't done it on purpose. His gaze drifted over her face, though he was careful not to venture lower. He knew that even a hint of what he was feeling would get him thrown out of the truck. Her eyes were devoid of anything but determination and a measure of fear. His gaze lowered to her lips, which were slightly parted, and he could almost hear the short, uneven breaths that signaled her discomfort with the situation.

No, Bethany Corbett hadn't meant to entice. She did it without knowing, a dangerous talent that Micah was sure brought her more trouble than she deserved. Or maybe she did deserve it, in ways that weren't related at all to the sensuality she radiated with every breath.

He didn't know and didn't care. The all-too-public divorce had broadcast her sins—everything from adultery to overwhelming greed, with enough lesser peccadilloes thrown in to convince everyone from the judge on down that Bethany Corbett was a woman who didn't deserve so much as a dime in settlement. Micah had watched with distaste the tapes Corbett had provided of the news coverage, only sitting through them because every detail was important when it came to tracking a person who didn't want to be found.

The woman next to him was a cool one—most of the time. He remembered how, with her reputation in shreds, Bethany had sat beside her attorney during the settlement hearing and listened to the judgment in stony silence—proof, the media implied, that she was guilty of everything her husband accused her of. The child-custody hearing that followed a few days after the settlement hearing had been pretty much a replay of the same theme, with the notable exception that the ex–Mrs. Corbett had displayed an emotional response Micah found puzzling—disbelief at first, followed by rage when her son was forcibly taken from her arms. Then there had been tears, silent tears, as she'd walked from the courtroom. She hadn't even waited for her attorney as she pushed through the throngs of spectators and disappeared into a passing cab.

Steven Corbett had taken advantage of the undivided attention of the press, posing for the cameras with a wide, confident smile on his face and his tiny son balanced somewhat precariously in the crook of his arm. He'd never been allowed to hold his own son, he'd informed his avid audience. It would take practice—something he intended to get a lot of over the coming months.

His charming admission of inexperience had won the hearts of Albuquerque's citizens, as well as going a long way to bolster his popularity in political circles. His power base was definitely expanding, and analysts were already predicting a run for the DA job in the coming elections.

Micah didn't give a damn about Corbett's so-called power base, partly because he was from Denver and just plain didn't care who was who in Albuquerque politics, and partly because he never let politics and influences therefrom sway him.

The Bethany Corbett he'd studied back in his office didn't match up with the woman he'd spent three days tracking, and not just because of the way he'd watched her care for her son in the diner. No, there was something in her eyes that was almost convincingly innocent of the seamy side of life where she'd supposedly dallied.

Innocent, almost to the point of ignorance. Micah

could have sworn that Bethany Corbett had but a fleeting knowledge of the sins she'd been accused of committing, a knowledge she had not gained by firsthand experience.

Now, though, staring down the barrel of the gun that obviously weighed heavily in her hands, he knew he couldn't afford to doubt a single rotten thing he'd heard about her.

Still, he couldn't help but wonder how it would feel to have Bethany Corbett focus all that incredible sensuality on him . . . deliberately.

Micah was beginning to see what had made Steven Corbett fall for the woman he'd made his wife.

THREE

"Does your hand hurt?"

As she asked the question Beth stared at the puckered red line that cut across the cowboy's knuckles and remembered how he'd worked under his car getting the tow rope set. She shivered and felt the guilt roll through her. It had been her fault he'd gotten hurt and she'd not even said a decent thank you.

"It's okay," he said without any trace of blame in his voice. "Just a little sore, but that shouldn't last."

"I'm sorry it happened."

He looked surprised, but eased whatever he felt with a shrug. "Me too. I wasn't in the mood for a brawl."

His casual response was so disconcerting, she shied away from the subject in favor of something more neutral. "Where are you headed?"

She almost laughed then, realizing he must think her an idiot for trying to make conversation when he was driving her truck through a steadily worsening storm with a gun aimed somewhere between his belly and neck. She couldn't seem to hold the thing steady, but even as the weight made it waver, she made sure to keep it pointed in his direction.

Her fingers cramped from the unnatural tension, and she could only hope they'd arrive somewhere—any-where!—before the heat inside the truck lulled her into the sleep she needed so badly. Damn, but it was hot! A surge of self-discipline made her straighten her shoul-ders, reminding her that she couldn't afford to give in to the exhaustion that had plagued her for the past few days. Nor could she turn down the heat, not with Jeremy needing every bit of the healing warmth.

Keep him warm, the doctor had said. His tiny system had suffered a shock and would benefit from a warm environment. And keep him safe, he'd added.

She hadn't needed to be told that last part. Just get-ting him away from Steven had removed the worst threat from his young life. Keeping Jeremy away from Steven's abusive rages was the only goal she had now.

That, and keeping herself a good distance from her ex-husband's brutal temper as well. Without taking her gaze off the cowboy, who drove her truck with a compe-tence she found calming, she slipped her free hand inside her coat to feel for the tenderness just below her left breast. A bruised rib or two, the doctor had told her. Painful, but bearable if she didn't lift or carry too much. Two weeks ago she'd been grateful to know Steven hadn't broken anything when he'd slammed his fist into her—a show of force to ensure her silence during the settlement hearing. Now she damned him every time she had to pick up Jeremy—with or without his carry cot.

She'd get over it, though. Just as Jeremy would sur-vive the bruises Steven had left on his arms and legs. As long as she could keep her son away from her ex-hus-band, the child would be safe. It didn't matter how many laws she broke ensuring it.

The cowboy cleared his throat, reminding Beth that her aim was much better with two hands than with one. She slid her hand out of her coat and curled her fingers around the butt of the gun as she studied the man next to her. Beneath several days' growth of beard was a face that matched his body in strength. To describe it in terms of dark eyes, brown hair that grew past his collar, and regular features sounded too tame, almost inappropriate. She tried to figure out why as she waited for him to tell her where he was going.

"I'm not headed anywhere in particular, not tonight," he said, his low, husky voice easily overriding the hum of the four-wheel-drive. "Frankly, I'd prefer to get out at the first motel." He shot her a look, then returned his attention to the road. "Do you have a problem with that?"

She shook her head, then realized he couldn't see her. "No. But I doubt you'll find anything this side of Monte Vista."

"That's about thirty or so miles ahead." He glanced at her again. "I'd think you should stop too. The roads are going to get worse before they get better."

She agreed, but knew she couldn't afford the luxury of stopping. Not if she wanted to get across Wolf Creek Pass before the storm shut it down. "I'll leave you in Monte Vista, then."

He nodded, and she watched as the fingers of his right hand glided over the wheel. The sheer nonchalance of his gesture was a reminder of simpler times, a different life—a time when she'd not known the meaning of rage, of abuse.

A time when she'd honestly believed the man who wooed her with such dazzling intensity was who he appeared to be. She'd met Steven at a fund-raiser, and not once over the next few months had he given her so much as a hint of his darker side. He was kind and funny and so incredibly sincere about his work and dreams that she'd had her hands full just looking at the package he presented. There hadn't been time or reason to look beyond.

His facade began to crumble almost immediately after the wedding. Steven didn't know when to quit—drinking *or* hitting. When she threatened to report his abuse, he countered with laughter, threats, and denials. He had an abundance of friends, important, powerful friends, who would believe him, not her. The academic community in which she worked was no match for the kind of political muscle Steven had at his disposal. Her credentials as a physics professor were insignificant when compared to his reputation as an upstanding community leader.

The only reason it had taken weeks instead of days for her to flee the marriage had been her own disbelief that he could be so cruel, so different. Even after she left him, she kept the sordid truth of her marriage from everyone, especially from her family in Boston. She was too embarrassed to admit she'd chosen so incredibly badly. And her father was too ill to be told the truth.

Once she was on her own again, she avoided filing for divorce, because to do so might trigger Steven's attention. She was relieved when he finally did the deed himself, even more so when her pregnancy became obvious and he ignored it. Just as he ignored the birth of their son.

Until it came time to settle the matter legally. Steven had bought her silence with the promise he'd lay no claim to Jeremy. So she had sat quietly in the courtroom and listened to herself being accused of a parade of sins she'd never imagined, much less committed.

All for a child she'd lost anyway. Legally.

Beth blinked back the tears that were all that remained of her innocence and concentrated on the world
at hand. The woman who held a gun on a man she'd
never seen before that night didn't believe in laws anymore. She only believed in what she knew to be right.

Micah decided then was as good a time as any to get
the gun away from her. He shot her a sideways glance to
make sure she was paying more attention to him than to
how fast they were going, then gradually slowed the vehicle until they were moving at half the speed of just
minutes before. With a prayer that her finger wouldn't
twitch at the wrong moment, he touched the brake and
sent the Explorer into a slight skid, throwing her hard
against the door. He had to admire the total silence of
her reaction. She neither screamed nor gasped as he corrected for the skid and guided the truck back onto a
straight path.

The fact that she didn't shoot him was also a plus.

He heaved a loud sigh and glanced with patent disgust at the gun that was still pointed in his direction. "If
that skid had been even a yard wider, lady, we'd have
gone off the road. I'd sure hate to get shot just because
the truck went bump and you accidentally squeezed the
trigger." He gripped the wheel and settled himself more
comfortably behind it. "I'm not going to be much good
at keeping this thing on four wheels if you shoot me
during a bad patch."

There was a long silence during which Micah slowly
accelerated back up to a speed he considered safe. They
were cruising along at nearly thirty miles an hour when
he saw her lower the gun to her lap.

"You have to take your finger off the trigger for that
to be effective," he reminded her.

She complied, folding her hands in a tense clasp over

the short barrel. "Drop your speed to anything under ten miles, and I'll pick it up again."

Micah hid his satisfaction, thinking she needed lessons in self-defense if she believed she was anywhere close to safe. Or in charge. He could simply hit her across the face and slip the gun from her lap before she recovered. Or put her to sleep for a few moments with a slight pressure to a certain artery. It would be child's play to go into another skid and take the gun without losing control of the truck.

He'd rather not have to hurt her, but didn't think she'd just give the thing to him if he asked for it.

He had decided to let her relax for a few minutes before finishing the job when the baby let out a surprised wail. Bethany looked over her shoulder, and Micah neatly slipped the revolver from her lap.

Her howl of outrage vied in decibels with the boy's. Micah held the gun against the wheel in his left hand and took his foot from the accelerator as he prepared to fend off any attempt to get it back.

When she didn't even touch him, he shot her an admiring look. "That's smart thinking, lady. I wasn't looking forward to ending up in the ditch a second time tonight."

Her voice was low and controlled, although he thought he detected a faint quaver. "I should have taken the chance of shooting you by accident."

"You shouldn't have stopped for me at all," he growled. "Taking your finger off the trigger was just another mistake in a whole string of them."

An indignant cry from the backseat interrupted whatever she was going to say. Micah stopped her with a heavy hand on her shoulder before she could respond to the child's cry. "Be very careful about what you do from now on, lady. I'm not in the mood to put up with any shenanigans." He felt her shudder, and knew when he took his hand away that she understood exactly who was in charge.

"Jeremy needs me," she said with surprising evenness.

Micah stole a quick look at her face and was satisfied that she wouldn't do anything stupid. Yet. Still, he kept a watchful eye on the rearview mirror as she slipped out of her seat belt and reached back through the gap between the front seats to dig into the bag on the floor. She pressed a pacifier into the baby's fingers, then stiffly turned back in her seat to stare out the windshield.

Micah stayed wary of any sudden moves on her part, only relaxing a fraction when she tucked her right hand under the flap of her coat and held it against her rib cage, just below her breasts—as though something hurt and the pressure of her hand alleviated the pain.

He remembered the way she'd winced a couple of times in the restaurant and wondered how she'd gotten hurt. Or if she'd been sick. Pneumonia sometimes caused pain, with your lungs pressing so hard against your ribs that you could hardly take a breath. And that would explain her voice.

He regretted that her husky voice might be a fleeting thing. Not that it mattered, he told himself. Pneumonia, though. He wondered how she thought she could take care of a baby when she'd been ill herself.

Not his problem.

He slipped the gun into his left pocket, then rubbed his neck in an attempt to relieve the tension that had been building there. At least the baby had quit crying. He tensed for a moment as she moved again, then relaxed when he realized she was applying more pressure to her rib cage as she took slow, shallow breaths. Micah revised his thinking from pneumonia back to an injury of some sort.

"You staged that accident, didn't you?"

He couldn't see any point in not telling her. Besides, the sound of her voice soothed nerves he'd thought long past soothing.

He nodded briefly. "You shouldn't kick yourself for stopping. It saved having to do this the hard way." When she didn't have anything to say to that, he pushed her into responding. "Why did you, anyway?"

"Stop?"

"Yeah."

"It seemed the decent thing to do." She sounded as though the decent thing was leaving a bad taste in her mouth.

Hearing the words aloud startled him, because he'd counted on her doing just that . . . even when there was nothing in her file to indicate she'd react that way. Staring into the herd of snowflakes that stampeded with futile force against the windshield, he wondered what it was about Bethany Corbett that had made him try the comparatively gentle way of stopping her versus edging her off the road with his car or any of the other tricks that would have suited his purpose.

The scene in the diner flashed through his mind, and Micah realized it was the scuffle with Sutton that had subtly altered how he perceived her. When the only thought he'd spared her was to notice she was on the floor and out of his way, she'd deliberately risked going for the knife in an effort to help him.

Because of that he'd been gentle with her when rough would have served as easily. Now they were even.

Exhaustion must be making him soft, he decided as he waited for her to ask how he'd found her. Or ask how much Steven was paying him. Or if, by some macabre chance, she'd picked up a man who had nothing to do with her at all. A stranger who meant her real harm rather than performing the simple recovery job Micah was there to do.

Didn't she know how stupid it was for a woman alone to do the decent thing?

When it came, her question was none of the above. "Will you let me come back to Albuquerque with Jeremy? He's so small and—"

She hesitated, and Micah firmly ignored the tears welling up in her eyes. False tears, he judged with harsh certainty. They would have done more for her in court than out here with a man who didn't give a damn about women who cried when the going got tough. She looked away for a moment, and he was nonplussed when she turned her face to him again and the tears had retreated to a mere glistening.

"I won't give you any trouble. It's just that he'll fret without me, and, well, you won't know how to comfort him." She gulped, then added, *"Please* let me stay with him." She lifted a hand as if to touch him, withdrawing at the last second with an expression on her face that said she hadn't meant to do that, not really.

But if it would help, she would touch him . . . and more. Micah realized that she was willing to do just about anything for her child. He also remembered Steven Corbett's warning that his wife—ex-wife—was extremely adept at getting her way. Sex was her tool of choice, Corbett had said, and Micah almost wished she'd use that instead of what she was doing now.

Bethany Corbett was begging. Micah hated how it made him feel. "You're assuming a lot, lady. What makes you think it's the kid I want . . . and not you?"

A sharp intake of breath was her only reaction. It hadn't even occurred to her, he realized during the silence that followed. Or it didn't matter, because the child was her entire focus. He would have admired such maternal devotion if he hadn't known that young Jeremy Corbett was only a pawn she was using against her ex. A living, breathing pawn that would net her the financial security she'd been denied in court. At least that was how Steven Corbett read Bethany's actions.

There wasn't an ounce of hope in her voice when she finally spoke. "You don't look like the kind of man who needs to kidnap women to get his kicks."

He shot her a disgusted glance. "Ted Bundy didn't look like a serial killer either."

A sudden wariness crept into her expression, and Micah felt a strange satisfaction at knowing she wouldn't make the same mistake twice. "Something to think about, isn't it?" he said softly, then went on before her growing panic made her do something foolish that would get them all killed. "But you're right, lady. I'm after the kid. Your ex gave me some papers that make it legal."

Technically legal, he amended silently. The New Mexico court system had awarded Steven Corbett custody, but they were in Colorado now. Taking the child from its mother without going through proper channels infringed on that state's rights to either assist or deny the transfer. While Micah knew there was no question of Jeremy eventually being returned to New Mexico, he'd agreed to do the job without the fuss of official assistance.

He hadn't taken on a case like this in years, and he wouldn't be doing this one either, except he owed a guy a favor and Steven Corbett was willing to pay the fee Micah demanded. Keeping his staff of private investigators interested and well paid required big bucks. The rent on the two floors of exclusive Denver high-rise that housed his offices wasn't cheap either, which meant cases like these rarely came his way anymore. Few distraught parents could afford him. Besides, Micah much preferred tangling with perpetrators of blackmail and fraud to getting mixed up in family disputes.

"Just because it's legal doesn't make what you're doing right."

He lifted his shoulders in an exaggerated shrug, wishing he could speed up so that he could dump Bethany Corbett and get on with the job before she used another word like *right* or *decent*. She'd lost big time in court over the meanings of words like those, and here she was using them with virtuous conviction.

"Legal's all that matters," he ground out. "And don't think you can bribe or cajole me into going back without the baby, because it won't work. I'm here to take the kid back and that's exactly what I intend to do."

"You're not bribable?"

"Just not in your price range," he shot back, angered by the obvious disbelief in her expression.

"So you *are* bribable," she said with a hint of speculation as she carefully shrugged out of her coat and folded it across her lap.

Micah was annoyed—at himself for saying something that wasn't true, at her because she'd believed him. He'd never let a quarry buy his or her way out of his grasp, and it irked him that Bethany Corbett assumed he might.

He was doubly annoyed that he was paying any attention at all to what she thought. Get the job done and go on to the next, he told himself. To hell with Bethany Corbett and the way her sweater lay across her breasts, skimming the curves in a way that hinted at their fullness and made him wonder what she'd look like in silk and lace.

He cleared his throat and remembered he was annoyed with her. "Your husband—"

"Ex-husband," she said distinctly.

He shrugged off her interruption. "Your *ex*-husband made sure I knew just how little you had in the way of available cash. End of negotiations."

A strangled sigh parted her lips. "Steven has always been a man consumed by details. *Cajole* was the other word you used. Does that mean I could talk myself blue and you'd not hear a word?"

Micah almost told her his interpretation of *cajole* was substantially different from hers. He didn't, though, keeping his mouth shut and his eyes on the road until she finally added her own conclusions.

"I would imagine the amount of money Steven can pay pretty much overwhelms any inclination you might have to listen to my side of the story," she said softly. "He always did say money could buy anything."

"Your side of the story is irrelevant. Corbett hired me to bring the kid back, and the courts back up his claim. I have a reputation for doing exactly what I'm hired to do." So faint that he could hardly see them, Micah picked out a pair of taillights just ahead. He slowed the truck to a crawl, and again wondered how he'd get the kid all the way to Pueblo on such miserable roads. Unable to see far enough into the night to chance passing the slow-moving vehicle, he reconciled himself to following the car the rest of the way into town.

"Why didn't you just take Jeremy from me at the diner?" she asked, her own gaze locked on the car ahead.

"We were never alone."

She lifted a single eyebrow in disbelief. "There was just a waitress, and she looked maybe a hair less exhausted than me. I doubt you'd have had to try very hard to fend off the two of us."

"I didn't want to have to hurt her if she tried to get in my way," he said, disgruntled because he'd told her the truth and she'd ignored it.

"But you'd hurt me?" It sounded more like a statement than a question.

Micah decided to let her think what she wanted. The more frightened she was, the easier she'd be to handle. "You're not an innocent bystander," he said.

"Lucky waitress," she snapped. Then the penny must have dropped, because she gasped softly and nodded almost to herself. "*Hurting* the waitress was never the point. Steven told you no witnesses . . . or police, didn't he?"

He nodded curtly. "I knew *you* wouldn't dare call the cops, but the waitress was bound to report a fight over the kid." He still hadn't figured out why Corbett wanted it done this way, and that bothered him. Micah had learned long ago that motive was a dangerous part of the picture when it wasn't obvious. In this case, motive was pivotal to everything, because Corbett was paying an exorbitant fee for a snatch that could have been done legally at no cost.

"Everyone's news conscious these days, even waitresses at deserted diners." The sarcasm was heavy in her voice. "I wonder what she's going to do with the man you left on the floor." Without giving him time to answer, she followed with another question. "And who was he anyway? If Steven sent you after Jeremy—"

"He was taking what I wanted. I stopped him." Micah didn't like knowing Corbett had hired another man without telling him. Still, it had happened before, especially when the client was too anxious for results to sit back and let the job get done right. But Sutton was the kind of man people hired when they didn't care what happened to the quarry. In this case, that included the baby.

The fact that Sutton had probably gone to Corbett instead of the other way around was Micah's problem. Sutton had been trying to get between Micah and his clients for months now, ever since Micah had gotten Sutton's private investigator's license pulled.

Micah was pretty sure Sutton's thirst for revenge wouldn't be satisfied by the wound he'd inflicted in the diner.

"Did Steven happen to say why he didn't want to involve the police?"

"He said he wanted to get his son back without the whole world looking on."

Bethany Corbett's snort of disbelief told him what she thought of *that* theory. "That kind of publicity would be icing on the cake." She clasped her hands together so tightly, Micah was surprised something didn't break. "No, I'm afraid Steven has other reasons for wanting Jeremy back without any fuss."

He was waiting for her to elaborate when she changed the subject.

"Did Steven tell you not to bring me back with Jeremy?"

Micah shook his head as he squinted through the flurries at a snow-blurred sign marking their approach to the dot on the map that was the tiny town of Center. "He's concerned about his son, not you. But I did not get the impression that Corbett would be happy to see you again."

"You don't seem like a man who cares if the Steven Corbetts of this world are happy so long as you get the job done and collect your money."

Micah didn't say anything, wondering if he was reaching the fine line between overly tired and totally exhausted. He'd nearly opened his mouth to say it made no difference whether she came along or not. Which was nonsense, of course. At least with the kid alone, he wouldn't have to be constantly on his guard against any little schemes she might concoct. Even if Jeremy Corbett screamed all the way to Pueblo, it would be preferable to trying to keep the woman in line without hurting her more than she already was. What with the way she tried to take shallow breaths and how she was trying to relieve a pain in her chest, Micah suspected she'd already taken enough of a beating from someone else. Maybe one of the "indiscretions" that had contributed to her divorce had objected to being made an instant daddy.

Micah hoped she had enough sense not to return to that man. A man who would beat a woman once wouldn't need much of an excuse to do it again.

Not even Bethany Corbett deserved that kind of life.

The car ahead slowed even more to turn off the road. They'd arrived in Center, he realized, and peered out at the handful of lights that lined the short main street. He steered the truck through the sleeping town, not surprised when they came out the other end without having passed a single twenty-four-hour business.

A sudden wail from the backseat was an almost tactile blow at the base of his neck. Micah winced and rubbed his neck, and was waiting impatiently for the baby's mother to do something about the steadily increasing racket when he realized she hadn't moved. *She wasn't going to do a thing!* He glanced into the rearview mirror at the red-faced screamer, then shifted his gaze to Bethany. She stared right back at him.

"He'll scream like that until I feed him," she said. "Or change his diaper. Or find his pacifier or Pookey or whatever else he thinks he wants."

"Do something now," he ground out, putting a lot of menace into it so that she'd act before he drove the truck off the road. His sanity was at stake, not to mention his eardrums.

"Take me with you to Albuquerque." Her demand was as implacable as his own. There was a strength underlying her words that Micah couldn't help but admire.

It suited him to let her win this round. He surrendered with a curt nod, figuring anything he said would be drowned out by the baby's howls.

She leaned back over the console and pulled a bottle from the diaper bag. Seconds later Jeremy was sucking greedily on his bottle in a glorious silence that was broken only by his mother's soft words of praise for his appetite. Micah had to strain above the hum of the engine to hear what she was saying. She'd do well to praise Jeremy's lungs, too, he thought, because they'd gotten her what she wanted.

"You can stay until I decide you're too much trouble," he said, thinking he should remind her there were conditions to everything. "Or until we get to Pueblo, whichever comes first." He was staring straight ahead, so didn't know if she was relieved or victorious or both. It didn't matter, he decided, as long as she kept the kid quiet so he could concentrate on driving.

"Why are you going there?" she asked. "Pueblo's the wrong direction if you're driving back to Albuquerque."

"We'll fly. There's a charter outfit there I've used before." Unless the airport was shut down by the storm. While reports had the blizzard heading straight south, a twitch to the left could engulf Pueblo with very little warning. Micah didn't want to even think about what he'd have to do then.

She actually laughed, a short husky note that didn't

have anything to do with being amused. "Steven's going to have a fit when he sees your expense account."

He almost opened his mouth to tell her the charge for the charter would be a relatively small entry on the overall accounting for this job, but figured that would lead to a discussion of how much money a man charged to separate a woman from her child. She'd probably bring up words like *right* and *decent* again, and that wouldn't do.

He wasn't in the mood to debate morals with Bethany Corbett, not even if it meant he'd have the pleasure of listening to her sweet voice.

A thud sounded on the floor behind him, followed by an unhappy cry. Micah waited with clenched teeth as the woman wiggled around in her seat to search for the bottle Jeremy had dropped. Faded jeans clung like a second skin to her butt, which brushed his shoulder as she stretched into the far reaches of the backseat. Where before he'd only imagined what form her soft curves would take under the long sweater, he now could see every perfect contour from the waist down.

Micah responded to those curves without any conscious thought, a purely masculine appreciation that stopped barely a breath short of total arousal. When she settled back in her seat with a pained wince, she looked so damned innocent that he was *almost* convinced she hadn't gone out of her way to entice him. Out of the corner of his eye, he watched as she straightened her sweater, tugging the hem down past her hips so that the loose-knit fabric tautened across her breasts. He must have made a noise of some sort, because she turned to look at him.

He returned her gaze, not bothering to tone down the sexual response he knew flared in his expression. She immediately looked away, but not before he saw the panic that flickered in her eyes. Confused, he checked the road ahead, then chanced another glance at her. In the soft glow of the dash lights, a deep blush on her cheeks signaled that she understood exactly what was on his mind.

Micah told himself he'd misinterpreted the look in her eyes, that a woman who went through lovers like peanuts would be used to men who looked at her the way he had. Even so, her "innocent" teasing had aroused him, a response that didn't particularly worry him because he'd never lost control around a woman in his life.

The fact that he hadn't decided whether he'd act on his response gave him something to think about.

Jeremy let out a couple of satisfied gurgles, and in the rearview mirror Micah watched as the baby waved Pookey back and forth, then threw him to land on the console between the front seats. He grabbed the toy and flipped it in Jeremy's general direction before his mother could even react.

"Keep his toys in the back," he muttered, his annoyance having everything to do with the mother and nothing whatsoever to do with the child. "And keep him quiet."

"He *is* quiet," she pointed out in that deep-throated voice that was an almost physical rub against his senses.

"Make sure he stays that way."

Micah knew his response to her was personal, *intimately* personal, and not merely the reaction of a man to sex in general. Bethany Corbett fascinated him in a way he'd never experienced. She was sexy and innocent without trying for either, it seemed. Just as she was intrepid and frightened and daring all at once.

According to her ex-husband, she was a whore.

Micah knew that, just as he knew that her reactions to him weren't those of a woman experienced in sexual encounters. He wondered which was the real Bethany Corbett, and why he cared one way or the other. With a grunt of impatience, he settled in for the drive to Monte Vista, determined to think of anything but the woman beside him.

He hated knowing that he desired a woman so many men had already enjoyed.

FOUR

The settlement hearing had turned her from a woman into a whore. Beth didn't think she'd ever get used to it.

Staring blindly into the worsening storm, she struggled against blurting out the truth. There wasn't any use, though. He wouldn't believe her; no one believed her. Not even her colleagues at the university, although they'd pretended otherwise. Men she'd once regarded as friends now looked at her with a kind of heated speculation that made her sick.

It was as though they wanted her to be the woman of Steven's lies, and the hearing had given them permission to dispense with the rules of polite society, in which she'd previously been treated with respect. The two long hours that Steven had filled with her sins and his innocence had changed forever how people thought of her.

The three days between the two hearings had been filled with unrelenting publicity that mocked her courtroom silence. She'd been tied to the deal she'd made, though, unable to explain anything as she awaited the custody hearing.

After that, it was too late.

Your side of the story is irrelevant. The cowboy's words summed up her situation eloquently. When the custody hearing ended, it had been too late to explain her silence to friends who were suddenly as deaf as the reporters Steven had manipulated.

She'd tried, though, after those few minutes of "justice" when she'd lost everything. But even the women she'd worked with over the past years were suspicious of her reasons for staying silent in the face of Steven's accusations. One woman, a friend, had gone so far as to ask the most obvious question.

How could Beth believe the courts would award custody of a small child to a woman of her reputation?

Because, she'd answered silently, she'd never imagined Steven wanted Jeremy. Because she'd believed that by smearing her reputation, Steven would achieve the appearance of purity that he sought, and wouldn't want more than that.

Because she'd bargained with the devil . . . and lost. She'd been too shocked at the first hearing to protest, too afraid he'd back out of his promise to let her keep Jeremy. In her naïveté, she'd been willing to do anything to keep her son.

It hadn't been enough.

The woman, her friend, had looked at her with pity and disbelief, then walked away. Beth hadn't blamed her, because hearing the words aloud had made her see how incredibly stupid she'd been to believe anything Steven said.

The administration at the university had reacted in much the same way, moving with unaccustomed speed to notify Beth that her contract would not be renewed the following spring. In the interim, they were reassigning her classes—pressure, they said, from trustees and parents who didn't want their children exposed to her questionable morals. She would be paid, but for doing nothing.

Beth had known the divorce would end her marriage. But she hadn't anticipated losing her friends, her job.

Her son.

She gave up trying to get comfortable in her seat, reaching with trembling hands to pick up her coat from where it had fallen on the floor. She hugged it to her breasts, hardly daring to breathe lest the man discover how incredibly frightened she was. It was strictly self-defense that drove her to maintain the facade of calm in front of this man who'd taken control of her life. Hers and Jeremy's.

Showing fear had made Steven even angrier, if such a thing were possible. She'd learned to conceal it, or try to.

At least this man hadn't said aloud what he was thinking, she mused, and wondered distractedly what had provoked the transition from disdain to desire.

Desire. She shook her head against the implications, her mind still reeling from his dark, hungry stare and all the wanting he'd put into it. Something deeper than fear tugged at her emotions, her senses. An endless shiver curled around her spine, spinning her nerves closer to the edge of total panic.

And awareness. Of him, the cowboy, the man. Beth's intellectual side knew her unacceptable interest in the man could be explained as the first signs of the Stockholm Syndrome. That knowledge didn't alleviate her self-disgust. It wasn't right that she feel a sexual response toward him.

It shouldn't even be tolerable.

She stiffened as a gust of wind nudged the truck into the oncoming lane. The man corrected for the sideways drift with such deft ease, she couldn't help but envy his control.

She'd have to get past that control if they were going to get away from him.

"Does the boy ever sleep?"

His sudden question startled her out of her thoughts. She glanced over her shoulder to see Jeremy staring right back at her, his cap of white-blond hair a halo in the dim lighting. Relieved that he seemed totally unaffected by the tension in the air, she forced a smile and said a few words of nonsense, which he replied to with delighted gurgles.

"He sleeps in spurts," she answered finally, avoiding meeting the man's gaze as she turned to face front. "He hasn't slept for more than an hour at a time since he was born." That was an outright lie, but she didn't want to get left at the side of the road when Jeremy finally settled down for a long sleep.

She thought she heard the man groan in response, but decided it must have been the wind, because when she glanced his way, his expression was untouched by any disgust or exasperation. That calmed her slightly, knowing he could control his emotions.

"No wonder you look like you've been hit by a truck," he said, surprising her with his observation. "I guess you've slept less than he has."

She almost told him she'd been lucky to get any sleep at all, since Jeremy mostly slept while she drove, and wanted to play when she stopped. Yes, she almost told him, but couldn't imagine why he should care. Then she knew.

"You don't have to worry that I'm too tired to take care of him," she said, and turned to look out her window so she could concentrate on trying to figure a way out of the mess her Good Samaritan act had landed them in. There was no way she'd let this man or anyone else take Jeremy back to Steven, but how was she supposed she stop him? He was bigger, stronger, and clearly someone who was used to getting his way.

Beth knew all about men like that, men like Steven, who had used his strength on her, then blamed her for the resulting bruises and injuries. It wouldn't have happened if she'd agreed with what he wanted, he'd said each time he'd physically lashed out at her during their brief marriage. She'd brought it on herself, he'd tried to convince her.

Just as Jeremy had brought Steven's wrath down upon himself by crying, or not sleeping, or some other insignificant event that had interfered with Steven's life.

Yes, Beth knew enough about men and their strength to be intimidated by this stranger. Which was why she didn't believe a word of what he'd said earlier when she'd asked him about the diner. *I didn't want to have to hurt the waitress if she tried to get in my way.*

And pigs flew. Beth was convinced he'd do anything necessary to get the job done. The waitress was just lucky Steven hadn't wanted a memorable scene.

"Scheming isn't going to help you any," the man announced in a flat voice. "I can stop anything you try, outthink any plan you devise. You'd be better off trying to get some rest."

She managed to reply with something that was neither a denial nor an acknowledgment of his assumption. "I need to stay awake, in case Jeremy needs me."

He shot her a sardonic look. "If one of his screams doesn't wake you, I'm sure I can manage something."

He had a point. Still, she had no intention of sleeping when there were plans to be made. His warnings against causing trouble were meaningless if her cooperation only meant leaving Jeremy with him in Pueblo. She had bought them a chance with her pleas to stay, and she had every intention of using it.

Besides, she wasn't supposed to be relaxed enough to sleep, not just inches from a stranger who threatened her entire world.

Resting her head against the seat, she closed her eyes and dredged up a map of southern Colorado from her memory. They'd soon be in Monte Vista, where the road south ended in choices of east or west. To get to Pueblo, the man would drive east, through Alamosa. She'd been heading the other way, to Durango. Opening her eyelids a mere slit, she snuck a look at the gas gauge. Slightly less than half a tank. That was good news, because only a fool would pass up the chance to fill the tank before heading out onto deserted roads in such a storm.

While nothing had been open in Center, Monte Vista was another story. Or Alamosa, she worried. It would be perfectly logical for the man to push those extra twenty miles before stopping. Twenty miles to the east. She couldn't afford the energy it would take to backtrack to the west. She'd have to convince him to stop in Monte Vista. Then she'd need to be prepared to do whatever it took to get away.

The doubts that assailed her were firmly squashed by the desperate knowledge that failure was unthinkable. They'd have to stop, and she'd somehow get Jeremy away. Remembering his words of warning, she knew she'd have to get it right the first time. And once they were away, she wouldn't make any more mistakes.

Taking small, even breaths to calm her jangling nerves, she stole another glance at the man beside her and wondered why it irritated her that she didn't even know his name.

"What do I call you?" she found herself asking, and was more than a little surprised when he answered.

"Blackthorne," he said, without looking at her. "If you're thinking the authorities will be interested, forget it. By the time they've dragged you through the courts for kidnapping, you won't even remember my name."

"I doubt anyone would be interested if I did, Blackthorne," she returned. "I've learned the hard way that anything I say in New Mexico is automatically discounted as a lie or an exaggeration." She stared into the flurry of snowflakes until she was nearly dizzy, certain she'd forget neither the name nor the man. Blackthorne. It fit him. Hard, cold, and merciless. Uncaring that what he was doing was essentially immoral, given the truth of her circumstances. But he didn't know the truth, she reminded herself. And she knew the truth wouldn't matter to him.

A job was a job, and he'd do it without moralizing. The only reason he'd come to her aid in the diner was to keep the other man from taking Jeremy. He'd said as much.

Blackthorne frightened her, though not in the way Steven did. Beth couldn't explain the difference, but she knew it had something to do with the way he'd kept her from picking up the knife. He'd been rough with her, but even then she'd realized he'd used only the force necessary to push her out of the way.

Her stomach clenched as she realized she didn't have the time to analyze Blackthorne's behavior. She was working through variations of how the gas-station scene would play out when Jeremy let go with an irritated cry. She knew that cry.

"What now?" Blackthorne demanded.

"I think he's wet." Jeremy's cries strengthened. On the off chance that she was wrong, Beth slipped out of her seat belt and wriggled around until she could reach the baby. Jeremy was indignant at the invasion of her hand as she groped inside his sleeper, but that couldn't be helped. A moment later she was fastening her seat belt again, her satisfaction at being right no comfort to an increasingly distressed Jeremy.

"He's still crying," Blackthorne growled.

Beth was so tired she nearly snapped at him. As it was, she barely kept herself from calling him a few names in between explaining what should have been obvious. "I told you he was wet, Blackthorne. What do you expect me to do about it?"

He looked at her with an exasperated frown. "Change him, Mrs. Corbett. *That's* what I expect you to do."

"In a moving vehicle? Forget it." She shook her head and reached back to give Jeremy a pat on a flailing limb that didn't help anything at all. "We'll have to stop, Blackthorne, and I don't see how we can without risking getting rear-ended or stuck. I guess you'll just have to put up with a little noise until we reach a gas station or something."

Jeremy's cries became screams as the tot imagined his situation was being ignored. She stole another look at her son, wincing when she saw his complexion was quickly deepening to the color of his fire-engine-red sleeper.

"I'll find a place to stop," Blackthorne muttered, both hands gripping the wheel as though he was finding the going tough. Beth tried to ignore her own frazzled nerves, content that Jeremy's screaming was putting Blackthorne off center.

Still, she wasn't prepared when he suddenly took his foot off the gas, turned the truck onto a side road, and stomped on the brake. The narrow, rutted road that curved through snow-laden sagebrush would lead to a ranch or reservoir or nowhere. She didn't imagine Blackthorne would ever find out, because he wouldn't risk leaving the highway. Not on foot, and that's exactly how she intended to leave him.

This was as far as Blackthorne was going.

Before he'd even set the emergency brake, Beth had already slipped from her seat belt. She was about to turn to release Jeremy when Blackthorne stopped her with his hand on her arm. She froze, then retreated against the passenger door, horribly aware that she was alone in the middle of nowhere with a man she knew better than to trust.

"I'll get the kid," he said, his deep voice barely audible over Jeremy's screams as he switched on the truck's interior lighting.

Her relief was written all over her face, she knew, and was grateful Blackthorne had already turned toward the back. He couldn't have seen the relief, or the fear that preceded it.

Then he touched her again, his hand on her shoulder, and she realized he must have caught her expression after all. The puzzled look on his face was all that kept her from pushing his hand away.

"This truck doesn't give us a lot of room to move around in, lady. As long as you behave, I'll leave you alone. But if you're going to faint every time I touch you, you're not going to be much good to me."

"I didn't faint," she returned, a bit wobbly but better than she'd expected. There was a lull in Jeremy's protests that she knew was only temporary.

"All but." He took his hand from her shoulder, sliding it onto the leather seat. "I don't hurt women. If I thought it would do any good, I'd remind you that you were the one who said I didn't look like the sort who'd kidnap women for kicks."

"And you're the one who brought up serial killers," she retorted. "Blame yourself if I'm a little edgy." She couldn't help but think, though, that there must be a grain of decency in Blackthorne for him to go to the effort of trying to soothe her.

"Edgy doesn't even begin to describe how you jumped," he murmured.

"Maybe I just don't like to be handled," she said without thinking. That should have been the end of it, except Blackthorne didn't reach for Jeremy. He was still staring at her, this time with the disdain she remembered from before.

"What's the matter, Bethany? Timing wrong?"

"Excuse me?" She stared at him uncomprehendingly.

"You forget your reputation precedes you, lady. Fainting at a man's touch isn't a normal response for a woman like you."

"A woman like me?"

"Tramp. Whore. Slut. Your husband went through the whole list more than once when we talked."

She understood then, and was thinking of scratching his eyes out when she realized he was only taunting her. It was understandable even, because he only repeated what he'd heard from Steven. Still, she had to tell herself a dozen times that she didn't care what he thought before she could manage a reply that wasn't both antagonistic and argumentative.

"You took me by surprise, Blackthorne. That's all." She lowered her lashes so he couldn't see the sick despair that filled her soul. "And I prefer *tramp*, if you don't mind. I've never been partial to the others, although Steven liked them all. He said they suited me." She spoke the last words in a near whisper, wondering why she found it necessary to encourage Blackthorne's already low opinion of her.

The silence between them was strangely harsh, as though the denials that filled her head had been spoken aloud and he'd reacted as she knew he would. As had all the others.

Her father would believe her, if she dared tell him. But his heart was too fragile, too weak for her to expect him to help her bear her pain. She could only be grateful he lived far enough from New Mexico that the horrible publicity wouldn't reach him.

Jeremy renewed his screams then, and Blackthorne moved, drawing her out of her thoughts and back to the present, where he was her single greatest threat. He reached back between the seats, managing to brush her arm in passing. She wished he'd stop touching her, because the warmth of his hand had penetrated her sweater, reminding her that he'd soon be freezing, perhaps dying, and it would be her fault.

His fault, she corrected as she watched Blackthorne unsnap Jeremy from his seat. She told herself she couldn't afford to be decent, not even to the man who was being so careful about how he handled Jeremy. The small child was safely balanced in hands that lifted him easily over the high-backed seats, and his cries hushed as he realized relief was at hand. Chubby arms waved his approval as Blackthorne levered him toward Beth, and it was all she could do not to laugh at the sight of his halo of stand-up hair against Blackthorne's big hands. Jeremy even gave Blackthorne a toothless smile as he was handed over to his mother.

Handing her son straight back to Blackthorne was the hardest thing she'd ever done, but Beth didn't see that she had a choice. In order to get Blackthorne out of the truck, she had to handle this just right.

"You'll have to hold him for me," she said. "On your lap so I can change him."

Blackthorne scowled and tried to give Jeremy back to her. But Beth was already on her knees and trying to pull the diaper bag through the gap in the seats. The effort made her ribs ache in protest, but she persevered.

"Why can't you put him on your own lap?" he asked, settling Jeremy in the crook of his arm as if he'd done it a million times. He grabbed a corner of the diaper bag and yanked it through the opening. The baby gave a delighted squeal, and Beth almost laughed at Blackthorne's disgust as Jeremy rubbed his drooling mouth on the man's coat.

"He's too big," she said simply. "And there's nowhere else." Unless she crawled all the way into the back —and the idea of that kind of strain on her ribs almost made her nauseous.

Blackthorne was looking from his lap to the baby and obviously trying to figure out how to get out of doing this, when a telltale aroma revealing Jeremy's true situation became all too apparent. Beth wrinkled her nose, carefully hiding her smile as she put the diaper bag on the floor and pulled a puddle sheet from it. She was about to spread it across Blackthorne's thighs when his fingers curled around her wrist, preventing her.

She jerked her wrist from his hold, knowing she could do so only because he let her. Swallowing over a fresh onset of nerves, she looked up at him in pretended exasperation. "Unless you want whatever Jeremy's done in his diaper all over your jeans, you'll need this on your lap."

Jeremy suddenly tried to grab the wheel, and would have fallen had Blackthorne not been paying attention.

Beth drew back her own hands, which had reached for her son, and she wondered how a man so obviously cold and uncaring could handle the child with such gentle care.

Blackthorne just stared at her, his dark gaze doing a thorough job of unnerving her before he finally spoke. "My legs are too close to the wheel; it won't work. You'll have to use the driver's seat."

Hope surged through her, but she forced herself to remain calm. "And where are you going to be in the meantime?"

He cocked his head toward the backseat. "Just so you don't get any ideas about driving off while I'm moving back there, I'll take the keys with me."

"And what if the truck won't start up again? It's been giving me trouble all day," she lied. She held her son close, not even minding the strain of his weight as she offered a solution she prayed he wouldn't take. "If you tilt the wheel all the way up, I might be able to manage without you having to get out."

Jeremy added his own two bits to the argument as he filled the air with an indignant howl, which was a mere warm-up to a whole series of shrill cries.

Blackthorne hesitated, giving her another of those long looks she was beginning to dread—the kind that made her worry he was at least four steps ahead of her and pulling away even farther. Even so, she kept her squirming internal and gave him a mutinous glare, standing her ground as though there weren't really quicksand beneath her.

His gaze suddenly lifted, and he surprised her by reaching back across the seats to snag Jeremy's heavy quilt. He waited until the baby was covered, then pushed open the door and got out in a flurry of wind and snow.

The door slammed shut, and it was all she could do not to reach for the automatic door lock.

Blackthorne would expect her to do something like that, she thought. By the time she hit the button, she'd be too late. All he had to do was open the back door—an easy reach for such a big man.

So she did nothing, waiting without appearing to watch as Blackthorne pulled open the back door and slid inside. He'd been quick, too, she noticed, although a part of her told her she'd have made it if she'd only tried.

The fact that she hadn't tried was a point in her favor. Taking a breath for patience, she laid Jeremy down on the seat and proceeded to change his diaper. True to form, Jeremy immediately quit screaming, knowing he had her full attention for the duration. She tugged his arms and legs from the soiled sleeper as she thought ahead to the reality of what she had to do to Blackthorne.

She had to face the fact that he might freeze to death when she drove off and left him stranded. He might die, she made herself admit, and knew she couldn't be swayed by that horrible truth. Her only priority was to keep her son safe. Blackthorne was a problem that had to be handled. End of debate.

So involved was she in her thoughts, she started when Blackthorne suddenly leaned forward to look between the seats. She shivered at his nearness, holding her breath as he reached for the map that was between her seat and the console. When he didn't immediately move back, she dared a quick look. He was staring at Jeremy, his expression hard as he scrutinized the nearly naked baby.

"What's wrong with him?" he asked, his voice low and hard.

"Nothing," she said sharply, then surprised herself

by daring to push Blackthorne aside with her shoulder. He let her—another surprise, although he stayed close, watching as she hurried through the business of dressing her son. Her hands shook under Blackthorne's scrutiny, but it wasn't until Jeremy was tucked into a clean sleeper and she'd put everything away that he spoke again.

"There are bruises all over him." Blackthorne shifted back out of the way as Beth pulled the diaper bag off the floor to return it to the back. "Who did it?" he asked, taking the bag and shoving it onto the floor near his feet.

She ignored his question, but it was too late to pretend he hadn't asked. She didn't want to talk about the bruises, didn't even want to think about them. . . . But that was practically *all* she'd thought about for the past three days—the bruises, and how easily Steven left his mark on those he claimed to love. Easily and frequently, although this was the first time for Jeremy.

And the last. She had to make sure of that.

"I asked you who did that to the child."

Her head jerked up, and she registered the anger in his eyes. All the fury that had been building inside her over the past few days exploded in a reckless admission. "*I* did it, Blackthorne. Why don't you come right out and accuse me of abusing my son? It's what you're thinking!"

His expression underwent a minuscule change that could have meant anything, then he shook his head. "Those bruises weren't made by anyone with hands as small as yours." He examined them again, dark blotches that encircled both Jeremy's torso and his upper arms. It was obvious someone had grabbed the baby with brutal force. "The finger span is too wide," Micah went on. "And the palm width." He glanced at her hands as if to confirm his words, then returned the full force of his gaze to her face. "Are you going to tell me or not?"

"Not." He wouldn't believe her, not with all the other lies Steven had fed him. And she couldn't afford to argue. The sudden rage had depleted her strength to a level where she knew she'd have to be very careful. "As long as you're working for Steven, I don't give a damn what you believe."

And she didn't, not really.

She lifted Jeremy from the seat, taking a moment to hold him close before placing him in the masculine hands that reached for him. With butterflies flapping madly in her stomach, she watched as Blackthorne secured Jeremy in his car seat and covered him with the quilt she handed back. Then a curious smile tugged at his mouth. She found herself thinking that his smile was every bit as intimidating as the rest of him as he reached across the truck and plucked his hat from the floor. By the crown, she noticed, and almost found herself smiling, too, as he set it carefully on the seat, just out of Jeremy's reach.

Lots of good it would do him there, she thought, then held her breath as he reached for the door and pushed it open. He didn't even look her way, trusting her, she imagined, because she hadn't done anything before. The second the door slammed behind him, she moved, fairly jumping toward the panel on the driver's side that housed the door-locking device. The ache in her chest sharpened as she knocked against the steering wheel, but it couldn't be helped. The button on the passenger door had been behind her, with fewer obstacles in the way, but a dead giveaway because she would have had to look around at it. Stretching across the wheel, she stabbed a finger at the button in a full panic, then hit it again in case it hadn't worked.

She could guess what he'd do if it hadn't.

It must have worked, though, because she heard a

dull thud and looked up to see Blackthorne's fist land for a second time on the window.

If he could get in, he wouldn't have pounded on the window. Her breath coming in short, uneven spurts, she dared to look beyond the fist to the man. Blackthorne drew back his hand as though getting her attention was all he'd wanted. Then he just stared at her, his expression impassive and all the more threatening because of it.

He was locked outside the truck, but she couldn't for the life of her see a gram of defeat in his expression. Instead, his steady gaze filled her with a foreboding that her strategy was doomed to failure. The storm swirled around him, bleaching his hair from brown to white, and still he stared at her. He was playing tricks with her mind, she thought frantically. *She had to get out of there before she succumbed!*

Wrenching her gaze from his, she grabbed the wheel and hung on to it as she clambered over the center console. A distant part of her noted the desperate cries that came from her lips, not Jeremy's. It was the pain in her chest, she imagined. But as her fingers closed around the gearshift she knew it was because she would be leaving Blackthorne out there to die.

It didn't matter that she intended to send someone after him once she reached Monte Vista, because they might be too late and it would all be her fault.

Nothing mattered, she told herself, except getting Jeremy away from Blackthorne. Away from Steven.

Sobbing in frustration because the seat was too far back, she leaned down and was fiddling with the lever to pull it forward when a heavy fist pounded on the window.

Unable to stop herself, she looked up . . . then wished she hadn't. Blackthorne was holding a gun in his hand. He wasn't pointing it, just showing it to her. She thought—somewhat irrelevantly, she admitted—that it was bigger than the one he'd taken from her. Much bigger, and much more threatening.

She was trembling like a leaf when she lifted her gaze to meet his. There was no anger in his expression, no frustration or impatience or any of the things she'd imagine he should feel.

There was only control, a dark, unrelenting control that frightened her beyond anything she'd ever experienced. Mesmerized, she watched as he backed up a few paces from the truck. Then she knew the meaning of real terror as he aimed the gun straight at her.

She couldn't help Jeremy if she was dead, and he knew that. Or he knew that she didn't want to die, not that night. Either way, he'd won, because even if she ducked and he missed—he didn't look like the type who missed—all he had to do was try again. And again if necessary. Or he could save himself the bother and just point the thing at Jeremy. A violent shudder nearly overwhelmed her, and she took her hand off the lever she'd been clutching, leaving the seat where it had been set to accommodate legs that were so much longer than hers. With fingers that were trembling, she reached for the auto lock and pressed it.

Blackthorne didn't budge, and she realized he was waiting for her to move. Without taking her eyes off the gun he kept trained on her, she edged out of the driver's seat and over the console. She didn't stop her slow retreat until she was back in the passenger seat with her hands folded in her lap where he could see them. Her passivity must have satisfied him, because he lowered the weapon and came back to the truck, tucking the gun out of sight somewhere before opening the door. She watched as he shrugged out of his coat and tucked it away on the floor behind the driver's seat. Then he climbed inside and pulled the door shut with a resounding slam.

He stared at her, and her face flamed under his steady regard. She was horrified to realize that she was almost as embarrassed as she was frightened—*embarrassed for not getting away with it*.

So misplaced was that emotion that she nearly missed his soft-spoken words, his first since he'd asked about the bruises. "What did you do, Beth? Forget I had your gun?"

The mild reproof in his tone made her blink, and she found herself replying without any of the nervousness in her voice that riddled the rest of her. "That wasn't mine."

He'd called her Beth, she realized, and shivered because it made what she'd tried to do that much more personal . . . more real.

Something that looked suspiciously like humor lit his eyes, leaving her feeling like she'd said something clever. "No, it wasn't yours." The humor was suddenly gone, and he reached out to cup the side of her face in his palm, which was damp from the snow. "Now then, Beth. Do I have to tell you what will happen if you pull a stunt like that again?"

"You'll put me out in Monte Vista?" she whispered, concentrating on not shrinking away from his touch and finding it not as difficult as it should be.

He shook his head, a slow movement that emphasized the grim candor of his gaze. "I'll do exactly what you were going to do to me."

She swallowed, and wished his hand weren't so warm against her face, so vital—a life force she'd actually considered ending. The reality of what could have happened frightened her almost as much as Blackthorne did. "I would have sent someone back after you."

"That's the difference between us, Beth," he said softly, then dropped his hand from her face. "I won't."

FIVE

Micah watched panic flare in Beth's eyes and knew she believed him. That was important, because the next time she tried anything, he'd probably have to shoot. Gunshots were risky because they were loud and not everyone ignored them.

He had a gnawing suspicion, though, that Beth Corbett was every bit as dangerous as any gun he'd ever handled. Beth. Somehow, it fit her.

He'd allowed her to lock him out of the truck in order to teach her a lesson. There were any number of ways to gain access to a vehicle, and several involved using a gun. He could have smashed in a window with the butt end, or shot through the glass to get at a lock. Pointing the weapon at her had been just as effective, not to mention a great deal less messy.

She needed to understand that there was nothing she could do to stop him from completing this job. He could only hope she wasn't a slow learner. Something in the way she clenched her jaw and avoided his stare, however, made him think that the first lesson hadn't made much of an impression.

Cursing under his breath, Micah put the truck into gear and got them back onto the road. "I suppose it would be a waste of time to warn you against trying any more stunts."

When she didn't reply, he continued. "This is where you tell me you won't cause any more trouble, Beth."

She was slow in answering. "I'd be lying. We both know that."

"Yeah, I guess we do." He was impressed that she'd at least learned he wasn't stupid. "Give me one good reason I shouldn't leave you in Monte Vista."

A knowing smile tugged at the corners of her mouth. "I saw the look on your face when I changed Jeremy, Blackthorne. The little aggravation you suffered back there in the snow isn't enough to make you want to take on that task for yourself."

"I've changed a few diapers in my time." Reluctantly, he admitted to himself, but baby-sitting for his nephews had involved more than playing peekaboo and watching football together.

"Pull the other one, Blackthorne." She snagged her coat up off the floor and held it tight against her chest. "If you've ever changed a diaper, it's been with a clothespin on your nose and your eyes closed."

Very nearly, he mused. He was about to ask if her ribs were giving her serious pain when she went and annoyed him again. "Besides, Blackthorne, you couldn't get rid of me even if you wanted to."

She spoke as though she had a choice. That irritated him because he knew better and had no time for people who couldn't face reality. Despite all that, he couldn't help but admire the determination that fired her rebellion, and he wondered where she'd gotten her nerve. She had more than most men he'd known—certainly way more than was good for her.

He didn't have to work at the disgusted look he gave her. "Just how do you plan to stop me?"

"I'll think of something. I have to."

"Give it up, Beth. You're out of your league here."

"I won't give up until I've tried everything."

The vehemence of her response startled him. Micah scowled into the swirling snow and methodically sorted through the options still open to her. There weren't many, but as long as she was indifferent to the risks, they were all dangerous. To her, not him, not as long as she needed to worry about the baby.

He figured it would be useless to point that out to her and resigned himself to staying alert. Someone had to keep Beth Corbett from hurting herself. Even though he knew her ex-husband wouldn't care either way, Micah would rather finish this job without her on his conscience.

The Explorer's headlights picked out a sign listing emergency radio frequencies for weather reports.

"Switch on the radio, Beth," he said, and gave her the frequency. She reached forward, her hands trembling, and he had to stomp on the flicker of compassion that provoked. Just as he was getting used to her bothersome brand of courage, she did something to remind him how truly frightened she was. Even though that fear made his control of the situation marginally easier, Micah found himself rooting for the part of her that was brave and foolish.

She finally located the station and fell back into her seat. They listened for several minutes to the twangy beat of country music before it segued into a weather report.

The storm had swerved east, closing the road to Alamosa as well as North La Veta Pass. Micah came close to beating his head against the steering wheel as the information crystallized in his tired mind. He couldn't go east, and west was out of the question in the shape he was in. The road over Wolf Creek Pass was a bitch, pure and simple. In this weather, he'd be a fool to try it. Even if he was lucky enough to make it in one piece to Durango, there was still that stretch south to Albuquerque that he'd heard was all but blocked with construction work.

He switched off the radio, then slouched deeper into the seat as the outskirts of Monte Vista filtered into view. The number of Beth Corbett's options had just doubled. He could almost hear the wheels turning in her head as she applied her own priorities to the weather report. He wondered how long he'd have before she tried something.

She didn't keep him waiting.

"If you try to get rid of me in Monte Vista, I'll go to the police."

He laughed aloud. "You wouldn't dare. They might be able to grab me on a technicality, but it wouldn't stick once I convinced them I'd always intended to get their help in returning Corbett's son across state lines." He shot her a disparaging look. "I'd be walking out the door while they were still booking you on kidnapping charges."

"But Jeremy would be in their care, not on his way to Steven," she said firmly. "At least they can stop you from taking him back."

"That's a stall, Beth, and you know it. They'd keep Jeremy only as long as it took to get a court order from New Mexico."

"There might be enough time—"

"For nothing," he interrupted, sick and tired of the what-if's and everything else that made him wish he'd looked closer at Corbett's motives before taking the job.

"Kidnapping isn't a game, lady. You'll be too busy lining up a defense for yourself to be of any use to your son."

"I won't give up, Blackthorne." Her sigh was a fragile counterpart to the howling wind. "I can't let it end this way."

"It's out of your control."

"Not yet."

He stole a look at her and saw the quiet desperation in her expression. It worried him, because he was beginning to believe her. Beth Corbett would do just about anything to stop him from taking her son, and she didn't give a damn what happened to her.

It made him curious as hell about who frightened her more than he did. The gentleness with which she treated her son almost persuaded him that protective maternal instincts were the driving force behind her actions, but he reminded himself that he knew better. Corbett had made it clear that his ex-wife had only taken the baby to extort money. Since the court hadn't awarded her a dime in alimony, she'd taken Jeremy to rectify that judgment. After reading and watching everything available about the case, Micah didn't see any reason to argue with Corbett's explanation.

Yet.

Things were beginning to add up to a different total, though, and Micah knew he would have to find the truth before letting the case come to a resolution.

If Steven Corbett or a member of his household had abused Jeremy, it was a logical explanation for his decision to handle the return of his son privately. In that event, Micah would have to rethink his role in all of this. But if someone else had inflicted the bruises, someone Bethany knew, the child would go back to his father and the ex–Mrs. Corbett would end up free and poor.

He'd be doing them both a service by keeping her

out of trouble. That included keeping her from going to the police. Micah couldn't let her do that.

Until he found out who'd left the bruises on Jeremy, he wasn't letting her go anywhere.

Beth stood between the two beds and watched as Blackthorne stomped the snow from his boots before easing Jeremy's car seat onto the small table next to the television. She'd been almost envious that Blackthorne hadn't had to transfer her son into something she could lift, but had simply unbuckled the belt that kept the car seat in place and hauled the whole thing inside without moving Jeremy.

As Blackthorne shucked his hat and gloves and turned to fiddle with the heat controls, Beth dug Jeremy out of his warm cocoon without lifting him from the seat —all the while working on her plan to escape. So far, all she'd figured out was that she'd have to get her gun back. Or get a hold of Blackthorne's. Either would do. She just needed something to point that he'd be forced to respect.

If nothing else, she'd learned that much from Blackthorne.

Just as he'd learned something from her. Since she'd locked him out of the truck, he hadn't allowed her to separate him from Jeremy again. She'd been the one to go into the motel office and register while he stayed in the truck with her son. Then Blackthorne had told her to wait inside the motel room as he unloaded the truck.

The muted click of a lock being turned interrupted her thoughts, and she looked up see Blackthorne sliding home the chain on the door. Without sparing her a glance, he sat down on the end of a bed and pulled her overnight bag between his feet. By the time she found the words to protest, he'd unzipped it and was digging through the contents.

"What do you think you're doing?" She grabbed at his shoulder, but he shrugged her off without even looking up. She let her hand fall back, the rational part of her mind understanding why he felt the search was necessary. The other part of her, though, hated him for invading her privacy so casually.

She watched impotently as he sorted through the various silks, laces, and flannel that composed the part of her wardrobe that was normally private. The ugly red slash across his knuckles contrasted vividly with the soft colors of her lingerie, and the knowledge that the wound was insignificant in his eyes sent a shiver down her spine. It hadn't even been enough to slow him down.

He didn't look up when he finished with her bag. Leaving the zipper open, he shoved it to one side, then reached for her purse and gave it the same treatment. He pulled out the bottle of pain pills the doctor had given her, read the label, and pocketed it. The diaper bag was next, and he was just as thorough with it as he'd been with the rest. He was stuffing Jeremy's diapers and such back into the quilted bag when resentment found her voice.

"Find anything your size?" she asked with a flippancy that reminded her of the person she used to be. Blood rushed to her face as Blackthorne slowly turned to look at her. He lifted a single eyebrow as though he wasn't sure he'd heard her right.

"You said what?" he asked quietly, coming to his feet.

She gulped and wondered what had possessed her. "Nothing, Blackthorne. You must be hearing things."

His gaze raked her from head to toe, then returned

to rest on her face. "You're pretty sassy for someone in your position."

"I didn't know it was against the rules," she shot back, knowing she was reacting without thinking but too exhausted to care.

"I'd think you would try not to annoy me," he murmured. "For Jeremy's sake, if not your own."

"If locking you out of the truck didn't get me thrown out into the snow, a few words aren't going to make much of an impact," she said, then bit her tongue. Reminding him of what had transpired out in the snow probably wasn't her best move.

He just shook his head and rubbed his eyes before leveling his tired gaze on her once again. "Do us both a favor and keep the smart remarks to yourself. You won't sleep very well with a gag in your mouth."

Prudence kept her from following up on that threat. Shivering because she was so completely out of her depth with this man, she just stood there and glared at him.

When his gaze narrowed on her, she knew he hadn't missed her body's reaction. "What's the matter? Nervous about sleeping in the same room with me?"

In truth, she couldn't deny it. She did try, shaking her head and ignoring his snort of disbelief. Of course it unnerved her to be with him like this—alone, if she didn't count Jeremy, and she didn't count him because the little darling didn't have a clue as to what transpired in the world of adults. She found her gaze torn between Blackthorne and the two beds that dominated the small, sterile-looking room. The beds implied an intimacy that teased her senses, and that surprised her. She'd been focused on survival for so long, nothing else had made much of an impression. Yet it was there, the awareness that Blackthorne wasn't only her enemy. He was also a man.

A very dangerous man. She'd do well to remember that.

"I want to know about the aspirin with codeine tablets I found in your purse," he said, his tone demanding her attention. "What are they for?"

"Pain." She didn't see the point in giving him any details.

He looked as though he were going to pursue it, but obviously changed his mind, because all he said was to tell him when she wanted some.

"You're afraid I'll take an overdose?" she asked.

He shook his head. "You're not the type to take the coward's way out."

His assumption surprised her. "So why did you take them?"

"Because I don't want to have to worry about you grinding them up and putting them in my coffee." He raked long fingers through his hair, then briefly massaged the back of his neck. "Just for the record, it wouldn't work."

"Why not?" she asked, for future reference.

"Aspirin tastes bitter when it's ground up. I'd know after the first sip." He opened his coat, then hooked his thumbs in the front belt loops of his jeans. "You couldn't give me enough to do more than slow me down. Just to be safe, though, I'll hang on to them."

"Suit yourself." She unzipped her own coat. "Speaking of coffee, I'm hungry."

"There won't be anything open for a couple hours. We'll get some sleep first, then eat."

Sleep. She couldn't afford even a nap. "I'm not tired," she said, then kicked herself because he'd likely wait for her to fall asleep first. She'd have to fake it, she realized, and tried to remember if one took deep or shallow breaths when asleep.

"The hell you're not tired. You're so exhausted, you can hardly stand up." He bent down to reach into his own duffel and took out a small leather case that she guessed held his shaving gear and other necessities. Her pills went inside it, then he pulled her gun from his coat pocket and discarded the heavy sheepskin coat on a nearby chair. Tucking the shaving kit under one arm and keeping the small gun palmed, he reached for Jeremy's car seat. He lifted the seat with the sleeping boy and headed toward the alcove. "We'll be just a minute. Don't go away." He shut the door behind him before she had a chance to tell him she didn't think he'd need a gun where he was going.

It occurred to Beth that her sense of humor was definitely misplaced, both in time and circumstance. She put it down to exhaustion, which also probably explained why she was still standing there when Blackthorne emerged several minutes later. The hair around his face curled damply, and he'd taken off his sweater. A chambray shirt stretched taut across his broad shoulders, tapering down over a solid torso to where it tucked into his jeans. Not an ounce of fat on him, she guessed, and decided it must be an optical illusion that made him appear larger even though he wore fewer clothes than before.

When he turned back from setting Jeremy on the table, her gun was still in one hand. But her gaze zeroed in on his other hand, where a trickle of blood oozed from the knife wound. The sickening feeling of guilt assailed her anew, and a whimper of distress escaped her lips before she could stop it.

"What?" he demanded, then followed her gaze to his hand. Shrugging, he wiped his knuckles on his jeans. "I cleaned it while I was in the bathroom. It won't bleed for long. If the sight of blood bothers you, don't look."

Her chin jerked up at the annoyance in his tone. "I feel guilty enough about that without you accusing me of being squeamish."

Micah looked at her in surprise. "Why should you feel guilty? The only reason I tackled Sutton was to get him out of my way."

"But I didn't know that then," she said with a catch in her voice. "I didn't know that, nor did I know how badly you were hurt. It doesn't sit well with my conscience that I ran while you were fighting my battle."

"I told you to," he said, his gaze narrowed on her face. "If I'd been smarter, I wouldn't have let him cut me at all."

The look on her face hinted that she wasn't going to let herself off the hook so easily. Dropping her gaze, she reached for the baby's bag and dug into a side pocket. A yellow tube was in her fingers when she turned back to him.

"This will help stop any infection," she said, holding the tube out to him.

He didn't take it, and told himself it was because he was curious to see how deeply the guilt went in her . . . even though he knew better. He wanted her to touch him.

He held out his hand, palm down. "You put it on, Beth."

She jerked her own hand back, and the disbelief he saw in her expression was quickly replaced by fear. "No."

"Why not?" he asked softly. "I thought you said you felt guilty."

"I do. I just—"

"Just won't, because the guilt isn't enough to make

you want to touch me," he said, lowering his arm to his side. "Never mind, Beth. Like I told you before, it was my own fault that I got cut." He was disappointed, and he was angry with himself for feeling that way.

The next thing he knew, she'd twisted off the cap and was squeezing the gooey antibiotic ointment onto her finger. When he didn't immediately offer his hand, she gave an impatient huff and grabbed his arm with a firmness that surprised him.

She turned his hand until she could see the red, swollen line across his knuckles and began to spread the antibiotic with a touch that was so gentle, he hardly felt it. Micah stood absolutely still, his gaze fixed on her bowed head, her silky hair brushing his arm. The tenderness with which she did the job bothered him, because he hadn't expected it.

The warmth of the fingers that skimmed across his hand bothered him too—deep inside where his masculine response to her touch didn't care that she was a whore. His arousal was quick and sure, and it was all he could do to keep himself from sliding his arms around her and bringing her hard against his hips.

He would have done just that if she hadn't looked up then with her mouth set in a brave, determined line. Micah realized how difficult she found it to touch him—difficult, he assumed, because he frightened her.

She'd done it, though. He had to give her credit for having guts. Shuttering his gaze, he concentrated on taking slow, even breaths so that his heart would quit slamming against his chest.

She'd done it. Beth took a deep breath and tore her gaze from Blackthorne's before he could see the surprise in her eyes. It wasn't so much that she'd dared touch this big man who scared the daylights out of her. No, that wasn't what made her fingers tremble even now, when she was no longer touching him.

She trembled because he was aroused and she hadn't had to look in his eyes to confirm it. She'd known by the way his breathing had gone low and harsh as she touched him, and by how her own nerves had jumped in response to the almost electric heat of his skin.

He wanted her, and the only thing she could think about was how the knowledge didn't disgust her. The relief that washed through her as he turned away without speaking was tinged by curiosity.

Why had he turned away? Even more important, why didn't his arousal frighten her? She didn't have an answer to either question.

She watched as he moved away from her, her eyes darting to the gun that was neatly holstered at the small of his back. The revolver was big enough that it would make a substantial dent in his back if he tried to sleep with it there. That reassured her, because she knew he'd have to put it somewhere else while he slept. Probably within reach, she granted, but that was better than having to figure out how to take it away from him.

He picked up his coat and dropped her gun back into a side pocket. Beth deliberately turned away and shrugged out of her own coat before kicking off her shoes. She was pretending to look for something in her overnight bag as Blackthorne carefully laid his coat on the floor beneath the windows.

Relief surged through her as she realized he was actually making it easy for her. All she had to do was wait until he fell asleep, crawl around the bed, and sneak her gun from his coat pocket. Once she had that, it would simply be a matter of pointing it in the right direction. Stealth and darkness would be on her side. He wouldn't have a chance even to reach for his own gun.

The plan was coming together.

"You've got five minutes before lights out, lady," he said. "Get a move on."

She moved, practically leaping into the bathroom, where she shut the door and leaned back against it before her knees gave way. She stood immobile, staring into the cracked mirror above the tiny sink and wondering how long Blackthorne would take to go to sleep.

The woman who looked back at her was only vaguely familiar. A worn-out version of the person she used to be, Beth decided, glancing from the bruised circles beneath her eyes to where her hair lay limp and tangled on her shoulders. She didn't look alert enough to outlast Blackthorne, she worried, then shut her eyes against the image because she couldn't afford to doubt.

A sharp knock at the bathroom door sent her flying across the linoleum. Without any more warning, the door opened and Blackthorne tossed her overnight case inside.

"Come in," she said, but the sarcasm was wasted. He'd already pulled the door closed. She was thinking Blackthorne would benefit from a lecture on manners and appropriate behavior when a grumbling reminder from the other side sent her into a flurry of action. Minutes later she opened the door to find Blackthorne with his fist in the air, looking as though he was ready to pound the door down. His gaze tracked over her, noting the jeans and sweater she hadn't changed out of.

"What took you so long?" Bracing his hands on either side of the doorframe, he looked over her shoulder in case she'd done something devious he needed to know about.

"Women take longer," she snapped, then ducked under his arm before he could stop her.

"You're not going to change for bed?" he asked from

behind her as she tugged the spread to the bottom of one of the beds, then pulled back the blanket and sheet. Taking both pillows, she arranged them along one side of the bed, ignoring Blackthorne as she did so because it seemed the prudent thing to do.

He wasn't an easy man to ignore, though, and it took every bit of her concentration to do so.

She stepped past where he leaned against the wall and went to Jeremy. She was unfastening the straps that held him secure in the car seat when Blackthorne asked, "Why didn't you change, Beth?"

"You didn't." She was suddenly terrified that he knew exactly what she was planning. Getting into a nightgown would hamper her escape plan, not only making it hard to crawl on the floor but necessitating a change of clothes before leaving.

Her fingers shook, and she had to take a breath and count to five before she was able to resume what she was doing. Gently, so as not to wake Jeremy, she lifted him in her arms and carried him to the bed, where she put him beside the pillow bolster. She'd sleep on his other side. *Not* sleep, she reminded herself. Either way, Jeremy would be safe from tumbling off the bed. Had Blackthorne not been such a suspicious man, she'd have left the baby in his car seat where he'd be easier to handle when the time came. If only Blackthorne hadn't brought the car seat inside, she silently raged. Lifting the heavy chair with Jeremy in it was going to severely strain her ribs. She'd just have to cope. Maybe she'd lock Blackthorne in the bathroom.

"But I don't wear anything to bed. You do." He edged her bag out of the way with his foot and walked past her.

She stared at him in disbelief. "You're not going to take your clothes off, are you?"

He turned to look at her, a curious glint in his eyes. "You act as though that would be a novelty. Are you trying to tell me you've never seen a naked man before?"

"My husband, of course," she said without thinking as embarrassment heated her face. "You're a stranger. I've never—"

"That's not what I heard, Beth. According to your ex, strangers were your specialty." He cocked his head to the side. "What's the matter, Beth? Afraid that flannel thing you brought won't turn me on?"

She felt the blood drain from her face, and had to look away because she couldn't bear seeing the disgust she knew would be in his eyes.

"Don't worry about it, honey," he said, his voice a low drawl that dragged across nerves already strung tight. "You can pretend you're as innocent as a peach if that's what excites you. Just don't bother me tonight. I doubt I could get up enough enthusiasm to make it interesting."

She blinked once, then again as understanding dawned. Blackthorne not only assumed her morals were as low as Steven had advertised, he fully expected her to put that rampant sexuality to work on him. And here she'd been nervous about being alone with him, nervous because twice he'd let her sense his arousal. Just as twice he'd banked that desire. Obviously, he was determined to steer clear of a sexual encounter.

She would have laughed if it weren't so absurd.

She would have cried if she'd had the energy.

Beth looked as though she'd been kicked. Micah pushed aside the irritating traces of guilt that nudged at his conscience and glowered at her. "Don't go near the door or my coat. Do you understand?"

She nodded, but he didn't miss the way her gaze measured the distance from his coat to her bed. He stopped himself from saying anything. Knowing her plan was better than spending the night wondering what she'd do.

He just didn't like what he'd have to do when she made her move. She probably wouldn't like it much either.

After a long sigh that did nothing to relieve his frustration, he sat down, pulled off his boots, and threw them into the corner. He got up to double-check the locks as Beth lay down beside her son, her back to Micah and her head cushioned on her arm because the pillows were down beside Jeremy. She was pulling up the covers when Micah grabbed the extra pillow from his bed and tossed it at her.

She didn't look his way, just took the pillow and dragged it under her head. He decided that suited him because he was holding on to his control by a thread and one more look into those big brown eyes might have been one look too many.

Simply being in the same room as Beth Corbett was an experience that was both erotic and disappointing: erotic because he couldn't help but respond to her, disappointing because he knew he was only one of many.

Or would be, if she'd bothered to try to seduce him. She hadn't, though, and that confused him. Sex was a weapon she wasn't supposed to be shy about using. Now Micah knew he looked a bit rough and ragged after three days on the road, but he'd looked that way a lot over the years and it hadn't done anything to discourage women's attention. Ego aside, he knew Beth Corbett wasn't put off by the stubble on his chin.

She wasn't thinking about sex at all—except how to stay out of his way so that it wasn't an issue. Instead, she was focused on making an attempt to get her gun back.

Lots of good that would do her.

Micah unclipped the holstered revolver from his belt and shoved it under his pillow. Then he stretched out on the bed, flicked the bedspread across his legs, and reached out a long arm to switch off the light.

He could only hope that she'd get it over with soon so that they could both get some sleep. While he waited he sketched a mental picture of the Beth Corbett he was coming to know, and wondered why the pieces didn't fit into the outline of who she was supposed to be.

Crouched on the floor, Beth glanced up at the end of the bed and hoped it was just her imagination that made the space between Blackthorne and his coat seem too narrow to negotiate. Swallowing her fears only succeeded in making her tongue stick to the roof of her mouth, so she edged around the corner, careful not to brush against his boots as she crawled along the rough carpet.

She'd waited forever, it seemed. But she'd had to be sure, and Blackthorne breathed so quietly, she hadn't been able to tell if he was asleep or not. Only when she'd caught herself dropping off had she known she couldn't afford to wait any longer.

The coat was within grabbing distance when something hard closed around her ankle and yanked her flat onto her belly. She'd hardly managed a breath when rough hands flipped her onto her back and dragged her away from her goal, back toward the end of the bed. Beth fought, not because she thought she could win but because she was so damned frustrated with losing. She fought him with everything she had left, swinging her arms in the hope that a fist would connect. Her bare toes rammed into something solid that could have been anywhere between shin and thigh, but she knew by his lack of reaction that the blow had hurt her more than him.

He wasn't solid all over, though, she realized, and was trying to get the leverage for a solid knee punch when he straddled her hips and captured her wrists on the floor beside her head.

She would have told him to be careful of her bruised ribs, but she suspected she'd surrendered all rights to fair play. The Blackthorne that glared back at her in the muted light of early dawn didn't look like he was in the mood to listen.

"How did you know, Blackthorne?" she demanded, trying to get a decent breath and blaming his thighs, which were like a vise against her sides.

"I'm not stupid." He pulled her arms high over her head and captured her wrists in a single grip. The stark vulnerability of that position made her renew her struggles. He countered by pinning her to the floor with his forearm against her shoulders. "Give it up, Beth. The only person getting hurt here is you."

The fight went out of her in a long, aching sigh. He eased his hold on her without relaxing his control, and she looked up to find his face just inches above hers. His eyes were dark and unreadable, and she could feel the warmth of his breath against her face. A distant part of her mind toyed with the knowledge that he could have hurt her, but hadn't. She could almost bet he wouldn't either, not unless she gave him no choice.

That knowledge gave her the courage to speak. "If you're so smart, why did you let me get as far as I did?"

"Because you wouldn't learn anything that way."

"Tackling me was supposed to teach me a lesson?"

He shifted his body against her, lessening the pressure of his legs without moving his arm from her shoulders or releasing her hands. His voice was a notch lower when he responded. "Yeah, Beth, this was supposed to teach you something. I just wish I'd thought ahead a little. I should have known we'd end up like this."

The arm that lay across her shoulders shifted, and she was astonished to feel the light caress of his fingers against her throat. She wet her lips, thinking she should say something, but not knowing what that should be. Too much was happening for her to sort it all out.

The back of his hand brushed her cheek. She jerked away from the unexpected warmth, but didn't get far because his fingers closed around her jaw and brought her back. "Be still, Beth. This will just take a second."

That was her only warning. The next moment his head lowered and he was kissing her, his lips dry and firm against hers.

Beth supposed she ought to be outraged and frightened. Instead, she could only think about how much gentleness he put into what he was doing. Kissing, she reminded herself firmly. Not something they should be doing at all.

She twisted her head aside, and the pressure of his mouth disappeared. His fingers tightened on her jaw again, forcing her to look up at him when she'd just as soon not. He was staring down at her, his head cocked as though there was something going on that he didn't understand.

She knew what he felt like. "Finished, Blackthorne?" she asked with as much annoyance as she could put into her voice.

"For now."

She sucked in a hard, painful breath and was about to tell him he'd better keep his hands—and kisses!—to himself when he reached across her to grab his duffel bag and delve inside. "The lesson is that you can't get through, past, or around me. The sooner you accept that, the easier things will be."

"You make it sound like we're going to be together for longer than a few more hours."

"If the weather doesn't clear, we're stuck with each other for another day. I don't want to have to go through this again."

Beth could have told him he was dreaming, but was distracted when his hand emerged from the duffel bag with lengths of cloth in its grasp. "What's that?" she demanded, though she was pretty sure she didn't want to know.

"Only silk. Nothing to worry about," he said, and proceeded to tie her hands together. "It won't mark your skin, not if you don't struggle." He finished with her hands, then moved off her hips as she brought her wrists into view and glared at the silk that bound them together.

"I can't take care of Jeremy like this."

"You'll manage." He half knelt beside her and slid his hands under her back. "On the count of two, breathe out."

"What?"

"Breathe out, and your ribs will hurt less when I pull you up."

"What do you know about my ribs?"

"One, two—"

She blew out a long breath, trying not to take it back in all at once as he brought them both to their feet and held her so that she wouldn't fall. She wobbled a bit, then backed up as he crowded her toward the bed she'd shared with Jeremy. Before she knew what was happening, she was on her back and Blackthorne was using another of those silken ties to bind her ankles together. When he was done, she wriggled away from where he sat at the edge of the bed.

He tugged the covers out from under her legs and

pulled them over her. "Maybe next time you get it into your head to take me on, you'll remember there are choices."

She strained at the bonds and scowled at him when the silk didn't give so much as a millimeter. "What choices?"

"You can either follow the rules, or be a little uncomfortable. It's up to you."

A glimmer of hope lifted her spirits. "What if I tell you I'm ready to follow the rules?"

"Maybe tomorrow, Beth. For now, just get some sleep."

She sagged back against the mattress. "How am I supposed to sleep with you in the next bed?"

"Easier than with me in the same bed," he retorted with a touch of humor.

"I guess that's something," she muttered, then couldn't stop herself from asking the one question she knew better than to ask. "Why did you kiss me, Blackthorne?"

"I wanted to."

"But why? Half the time you look at me as though you can't stand to breathe the same air as I do." She knew he wanted her. She just didn't understand why. Swallowing back emotions that were ragged and beaten, she held her breath and waited for his answer.

"You're making this too complicated." He shifted on the bed, the movement pulling the covers tight across her shoulders. "I can't be the first man who's wanted to kiss you. A woman like you—"

She didn't want to hear him say it. "And you know all about women like me, don't you? Steven told the whole world what a tramp he'd married. Kind of makes you wonder about his taste in women, doesn't it?" she finished bitterly.

"I was referring to how you look, not how you act. You're a beautiful woman, Beth. I'm surprised you aren't more at ease with that."

His calm response startled her into silence. There was a long pause before he continued. "Don't let what I think or believe keep you awake. It's not worth it." His weight lifted from the bed and her eyes tracked him as he went to lie down on the other.

The first tears she'd allowed since the nightmare had begun streamed down her cheeks as Beth lulled herself to sleep to the silent litany of, "I'm sorry, Jeremy. I tried."

SIX

Micah slipped the last knot from the silk bonds, then tucked the cloth into his pocket as Beth stirred. Impossibly long lashes fluttered over her soft brown eyes as she slowly came awake. He didn't move away, entranced by the innocence of her gestures as she rubbed her eyes with her fists, then stretched with the lazy grace of a cat. It was all he could do not to flinch when the sleep left her eyes and her expression took on that hunted look he was beginning to hate.

"What do you want now?" she asked.

"It's the baby."

Her eyes flew wide open as she bolted upright. "What's wrong with Jeremy?" she demanded, her gaze flying to where Jeremy lay beside her, trying to stuff his foot into his mouth.

"He's awake." Micah turned and walked to a chair as Beth reached for her son. If possible, the baby's hair was fuzzier than before. It occurred to Micah that the white-blond color was at odds with his mother's rich brown hair. If it hadn't been for the way Jeremy's nose tilted at exactly the same angle as his mother's—not to mention the eyes that were a precise replica of the sherry-brown hue in hers—Micah would have wondered if she'd kidnapped the right kid.

Jeremy allowed his mother to hug and kiss him for several moments before grabbing a handful of hair and yanking.

She looked over at him. "Nice job, Blackthorne. Does Steven pay you extra to scare me half to death?"

A smile kicked at the corner of his mouth, but he gritted his teeth to control it. "If I hadn't wakened you, Jeremy and I would both starve."

Still holding the baby, Beth got up from the bed and grabbed the diaper bag. She put both Jeremy and the bag back on the bed and proceeded to get the child ready for the day. Jeremy cooperated with good humor, making the task as difficult as possible by turning onto his tummy every time Beth took her hands off him. Micah studied the marks on the baby's skin, and knew by the way Beth's fingers fluttered across the bruises that she couldn't ignore them either. But she let none of her distress communicate itself to the baby, replying in real words and sentences to Jeremy's unintelligible babble as though she knew exactly what he was saying.

By the time she'd managed to dress him in a royal-blue outfit that snapped all the way to his toes, Micah thought she looked a bit winded. She pushed her hair out of her face with one hand and rubbed the small of her back with the other. "Are we going out for breakfast, Blackthorne?"

"If you think you can behave." When she nodded, he said, "It will be better if you call me Micah."

She glared at him. "Better for whom? I was just getting used to Blackthorne."

"Better for you, naturally. I wouldn't want anyone to

hear you call me Blackthorne. It wouldn't fit with the happy family scene I have in mind."

"Why on earth should we pretend to be a family, much less a happy one?"

He stretched out his legs and crossed them at the ankle. "Because we'll blend in easier that way. It would be inconvenient if someone remembered us enough to answer any questions that might be asked."

She leaned across the bed to arrange the pillows around Jeremy so he wouldn't roll off the edge. "Why would that matter, unless you think that man from the diner might come after us?" She looked at him, her body suddenly tense. "Is that it?"

"That's doubtful. I arranged for him to be detained. I just don't like taking chances."

She shrugged, and Micah thought he detected a slight relaxing of her muscles. "As far as I'm concerned, it's a moot point. If he was here instead of you, I might not have had to spend the night tied up."

Her naïveté appalled him. "The man you're talking about is Jack Sutton. He's mean enough to tie you up, rape you, then walk out the door with your son and leave you on the floor naked for the maid to find."

"You're exaggerating." Still, she straightened from what she was doing to stare at him.

He shook his head and noticed how her body went all tense again. "Sutton's not the type to give up and go home without anything to show for his time."

She licked her lips nervously. "You want to get paid too badly to let anyone interfere, Blackthorne."

"It's Micah, Beth. And you're right, but I'd rather get paid without any more hassle from Sutton."

Jeremy chose to interrupt with a scream of displeasure. Beth gave him his pacifier, but he spat it out and yelled louder, beating his tiny limbs against the mattress.

"He's hungry," she said.

"So go and get changed," Micah shouted over the din. When she glanced at Jeremy's beet-red face and hesitated, he grabbed her overnight bag and handed it to her. "I'll watch the kid. Just wash your face and comb your hair so we can get out of here."

She ran her fingers through her hair. "Shower?"

"Later, after breakfast."

She stole another look at the screaming baby, then retreated to the bathroom.

Micah decided to give her five minutes. He grabbed Jeremy's yellow snowsuit from the top of the bureau and proceeded to stuff the bawling kid into it. Gently. He was patient because he knew it wasn't Jeremy's fault that he was hungry and uncooperative. Fitting the hood of the snowsuit over the cap of electrified hair gave him more problems than the wiggling limbs, but he just kept pushing the fine strands behind the elastic until it had all disappeared.

By some miracle, Jeremy took the added clothing as a good sign. He quit screaming and started to gnaw on the mittens of his snowsuit. Keeping one hand on the squirming baby, Micah grabbed the bedside phone and put in a call to his office. When Beth came out of the bathroom in clean jeans and a light blue sweater, he'd finished the call and was standing over Jeremy as he pulled on the thick sheepskin coat. He tossed Beth her coat, then picked up Jeremy and buckled him into his car seat. The baby promptly started screaming again. Micah assumed it was because he couldn't grab his foot any longer.

"He's screaming because he's hungry," Micah said when Beth looked at him with a question in her eyes. "I didn't hurt him."

"I know that," she said, and pulled on her coat. "I

just didn't realize you knew one end of a baby from the other."

He couldn't stop himself. "One smells, the other yells."

She grinned. "Humor, Blackthorne? I wouldn't have thought you were capable of it."

"There's a lot you don't know about me, Beth," he said, and led the way out into the storm before she realized she'd said much the same thing about him just hours earlier.

Beth looked across the table at Blackthorne and thought the shave and shower he'd had made him look almost civilized. Not entirely, though. There was something about him that was as untamed as the storm that lashed at the restaurant's windows.

At odds with that assessment was his kiss the night before. It had been filled with a gentleness that had slipped past her panic, coaxing a response she might have revealed if the kiss had lasted a moment longer.

She couldn't afford to let him know she didn't loathe his touch. Things were tense enough between them without the added friction of sexual awareness. As long as he didn't know, he'd leave her alone.

In the meantime, here they were, acting out a family scene when it was the furthest thing from the truth, eating breakfast as the rest of the customers in the restaurant ordered lunch. Nothing was normal or ordinary, yet sitting across the Formica table from Blackthorne felt almost natural.

Micah, not Blackthorne. There was something about the matter-of-fact way he'd told her about Sutton that made her believe he wasn't making up stories about the man just to frighten her. More than that, she hadn't forgotten how the blond man had thrown her to the floor with less expression than most people had when watching the numbers light up on an elevator. A shiver inched its way up her spine, and she knew that when she ditched Blackthorne, she'd be losing whatever protection she had from the man named Sutton.

It amazed her to realize she trusted Blackthorne to be who he said he was.

Micah, not Blackthorne. It would take a while to get used to.

She reached for the coffeepot the waitress had left at the end of the table, but Blackthorne anticipated her move and was there before her. "Afraid I'll spill something hot in your lap?" she asked as he poured her coffee before setting the pot down out of her reach.

He just resumed eating, digging his fork into the mountain of hash browns, eggs, and ham he'd ordered despite her snide remark about cholesterol being more of a risk than she was. She took a cautious sip of the steaming coffee, then tore off a crust of toast and handed it to Jeremy. Finished with his own breakfast of oatmeal, peaches, and juice, the baby latched onto the treat as though he hadn't eaten in a week.

"What are we doing here if you're so worried about your pal Sutton catching up?" she asked.

"I'm not that worried," he said. "Besides, we have to eat."

Beth thought that was all he was going to say, but he surprised her by adding, "One of my people got to the diner before Sutton regained consciousness. They're probably halfway to Denver by now."

"How do you know that?" she asked, nerves on full alert again. It took all her acting skills to keep those nerves from showing in front of Blackthorne. She didn't know why she bothered except that she couldn't help but believe that the less he understood her, the better chance she had of getting away.

Blackthorne declined to answer her question, and she knew by the look on his face that no amount of badgering would get one. He pushed his empty plate aside, then leaned back in the booth and took a long swallow of coffee. "For a baby that only sleeps in spurts, last night must have been a record breaker."

She squirmed under his gaze. "Seven hours is rather a lot for Jeremy."

He didn't look as though he believed her. She didn't blame him. She concentrated on finishing her oatmeal, thinking that perhaps he knew more about babies than she'd given him credit for.

A lot more, as his next observation proved.

"I haven't seen you breast-feed him. Why not?"

The red flush of her reaction was impossible to stifle. "None of your business, Blackthorne." It occurred to her that she'd said that a lot since meeting him.

"Micah," he said softly.

"Micah," she said, stressing both syllables so he'd know how difficult she found it. "Maybe I need a little more privacy than you've allowed."

He shook his head. "I don't think you breast-feed him at all. Your breasts would be swollen and hurting by now if you did."

She could feel the flush spread and deepen. "Your concern astonishes me."

"The more I know, the fewer mistakes I make." He helped himself to some more coffee, then wrapped his fingers around the cup and stared at her over the rim. "If I'm wrong, you need to tell me."

She pretended she hadn't heard him. Cutting a piece of melon with the edge of her fork, she tried to think of something—anything!—to change the subject.

He didn't give her the chance. "Do you or don't you?" The demand in his tone was implacable.

She gritted her teeth and rethought her assumption that Blackthorne was even partially civilized. Civilized implied manners; Blackthorne didn't have any. "I can't, so I don't," she said evenly. "Happy?"

He shrugged. "You just seem the type that would."

"You've known a lot of tramps who breast-feed their babies?" She could have sworn he looked uncomfortable that she'd thrown his description of her back at him, but the feeling was gone before it yielded any real satisfaction.

Jeremy gurgled and threw the mushed-up crust onto the table. Beth reprimanded his manners with a wag of her finger and handed him another bit of toast to test his gums on.

"My sister has two kids," Blackthorne said. "She breast-fed them both." He put his cup down and crossed his forearms on the table. "The care you take of Jeremy reminds me of her."

"You sister is a tramp?"

The flash of anger in his eyes was unmistakable, but she didn't back down because she wasn't tired anymore, at least not as tired as she'd been several hours earlier when he'd wrestled her to the floor and kissed her. She'd like to see him get away with that trick now that she had the energy to fight back. As she held his gaze she stifled a dozen or so embellishments on the tramp theme, waiting for Blackthorne to reply to her first. It was sure to be something scathing, at least equal to Steven's level of crude insults. She waited, feeling stronger than before . . . feeling like a fight.

He ruined it all with something that bore a startling resemblance to an apology. "Repeating your husband's words represents a lack of discrimination on my part."

She looked at him suspiciously, forgetting all about the substance of what they were discussing in favor of the finer points. "You're talking like a lawyer, Micah." She hardly noticed how easily his name came out that time.

He surprised her by grinning. "You don't call me names, and I won't call you any either."

"Are you a lawyer?" she asked, thinking this was another strike against him. It was a conspiracy of lawyers that had landed her in the fix she was in now.

"Not anymore."

She was relieved. "I've been assuming you're a private detective of some sort. Knowing Steven, though, you could as easily be an ex-con who owes him a favor."

"Sutton is the ex-con. I'm just a simple private investigator."

"I've got the feeling you're not a simple anything," she said, and wished she didn't believe the things he'd told her about Sutton. The blond man already gave her the creeps, and the idea of meeting up with him again terrified her. "Are you going to tell me why you're not a lawyer anymore?"

Blackthorne surprised her by answering her question. "I like things simple. The legal system tends to bog itself down with too many technicalities."

"Which makes this job perfect for you," she said smartly. "You snatch Jeremy and take him back to his father without bothering about little nuisances like jurisdiction and proper channels. Nice work if you can get away with it."

"Getting caught wouldn't net me more than a slap on the wrist, and I will have saved everyone a great deal of trouble." He shook his head. "You took a child who doesn't belong to you. No matter where you study law, they call that kidnapping. Law enforcement types get all hyper over cases like this. I doubt you'd be sitting here having a nice meal if they'd caught up with you."

"You sound like I should be grateful Steven hired you instead of calling the cops."

He hesitated before replying, then looked across the table to capture her gaze. "Things could be worse, Beth. If you're lucky, you'll only have me to deal with. Not Sutton, and not the person who hurt Jeremy."

Blackthorne sounded almost human, she thought. So human that she was suddenly tempted to tell him the truth. She thought about it for a moment, then decided to go ahead and give it a shot. Not having tried everything would haunt her someday if she failed to keep Jeremy away from his father.

"What if I told you it was Steven who abused Jeremy? Would you be so dead set on taking him back to Albuquerque?"

He regarded her with eyes so expressionless, she felt she was looking at a total stranger and not someone with whom she'd discussed breast-feeding, tramps, and lawyers. "If that's true, why didn't you go straight to the cops? They'd have to do something. The bruises are pretty powerful evidence."

"You're assuming they'd believe it was Steven and not one of the thousand lovers I've had just this year alone." She shook her head in disgust. "Sorry, Blackthorne, I can't depend on the police believing me. I got burned once already trusting someone I shouldn't have. I won't risk that happening again."

"Who was that?"

"My lawyer." She gave a humorless laugh, remembering the naïveté with which she'd allowed him to guide her through the divorce proceedings. "I suppose I should have realized Steven could afford to pay him more than I could." When Blackthorne didn't comment, she continued. "I can't assume the proper authorities will do the proper thing. That includes the police."

"You sound as though every cop and lawyer in Albuquerque is crooked."

"Probably not. But I'm not stupid enough to think I'd know the difference just by looking at them. Not anymore, anyway." She almost smiled. "Besides, not even an honest cop will do me much good. If the police believed me—which, for the record, I doubt because no one's listened to a word I've said since the settlement hearing—but if they did, they'd likely put Jeremy into foster care."

"At least he'd be safe," Blackthorne said.

"And I'd never see him again." She finished her coffee in one long gulp, then looked up to find he was once again studying her. "It's my reputation, you see. Even if Steven loses custody, they'd make damn sure I didn't get Jeremy. Steven might lose, but he's got enough contacts to make sure I don't win."

She put her cup down and hid her shaking hands under the table. "That's not the way this is going to end, Blackthorne. Jeremy is my son. I won't let anyone take him away from me."

Jeremy vocalized a demand for attention, and Beth was digging in the side of his car seat for his pacifier when Blackthorne spoke again.

"I've got a couple problems with that story."

She looked up, not speaking. She'd said enough. Too much, even, because he'd found a way not to believe her and it had all been a waste of energy, of time.

Of hope.

She should have known better than to waste her efforts on a man who wouldn't get paid for doing the decent thing.

"You only ran as far as Colorado," he said, "and then

spent three days hovering around Denver before heading south . . . back toward Albuquerque." Blackthorne
drummed his fingers on the table and shook his head.
"Any sensible person would be a thousand miles from
here, or try to be. Can you explain that?"

She could, but knew better than to share that detail
with Blackthorne. He'd know then where she was
headed. By the look on his face, he was the last person
she could trust with that information.

"Maybe I ran out of money," she said, thinking that
wasn't far off the truth. She'd only dared use her credit
cards in the very beginning, knowing they'd leave a trail.
Her cash was limited to what was left of the thousand
dollars she'd drawn from the bank before leaving Albuquerque.

"Right story, wrong chapter," he shot back, then
continued when he saw the puzzled look on her face.
"Corbett said you had enough to get by on, but not
enough to outbid him. No, Beth, you stayed close so that
when Corbett gave in, you'd be able to make the exchange without losing any time."

"Excuse me?" She couldn't believe what he was sug-
gesting.

Blackthorne signaled the waitress for the bill.
"You're using Jeremy to extort money from Corbett. He
said as much when I met with him."

She just stared at him, speechless. Steven had found a
way to discredit her by simply building on the lies he'd
already told. "That's not true," she whispered.

"So what are you doing so close to Albuquerque?"

She couldn't tell him, and knew that her silence confirmed his theory. She took a deep breath and tried another tack. "What about the bruises, Blackthorne?
Somehow, I got the impression they made a difference."

"To you, maybe." He slid out of the booth and

shrugged into his jacket. "*If* he did it—and you haven't convinced me of anything yet—you should be able to get something from him for keeping quiet."

Beth couldn't respond because there simply weren't words in her vocabulary to adequately express her rage. In any case, Blackthorne didn't give her the opportunity. Instead, he told her to get Jeremy into his snowsuit, then went and paid the check.

It wasn't until they were back in the motel room that Beth admitted to feeling disappointment as well as fury. Disappointment in a man she'd naively assumed was decent because he'd handled her son with such gentle care.

She'd almost begun to trust.

She was unwrapping Jeremy from his cocoon when Blackthorne spoke.

"I have to call Corbett and tell him. What should I say you're going to do?"

She nearly gagged on the bile that rose from her stomach. "Do about what?" she managed to say.

"About the bruises. You've said you'll go to the police, which means you think you've got some sort of proof. I assume Corbett will want the opportunity to talk about that."

Her hands were shaking so badly, she didn't dare try to pick up Jeremy from his car seat. She left him where he was, secure for the moment within the safety straps, pulled Pookey out of her pocket to give him, then directed her full attention to the man who watched her more closely than she liked.

"You're a bastard, Blackthorne. Don't you realize he'll kill him?"

"Save the dramatics for your ex-husband, lady. They might get you a few dollars more if you play your cards right, but I'm not buying anything."

"I have nothing to say to Steven," she said evenly. "If

you want to call him, I can't stop you. But if you try to take Jeremy back to Albuquerque, I'll go to the police and scream as long and as loud as it takes for someone to listen to me."

"You won't have another chance like this, Beth. I doubt Corbett will be as generous once he gets Jeremy back. The proof will disappear with the bruises, and you won't have anything left to bargain with except your word against his."

She glared at him, her hands fisted at her sides. "Go to hell, Blackthorne, and take your revolting suggestions with you."

She wasn't after money, Micah realized. At least, not if she had to use the kid to get it. He was convinced, and not the least bit ashamed of the brutal tactics he'd used. They'd gotten him the answers he needed. Beth's disgust at his suggestion was so unequivocal, he knew it was time to reevaluate everything Corbett had told him. Everything, not just the parts about Jeremy.

He couldn't take the child back to his father until he knew the truth—and he wouldn't take Jeremy back if the charges proved true. Nor could he let Beth disappear with Jeremy. She might not be the one who'd abused the child, but the kind of life she'd reputedly led didn't encourage him to believe she'd give Jeremy the home he deserved.

His instincts told him she was no more a tramp than his sister was. His common sense, however, told him he was too attracted to her to be able to rely on those instincts.

One way or the other, he intended to get to the truth.

He stared at the silent, fuming woman standing in front of him and cursed under his breath. He wished he'd never gotten involved in this case, yet knew he couldn't just walk away because he *was* involved.

It was a mess any way he looked at it.

A very expensive mess, he thought wryly, knowing his accountant would be grumbling about it for months. He hoped he was right about Beth Corbett, because she was about to cost him a great deal of money.

"If it's not money you're after, why are you hanging around?" he asked. "I might not have found you if you'd gone to Canada or someplace like that."

She shook her head. "I've been stupid enough lately without telling you my plans. It's clear you'll just tell Steven."

He didn't enlighten her—didn't plan to until he got a couple of steps ahead of her. And that would take a few calls and a day or two at the very least.

"Go take a shower, Beth. We'll still be here when you finish."

"How do I know that?"

He couldn't blame her for doubting. Digging into his pocket, he pulled out the keys to the truck and handed them to her. "Take these with you into the shower."

Her fingers curled around the keys, and she looked at him as though he'd done something she hadn't expected. Then she turned and started to fuss with the straps that held Jeremy. Micah reached out to pull her away from the baby, but stopped himself in time. He knew better than to touch her.

She didn't want him to.

He wanted to too badly.

"I'll take care of Jeremy, Beth. You need to take care of yourself right now."

Her reply was reassuringly sassy. "You're saying I need a shower, Blackthorne?"

"It's Micah," he returned. "Remember that, or you'll have to settle for takeout for dinner. I may have Sutton under control, but all it will take is a leak from Corbett's end and the cops will be all over the place. If they get wind of this, he won't be able to stop them."

A new kind of distress clouded her expression. "And they'd know where to look because you told Steven."

Micah nodded. "Corbett doesn't appear to have much control over who knows what. I assume that's how Sutton found us—through him."

She let that remark go in favor of another question. "How did *you* find me? I didn't tell anyone I was even going to Denver."

"Someone in Albuquerque told your husband they'd seen you at the airport. When he found out where you were headed, he came to Denver and hired me." He couldn't see any harm in telling her where she'd made her mistakes. "You used your credit card at the motel out in Aurora."

She shook her head. "I paid cash."

"But they still took an imprint of your credit card. Any respectable place does that to have a trail in case you destroy the room."

"But I watched the clerk tear it up the next morning," she murmured.

"It was too late, Beth." He walked over to the car seat and unsnapped the safety harness. She was still standing there when he lifted the gurgling baby into the crook of his arm. "My office sent out a notice on your card, faxing it or delivering it to the local hotels and motels. The day manager called us ten minutes before you checked out. He also told us what you were driving."

"You followed me from the hotel?"

Micah shook his head, and went to sit in the chair as

Jeremy grabbed his collar and tried to hoist himself higher. "Tracked, not followed. I didn't get there soon enough." He settled Jeremy on his knee before the little bugger pulled his ear off. "It was pretty smart of you not to tell the friend whose truck you borrowed where you'd be."

He glimpsed the panic in her eyes, though she tried hard to hide it.

"You saw Karen?" she asked.

Micah wondered what Karen Robertson knew that she hadn't told him. He'd have to send someone over to talk to her again. "I saw her, but she wasn't any help. She said you were keeping in touch, not the other way around."

"Even knowing what you did, I'd still think it would be impossible to find someone in a city like Denver."

"With enough people and resources, it can be done." He gave her a wry smile. "I have to admit you kept us jumping, though, with all that backtracking. It took us a while to figure out you were trying to stay lost without leaving the area. If I hadn't caught up with you when I did, I'd have lost you when you suddenly headed south."

"You were behind me all the way from Denver?"

He nodded. "It just took me a while to get you stopped."

She shook her head and was half-turned to go into the bathroom when she looked back at him. "Why would Steven hire Sutton if he was already paying you?"

"Sutton probably negotiated a better deal. I don't work as cheap as he does, and I don't get paid until the job is done."

"Why would Sutton target this job?"

Micah shrugged, knowing it was his fault for not taking care of the man months ago. "He's been nipping at my heels for a while, trying to slip in at the end of a job and grab the paycheck without doing the work."

"But why?"

"He was on the wrong end of a blackmail deal I busted up a while back. While I was busy digging past him to who paid him to front the scheme, he managed to plea-bargain the charges down from extortion to petty theft. He got off, but not without losing his investigator's license." He looked grim as he said it. "He blames me for that."

"Which explains why he's not a fan," she murmured, then looked confused again. "But how did he know to call Steven?"

Micah shrugged. "With all the flyers we distributed, he would have figured out pretty easily who I was working for." He thrust his fingers through his hair in frustration, then leaned over to pluck Pookey from the floor where Jeremy had tossed him. "I assume Sutton called your husband."

"So Sutton has been on your tail for three days and you didn't notice?" The disbelief in her voice was unmistakable.

Micah almost laughed at her faith in his abilities. "He was never on my tail, not in the way you think. But I knew he was sniffing around, because someone who works for me was keeping an eye on him. I don't like not knowing where he is when I'm working."

"But how did he know to come to the diner?"

"Because I made a mistake." Micah rose and put Jeremy down among the pillows on the bed, then returned to stand in front of her. "I called Corbett from my car when I picked up your trail south of Denver. I told him exactly where we were and what you were driving. It doesn't take a genius to figure out where you might have been headed. There are only so many options."

"Steven told Sutton," she murmured. "Obviously, Steven doesn't realize you're every bit as ruthless as Sutton, or he wouldn't have bothered with the second string. He should have known better."

As he watched her walk away from him Micah told himself he didn't care what Beth Corbett thought of him . . . and knew that for the lie it was.

SEVEN

Beth dawdled over her shower, secure in the knowledge Jeremy would be there when she got out. Blackthorne, too, but she couldn't do anything about that.

Not so long as they were stuck in the room together. She'd learned that much last night. But there *was* something she could do once they got back on the road again. It was risky, but anything was better than letting him take Jeremy back to Albuquerque.

In the meantime, all she had to do was keep her emotions in check and stay out of Blackthorne's way. She didn't think that would be difficult, not with a baby to entertain. Reassuring herself first that Jeremy was still there by listening at the door until she heard his baby gibberish, Beth switched on the hair dryer and began the laborious process of drying her thick waves of hair. By the time she'd given her hair a final brush and pampered her face with a layer of moisturizer, she was beginning to feel human again. A bit of powder on her nose and clear gloss for her lips completed the transformation.

She came out of the bathroom just as Blackthorne was putting down the phone. "The pass on the other side of Alamosa is still closed," he said, "but the storm bypassed entirely the road to Durango. If we leave now, we can get over Wolf Creek Pass while it's still light and be in Durango for dinner. Depending on the roads, the trip shouldn't take more than three hours, give or take. I'll figure out tomorrow whether to drive or fly the rest of the way to Albuquerque."

Beth looked down at her watch so that he wouldn't see the excitement in her eyes. Durango! She'd be half-way to a solution to this mess once she got there and met the man she'd been sent to see. Karen Robertson's brother would help her, and she could trust him—even though he was an attorney. Karen had been a friend too long to be swayed by the publicity over Beth's divorce, and Beth had faith that Karen's brother, Alan, would listen and believe. And help.

The only reason she wasn't already in Durango was that Alan had been on a ski trip in Canada the previous week. Beth had decided to spend the interval in Denver, thinking it was easier to disappear in a city than a remote town like Durango. Her only comfort in being wrong was that once she got rid of Blackthorne, he wouldn't have any reason to connect her with Durango. By the time he found her—and she didn't doubt for a second that he would—she'd be ready to go back to Albuquerque on her own terms. With Alan's assistance, Steven would not only relinquish any claim to Jeremy, he'd make damn sure the court awarded her custody.

Beth knew that if she failed to reach Alan, his sister would make sure he caught up with her in Albuquerque. That wasn't good enough, though, because if Steven got his hands on Jeremy again, he'd only have to threaten to hurt him and Beth wouldn't be able to do a thing.

She knew better than to believe that Steven wouldn't follow through. The fading bruises on Jeremy's body were proof of that. She had to get to Durango, and she had to lose Blackthorne somewhere along the way.

"Beth?"

A shiver of anxiety crawled up her spine as she looked at Blackthorne. Things were going to happen now, and she couldn't allow herself to be swayed by the dangers involved. "What?"

He held out his hand. "The keys. I'll get the truck warmed up while you get your things together."

She dug them out of her pocket and handed them over. "Are you sure it's safe to go out in this? The storm doesn't sound like it's letting up any." A little reluctance wouldn't hurt, she decided, then wondered if she shouldn't really be insisting they stay a bit longer when a hard gust rattled the windows.

"The highway patrol says we break out of this about ten miles west."

"But it will be dark soon."

"It's just three now. We've got two hours easy before night falls." He pushed his arms into his coat and buttoned it. "Don't worry, Beth. I'll be driving, and it's a whole lot easier to get through stuff like this in daylight than it is at night. We'll be on the other side of the storm before you know it."

"Why are you all of a sudden in a rush to leave?"

He hesitated, then looked at her, his expression blank. "There was an accident on the highway just south of Denver—a semi jackknifed across the road. Sutton got away while my man was helping the emergency crews. I have to assume he'll head this way."

"And when you called Steven, you told him where we were," she added in a voice that sounded weak even to her ears. "He'll tell Sutton—"

"I didn't call Corbett."

Her chin jerked up, and she stared at him in disbelief. "You said you were going to."

He shook his head. "There's nothing I can tell him that I want Sutton to know. On the chance Sutton wasn't the only second-stringer he'd hired, I didn't call." He sighed and shifted his feet with an impatience she couldn't miss. "But even though I didn't call, Sutton will know there's only one road open to us. We can wait here for him, or take our chances on the road. I'd rather hit the road. The greater distance between us, the better I'll feel."

"You're not going to let anything stop you from getting paid, are you?" she asked.

He shook his head, and she had her answer. "Just get ready, Beth. I want to leave now."

"We'll need to pick up a few things for Jeremy before we leave town. Is there time?" She riffled through the supplies in the diaper bag, making a mental list of the necessities, then doubling it. Once she'd ditched Blackthorne, she didn't want to have to stop again.

"There's a store in the next block," he said. "We'll drive over and you can get what you need." He snagged his hat from the table and put it on, tugging the brim low on his forehead. From a pocket he pulled out a pair of gloves that he put on before going out the door.

When Beth looked out the window a few minutes later, Blackthorne had just finished scraping snow and ice off the truck windows. By the time he came back inside, she had everything ready, Jeremy included.

He pulled some money from a pocket and held it out to her. "Go check us out of here, Beth. I'll get everything loaded."

When she hesitated, he sighed his disgust. "If I was going to run off and leave you, I'd just tie you up and lock the door. Or I could have left earlier, when you were in the shower. The lock on the bathroom door is worthless, and you should know by now that if I'd wanted the keys, I would have come in and taken them. Jeremy and I could have been five miles away before you'd even gotten your clothes on."

It had never occurred to her that she'd been so vulnerable in the shower. The realization brought a flush to her face that made Blackthorne just shake his head at her. "You don't think things through, Beth. That's going to get you into trouble someday."

"Like I'm not in trouble now?" she retorted, then clicked her tongue in frustration. "So why are you taking me with you, Blackthorne? I've watched you with Jeremy. You don't need me." Not to change diapers, anyway. In packing the diaper bag, she'd realized Blackthorne must have changed Jeremy while she was in the shower.

His gaze narrowed on her face. "Maybe I don't like the idea of Sutton catching up to you. He'll be spitting mad as it is, and finding you without Jeremy will infuriate him. You don't want to be around him when he gets like that." He reached for her hand and put the money into her palm, then closed her fingers over it. "I don't want to have to explain myself every time I tell you to do something, so get over to the office before I decide you're not worth the trouble."

She brushed past him and ran through the drifts, not caring that her shoes filled with snow. By the time she finished and got back to the truck, they were waiting for her. He drove the block to the store, then sat with Jeremy in the truck as she made her purchases.

Blackthorne got out to help her put everything away in the back end, and when he grumbled about why she'd bought so much, she grumbled back with the list of what-if's she'd composed while shopping. He lasted through "what if the storm changes course and we get stranded," and "what if the truck breaks down and we get stranded." She was getting started on "what if Jeremy gets diarrhea while we're stranded" when he told her to get into the truck.

They stopped for gas, and he made her get out with him as he filled up the tank. When he sent her inside to pay, she obliged willingly because she wanted to buy them something to drink. Coffee, to be specific.

She got Blackthorne the traveler's special, about half a quart. When she returned to the car and handed it to him, he looked at her suspiciously.

She frowned at him, pretending exasperation. "I thought we needed something to drink. I didn't put anything in it."

"Then you won't mind trading with me," he said, making the switch before she had a chance to argue.

"Mine has cream in it," she muttered. "Yours doesn't."

"I don't mind." He took a swallow through the hole in the plastic top, then put the huge container into the cup holder near the stickshift.

Beth groused audibly for as long as it took Blackthorne to get the truck into gear and on the road. When she subsided, it was all she could do to suppress a smirk of victory.

To know him was to outwit him, she mused, giving herself a mental pat on the back for buying a traveler's special for herself.

Now all she had to do was wait.

Breaching the storm into the crisp, clear afternoon beyond it was nothing less than dramatic. One minute they were trudging along at thirty miles an hour in almost zero visibility, and the next they were completely out of it. Not that the day they drove into was anything close to one of Mother Nature's spectacular numbers, but the overcast skies and mildly gusting winds were a far sight more welcoming than what they'd left behind.

Beth felt the tension of the last half hour drain out of her. She'd been horribly worried that Blackthorne hadn't been right about the storm, and that she'd have to drive over Wolf Creek Pass by herself in weather that made even a straight, flat road treacherous.

Now all she had to worry about was how long it would take before the coffee hit Blackthorne. Or, more specifically, Blackthorne's bladder. She hoped it was soon because she wanted to get rid of him this side of the pass. What he'd said about Sutton now applied to him: The more distance between them, the greater the cushion of safety she'd have.

Jeremy started chattering about something obviously important, and she turned in her seat to entertain him for a few minutes. Her ribs were definitely on the mend, she realized, thankful she was able to move so easily. Just having Blackthorne heft Jeremy around for her had probably done more than anything to speed the healing.

She slid back into the seat and nearly missed the sign advertising a rest stop five miles ahead. "Can we stop there?" she asked, waving a hand at her nearly empty coffee container. Blackthorne had finished his just five minutes earlier. "I shouldn't have bought the large size."

"If it's open," he said. "They sometimes close these things down in the winter."

She prayed they hadn't. Five miles later her prayers were answered as Blackthorne pulled off the road and parked in front of a squat brick building with a door at either end. The rest stop was deserted save for a pickup at the far end that looked decrepit enough to have been abandoned. There was certainly no one around, and the rare vehicle they'd passed would lessen Blackthorne's chances for a ride.

Beth looked up to find him staring at her. "What?"

"I thought you needed to go."

She nodded, but Jeremy hollered and she let herself be distracted. Making a great show of it, she turned in her seat and pretended to check if he was wet. She knew he wasn't. It had been his "I dropped something" howl, but Blackthorne wouldn't know that.

"He's wet," she said. "Why don't you go ahead while I change him."

He shook his head. "Jeremy goes with me."

Beth feigned impatience. "Oh, for heaven's sake!" She dug into the diaper bag for a clean diaper, then looked back at Blackthorne as though she'd had enough of his orders. "Take the keys, Blackthorne. You didn't seem to have had any trouble starting the Explorer today. It's probably one of those chauvinist vehicles that wouldn't dare go dead with you in charge."

She looked away from the gaze that seemed to pierce her soul, so she only knew her plan was working when Blackthorne reached past her to lift Jeremy from his seat. He handed her son into the crook of her arm, then grabbed his coat, switched off the engine, and got out.

Beth waited until he'd disappeared inside the building, then moved faster than she'd moved in her entire life. After practically throwing Jeremy back into his seat and fastening the belt, she opened the ashtray, pulled out the spare set of keys, and dove into the driver's seat. It took precious seconds to lever the seat forward, and her hands were trembling so badly, she could hardly fit the key into the ignition, but she managed finally. Knowing Blackthorne would hear her no matter how quiet she tried to be, she started the engine and backed out of the parking slot with a squeal of rubber on concrete. Then she put the truck into first and hit the gas.

Micah stood in the shadows of the door, shaking his head. He waited until she'd gotten the truck straightened out, then lifted his right arm and shot out the Ford's left rear tire.

EIGHT

Beth was still trembling when Micah got back into the truck after changing the tire. There was a heavy feeling in his stomach because he hated seeing her like that. It couldn't be helped, though. It was probably the first time she'd been shot at. He doubted any comfort offered by the shooter would make much of an impression on her.

Nor did he think telling her he wasn't taking Jeremy to Corbett would help, not when he followed it with the news that he'd made arrangements for Jeremy to be taken away from her the next morning and stashed somewhere secure until he got this mess figured out.

Micah put the truck into gear and got them back on the road, weary beyond measure of the struggle between doing what he wanted and what he had to do to keep her and the boy safe.

He wanted to take her into his arms and tell her everything would be all right. He wanted her to trust him. He wanted to believe in her innocence.

He wanted to shake her until her teeth rattled for the

risk she'd taken in trying to drive off without him. *Hadn't she listened to a word he'd said about Sutton?*

Beth would be a sitting duck for Sutton if Micah let her get away. The only way he knew to keep her safe meant keeping her frightened of him. Until he knew more about her, he didn't dare allow her inside his defenses.

The well-being of a small baby depended on him. For that very important reason, Micah knew he couldn't afford to let his emotions sway him. Facts were essential. He was depending on his efficient staff to provide them.

He'd soon learn if Beth Corbett was the lying slut portrayed by her husband, or the innocent victim of a smear campaign. Then he could decide what he was going to do about her.

"Why did you do it?" she asked, surprising him. He was beginning to think she was never going to calm down enough to speak. "You knew about the keys all along, didn't you."

He nodded. "I figured there had to be another set. I just hadn't gotten around to looking for them."

"So why shoot? You could have killed us." She ended on a whisper, clearly still shattered from the experience.

"There was never a risk, not at the speed you were going," he said reasonably. "And I did it for the same reason I let you lock me out of the truck and let you try to get your gun back."

"More lessons, Blackthorne?" she said bitterly. "Seems like changing a tire is a lot of trouble to go to when you could have prevented the whole scene by looking for the keys."

"Finding the keys might have taken longer than changing the tire," he returned, gearing down as the climb into the mountains steepened. "And you wouldn't have learned anything."

"What I can't figure out is why you've bothered teaching me," she said, her voice stronger now. He noticed the trembling had nearly ceased too.

"I had a choice of keeping you in line or taking care of Jeremy by myself. Teaching you the rules looked easier than changing diapers."

"Your patience astounds me," she said, and glanced over her shoulder to check on the sleeping baby. "You haven't even raised your voice. Given everything you *have* done, I find that rather remarkable."

"It's not your fault you don't know your limitations in situations like this." He punched the button for four-wheel-drive as the roads became more consistently snowpacked in the rising altitude. "There's something else you should know, Beth."

"What's that?"

"You've had your last lesson." He glanced aside to find her looking at him. "With Sutton behind us, I don't have time to worry about what you'll do next. If you so much as look as though you're going to pull another stunt, I'll leave you for Sutton to play with."

Her breathing was labored as she tried to assimilate his threat. "You're assuming I'm going to try again?"

"I'm assuming you won't," he said firmly. "You might be a slow learner, Beth, but I doubt you're stupid. If you want to stay with Jeremy, you've got to know you've just had your last free mistake."

Traffic thickened around the ski area near the top of the pass, but otherwise the drive was smooth and uninterrupted. Beth was so lost in thought that the spectacular view on the other side of the pass totally eluded her. Thankful that Jeremy slept on, she got her nerves under control and conceived a plan that wouldn't antagonize Blackthorne any further. She didn't dare attempt another getaway—partly because of what he'd threatened, but mostly because she'd already used up all her good ideas. If they hadn't worked, the plans she'd rejected weren't likely to either.

Blackthorne had said he would either drive or fly with Jeremy out of Durango. She had to assume he intended to leave her behind as the trip wouldn't take more than a few hours either way. She also had to assume they'd spend the coming night in another motel.

She would just have to find a way to call Alan Robertson and get him to meet her. Maybe *he* could convince Blackthorne that taking Jeremy back to Steven was tantamount to murder. She doubted that, but having Alan handy would greatly improve her chances of getting a fair hearing from the authorities. He could also get to work on the one witness she'd been too afraid to talk with for fear Steven would learn about it and do his thing with intimidation, money, threats, or all three.

Yes, having Alan on her side would be a relief. She'd have to wait to call until they were in the motel room, because she'd likely only get one chance, and it wouldn't do any good to waste it before she knew where to tell Alan to come.

She couldn't imagine why she thought Blackthorne would allow her to meet with Alan, but something inside her kept pointing out that despite everything, Blackthorne was actually a reasonable man. He could have been harsh and cruel; instead, he'd been firm. While she deplored the methods he'd employed to abort her plans, she was realistic enough to know he was being as gentle as he knew how.

He could have hurt her, and he'd gone out of his way not to. She knew that, without understanding why.

She also knew that he affected a part of her that she'd thought dead and buried. In the quiet moments—when

he wasn't shooting at or otherwise terrorizing her—
she'd found herself looking at him and wondering what
it was about him that drew her interest. When she
should have been consumed by the task of freeing her
son, she was thinking about Blackthorne and what it
would be like to know him well.

He'd kissed her with a gentleness and restraint she
couldn't deny . . . just as she couldn't deny she had not
hated the taste of his lips on hers.

And now, each time she looked at him, she was reminded of how his body had fitted above hers, touching
without lying fully against her. Even in her panic, she'd
sensed a curious comfort in his warmth, his nearness.
Comfort, and a delicate pricking at her sensual responses
that had made her want him to come closer so that she
might know him better.

In the close confines of the Explorer, she became
attuned to his patience and his restraint. She would have
preferred his anger, because at least then she'd have an
emotion that was closer to the turbulent feelings that
surged through her.

She relived his kiss, knowing—and regretting—it
might be the only one they ever shared.

It was madness, she knew. But wasn't everything anymore?

Her intuition told her Blackthorne was a good man.
His determination to take Jeremy back to Steven contra-
dicted that.

He hadn't hurt her or Jeremy, which was more than
she could say for the man she'd married. And though
Blackthorne frightened her, he'd done so deliberately.
She understood now that her fear was as much of a tool
as his gun. He'd frightened her to keep her in line, and
when it hadn't worked, he'd done it again. And again.

She'd gotten so used to being afraid of him that she'd

been incapable of separating her fears for Jeremy from her fear of Blackthorne. But things were changing. Her fear of Blackthorne had evolved into a level of trust: She knew he wouldn't hurt either of them, not by his own hand. She also knew he would do exactly as he'd said if she tried to thwart him again.

Regardless of her feelings toward Blackthorne as a man, they were on opposite sides of a war, a war she had to win.

Jeremy was counting on her, or would be if he had any idea of the evil that threatened him.

She could only give thanks that he didn't.

They stopped in Pagosa Springs to pick up a new tire. Micah was uneasy about the amount of time it would take for the tire to be mounted on the wheel and balanced, but knew it was a necessary risk. Driving without a spare was irresponsible in normal circumstances, sheer idiocy in the situation they were in.

He took the precaution of making sure the truck was parked out of sight inside the garage and promised the mechanic a bonus for a quick job. Then he took Beth and Jeremy to wait in a café across the street. He called the office from a pay phone near the entrance, where he could keep an eye on the pair as well as watch the street. The news was good and bad: The good part was that the man he'd sent for had landed at the Pagosa Springs airport a few hours earlier and would now be told where to meet them. Micah felt a hell of a lot better knowing Andrews would be there if needed. The bad news was that Sutton had also headed out by air.

Micah went back to the booth where Beth was feeding Jeremy and slid into the seat facing her. There was a calmness about her that suggested she'd come to terms with his ultimatum. He hated having to ruin whatever peace she'd found.

"Sutton chartered a plane out of Denver instead of driving."

The hand holding the spoon froze in midair. "I thought he'd come by car." Jeremy prompted her with a demanding yowl, and she resumed feeding him, her movements mechanical and jittery.

"He must have realized the storm would push us in this direction. Instead of wasting time following, he's apparently decided to intercept us." Micah checked his watch, then reached for the coffee she'd ordered for him and took a large swallow. "He'll either land here at Pagosa Springs, or go to Durango and backtrack."

"When?" she asked, the tremor in her voice telling him that at least she was treating Sutton as a real threat. "How long before we have to start looking over our shoulders?"

"Anytime now. We'll get back on the road as soon as they finish the tire." He put a note of confidence into what he was saying, anything to get rid of that hunted look in her eyes. "Once we're in Durango, we'll be able to get lost among the ski crowd."

She shook her head. "I'm scared, Blackthorne. If he catches up with us—"

Micah reached across the table and took her free hand in his, forgetting all about how he was supposed to treat her and doing what he wanted for a change. He was surprised when she didn't pull away. "I told you that I won't let him interfere, Beth."

She stared down at their joined hands, then looked up at him with an expression that was a confusion of despair and frustration. "Why should that make me feel better when I know you're still determined to take Jeremy back?"

He couldn't tell her, not all of it. But with Sutton more of a threat than he'd anticipated, he needed to be able to count on her if things got complicated. "Trust me, Beth. I won't let anything happen to Jeremy."

There was a brightness in her eyes that she stopped to blink back before replying. "What are you telling me, Blackthorne?"

"Not any more than that. Just take my word for it that your son will not be the one who loses in this mess."

She didn't say if she believed him, but he hadn't expected her to. "What about me, Blackthorne?"

"I haven't decided yet." He clenched his jaw against the urge to say more. "And call me Micah."

"Why?" She glanced around the empty café. "There's no one around to hear what I call you."

"You need to get into the habit so that when it does matter, you won't screw up." Besides, he wanted her to.

"I don't think it makes any difference." There was a wry smile on her lips as she looked him up and down. "You're not exactly the type people forget easily. All he has to do is describe you, and bingo, you're tagged."

"Sutton doesn't know for certain that I'm with you. It could just as easily be any one of my men." He liked knowing she found him memorable.

"But you told Steven—"

"I told Corbett I'd have one of the others take over once I'd got you stopped. That was before I caught up with you at the diner." He shrugged. "Sutton won't have any reason to think I've changed my plan."

Her eyebrows drew together in puzzlement. "So why didn't you have someone else take over?"

"The man backing me up got stuck with Sutton. I got you." He didn't add that he wouldn't have turned her over in any case, not once she'd pulled a gun on him.

He'd been intrigued by her audacity, her will to survive.

He rubbed his thumb across the velvety skin on the inside of her wrist and wondered how someone so delicate could be so incredibly strong-willed. "Every time you say Blackthorne, it sounds like a challenge. People are going to remember that. All I want is for us not to stand out any more than we have to."

"What makes you think I'd say Micah any differently."

"You just did." The smug satisfaction he felt was doubled when he saw the beginnings of a blush color her cheeks. He let her hand slip from his grasp and pondered how bereft that made him feel as he watched her scrape the last of the cereal from the bowl and trick Jeremy into swallowing it in one go.

She'd hardly put the spoon down when he stood up and helped her throw all the bits and pieces into the diaper bag. He knew she sensed his urgency as he hustled them all out the door, pausing first in the shadows to check the street. Not much was moving in the early-afternoon gloom of the resort town that boomed in the summer months, but he felt better once they'd crossed over to the tire store and retrieved the Explorer.

He didn't tell Beth about the dark green Chevy Blazer that pulled out behind them, because Andrews was there only to protect Jeremy.

From his own mother, if necessary.

Ten miles east of Durango, Beth asked Micah to pull over at a gas station so she could use the rest room. When he told her she'd have to wait until they reached Durango, she crossed her legs and told him waiting wasn't an option.

Micah checked the rearview mirror once again, then

reluctantly pulled off. The station was adjacent to a gift shop featuring Indian blankets, grass baskets, and clay pots. At least a dozen cars were scattered around the pumps and in front of the shop. He followed signs for rest rooms, driving around to the back of the station where vehicles belonging to employees had been parked. Beth got out and dashed for the ladies', pulling on her coat en route. When the door wouldn't open, she ran around the corner to the front of the building before Micah could stop her. He didn't start breathing again until she returned with a key that dangled from a foot-long board.

He kept the truck running, turning once to hand Pookey to Jeremy when the bear came flying over his seat to land in his lap. The rest of the time he drummed his fingers on the wheel and kept a close watch on the building and anything that moved toward the front. There wasn't any activity where they were parked, leading Micah to believe there must be another rest room inside the station or the gift shop. Still, he wished she'd hurry because he didn't like the chance they were taking. He hadn't been able to tell if they were being followed for the last half hour or so, because the road was narrow and rarely allowed for anyone to pass. Traffic was substantial, most of it skiers obviously headed for Purgatory, the ski area north of Durango.

Even knowing that Andrews was parked around front didn't make him feel any less edgy. Andrews's orders were to protect the baby, *only* the baby. When Beth finally came out of the rest room, Micah opened the window and said, "Leave the key in the door and get in the truck."

She shook her head, then scared the life out of him by walking toward the front of the station.

He came halfway out of the truck and yelled. "Beth! Get back here!"

She shouted over her shoulder. "I had to leave a deposit. Guess they lose a lot of keys." She skipped around the corner and disappeared from sight.

Micah almost went after her, but knew better than to leave Jeremy. Instead, he got out of the truck and slammed the door, cursing freely in the frigid dusk as he waited for her to reappear.

When she did, she wasn't alone. Sutton was with her, his arm tight around her shoulders and his hand pushed up against her side, a wool scarf hiding the gun Micah knew would be there. He glanced beyond the couple and saw that Andrews was maintaining a discreet surveillance from the shadows near the building.

He'd interfere only if Micah signaled him. Micah hoped he wouldn't have to because that would mean things were getting out of control.

At the moment they were merely a bit tense. He thought about reaching for his gun, but knew Sutton wouldn't hesitate to use Beth as a shield. So he forced himself to stay perfectly still, waiting for Sutton to make a mistake.

The trouble was, Sutton rarely made any.

As they neared the truck Micah forced himself to ignore Beth and focus on the blond, gray-eyed man who held her. He couldn't afford to look at her, fearing Sutton might see something in his expression that would make him realize she was more than a job to Micah.

They stopped when they were about six feet from the truck.

"I always said that decent streak of yours would be your downfall," Sutton said, then pulled the scarf from his gun and aimed it straight at Micah. He kept Beth hard against him and indicated by waving his gun that

Micah should move away from the truck. With Sutton's back to the front of the station, Micah knew no one would notice anything amiss.

Which was just as well, because things were difficult enough without a bunch of nosy bystanders to worry about.

He edged away from the truck, then cleared his throat and spoke before Beth could say something that would complicate things. If she opened her mouth and called him Micah, he'd lose the only edge they had of resolving things the easy way. "I knew better than to let the witch out of my sight." He shook his head in self-reproach, hoping his words would give her the clue to keep quiet.

"Blackthorne—" she began, and he cut her off by growling a harsh "Shut up."

She did, and he glared at Sutton. "What's wrong, Sutton? Can't find another line of work?"

Sutton's mouth stretched into something that was half grimace, half smile. "Too much money in this one, Blackthorne. Now why don't you turn around and pull out that gun you carry in your belt before I get nervous."

He hadn't expected Sutton to let him keep it, so he did as he was told, using his fingertips and putting the revolver on the ground before he turned back around.

"Kick it over here, Blackthorne. I'd hate for my spot of good luck to be marred by an incident."

Micah complied, then watched carefully. If Sutton bent down to pick the gun up, he'd have to take the chance and jump him. But Sutton didn't pick it up, just left it where it lay at his feet.

Micah saw the look in Sutton's eyes and knew the other man would be extremely careful as long as Micah was anywhere nearby.

"You're going to need a lot more than luck to see you through this one," Micah said. "Speaking of which, how did you do it? Sit at a crossroad and wait until we drove by?"

"There are certain advantages in knowing which road you had to use. The only risk was gambling that you wouldn't hang around in Monte Vista waiting for the road east to open." He tut-tutted at Micah's frustrated expression.

"I still think you're biting off more than you can chew, Sutton. Between the woman's nonstop whining and the kid screaming in my ear, I've been lucky to make it this far without driving into a ditch."

"So why bring her along?" Sutton asked. Beth started to struggle then, babbling all the things about Jeremy that Micah had heard already. He watched without reacting as Sutton twisted her arm up behind her back. Judging by her grimace of pain and the way she was suddenly still, Sutton had applied enough pressure to nearly pull the arm from its socket.

Micah would make him pay for that someday soon. In the meantime, it was important that Sutton believe he didn't care one way or the other if Beth was hurt. "I brought her along to change diapers, Sutton. It certainly wasn't for sex, although I have to admit it was a step up from paying for it." He heard Beth's gasp and shot her a disgusted look that was effective in stifling anything she might blurt out. Before he returned his gaze to Sutton, he saw what he hoped was the beginning of comprehension in her eyes.

Sutton's brows lifted in surprise. "She's not any good?"

"Not good enough to make all the aggravation worthwhile."

"That's a pity." Sutton sighed, then brightened as he

thought of something. "Never mind, Blackthorne. I'm sure I'll find something interesting to do with her. After all, I'm not burdened by that decent streak of yours."

Micah lifted a hand and rubbed his jaw to hide its almost painful clenching, the only visible sign that he was close to attacking Sutton and to hell with the gun he held. It was all he could do to sound reasonable when he spoke.

"You're taking the woman?"

Sutton nodded. "That's good advice about the diapers, and you've got me intrigued about the woman. I'm sure I can find a way to keep her quiet."

Micah fisted his hands at his sides. "If I hadn't already sunk a fortune into this job, I'd almost wish you well."

"Better luck next time, Blackthorne." Sutton let Beth's arm drop and told her to get into the backseat of the Explorer. She hesitated, and Sutton pushed her so hard she stumbled. Micah heard rather than saw her open the back door and get inside. "We'll be leaving you, Blackthorne. I hope you don't mind, but we'll keep the Ford, since it's already loaded with what I came after. We don't have that far to go that I'm worried about one of your people giving me any trouble."

"You expect me to stand here and watch you drive away?"

"No, I expect you'll still be unconscious then."

Micah cursed, then said loud enough for Beth to hear, "At least let me have my coat, Sutton."

Clearly, Sutton was in a good mood, because his eyes lightened and he nodded graciously. "Of course, Blackthorne. When they find you, perhaps they'll just think you're a passed-out drunk." He shouted at Beth to get the coat, calling her a name Micah knew would make her cringe.

The opportunity to get her gun from his coat pocket died when Sutton told her to bring the coat to him. "No sense in taking chances, Blackthorne," he said, without taking his eyes off Micah. "I'll just check for anything you might find useful."

Micah was just about to signal Andrews when Beth walked over to Sutton, handed him the coat, then brought out the gun she'd hidden in the folds of her sweater and pointed it at him.

"I can't miss at this range, Sutton," she said so quietly that Micah hardly heard her from where he was standing.

As Sutton hadn't dropped his own gun, Micah knew better than to move. He stood calm and attentive and let Beth handle things.

He hoped she was thinking clearly enough to know there were only two sides to this, and that he was on hers.

Sutton split his attention between her and Micah. "Have I missed something interesting between you two?" he asked.

Micah was grateful that Beth had the sense to evade the question. "Drop the gun, Sutton. My baby isn't going anywhere with you *or* Blackthorne. I'll shoot both of you if I have to."

"Or I could shoot Blackthorne," Sutton offered. "Save you a bullet."

"Works for me," she said, and smiled.

NINE

Micah left Sutton unconscious on the floor of the ladies' bathroom and threw the key into a Dumpster at the far corner of the parking lot. He figured it would be a few hours before Sutton came to or someone found another key. Just to make things more difficult, he passed Andrews the keys to Sutton's car, knowing that Andrews would lose the car before resuming his watchdog duties.

Sutton would have to borrow or steal another vehicle before coming after them. That is, if he could walk. The kick Micah had delivered to his groin would definitely be a factor in how fast he moved.

Micah would have done more, but he was reserving that pleasure for another time when he'd have the luxury of giving Sutton his undivided attention. The groin kick had been an invitation he knew Sutton wouldn't ignore.

It was time he got Sutton out of his hair, once and for all.

First, though, there was Jeremy to take care of. And Beth. They'd both have to be sent away—in different directions, of course. Until he heard back from the man he'd dispatched to Albuquerque, Micah knew it would be irresponsible to send them away together.

In the meantime, they could sleep easily that night knowing Sutton wouldn't have any way of finding them. By the time he got loose, they'd be tucked away safe and sound in Durango. The house they were headed to was being loaned to them by the aunt of one of his operatives in return for a hastily arranged vacation in Mexico. Micah reviewed the directions in his mind and kept a careful watch on the street signs as they cruised along the brightly lit highway that bisected Durango.

He glanced at Beth. "I still haven't decided why you didn't take your chance and run. Once Sutton dropped his gun, you had the opportunity."

"You taught me to think things through, Blackthorne. I couldn't figure out how to pick up both guns and get into the truck without one of you jumping me." She sighed out loud and rubbed her temples with both hands. "Any way I looked at it, I knew I'd end up having to shoot."

She didn't look at him, but at least she was talking. She hadn't done more than speak in monosyllables since they'd left the gas station. He couldn't decide if she was angry that she hadn't done something different, or traumatized by what had happened.

He was a little traumatized himself, given Beth's wholly believable glee when Sutton had offered to shoot him.

"You could have just shot us before getting into the truck, or didn't you think you could shoot a man?"

"I knew I couldn't shoot *both* of you. You were standing too far apart, and I'm really not that good with a gun."

That sobered him for a minute. "You could have let Sutton shoot me. He was willing."

A little smile tickled the corner of her mouth. "If I hadn't seen that guy watching us when I got into the truck, there's no telling what I might have done."

She'd spotted Andrews. That surprised Micah. He'd thought she'd been too rattled to look beyond what was happening. Then again, she'd been the one to get the drop on Sutton, and that had taken courage and initiative.

It was a good thing they'd soon be surrounded by people he trusted, he decided. Beth was learning the game faster than he'd anticipated.

He would have been a lot happier, though, if she'd said she wouldn't have shot him, Andrews or no Andrews.

"Who was that man?" she asked, suddenly turning to look at him.

Micah was thinking about how embarrassed Andrews was going to be when he told him. "Andrews. He's been with us since Pagosa Springs."

"So why didn't he pitch in and help? I assume that's what you brought him in for."

He shook his head, then slowed the truck and turned left. "He was there to protect Jeremy. He wouldn't have let Sutton leave with him, one way or the other."

"But he would have let Sutton kill you?" she said as though it were the most absurd thing she'd ever heard.

Micah answered without answering. She'd had enough for one night. "It wouldn't have come to that. Sutton knew better than to make noises that would attract attention. The worst he'd planned was exactly what I did to him." He hoped.

She snorted her disbelief, then looked curiously at the passing row of houses. "Where are we going?"

"Somewhere safe." He explained about the aunt, then made a right turn and pulled into the first driveway on the right. The garage door at the end of the drive was open, and he didn't stop until they were parked inside. He killed the engine, then told Beth to stay put as he got out and went to pull the door shut. Then he walked around to her door and opened it.

"Go on inside, Beth," he said, nodding toward the door that opened into the kitchen. "Stay away from the windows and doors. I'll be right behind you with Jeremy."

She didn't move, just turned her head to look at him. "I didn't shoot you, Micah. That should count for something."

He leaned his arm on the Ford's roof and sighed. "I've already told you I won't let anything happen to Jeremy."

"That's not enough," she said, her husky voice quieting to a whisper as she lifted a hand and hesitantly laid it against his chest. "I want more."

His body thrummed to the beat of a heart shocked into double time by her touch. He wanted her. And all he'd have to do was promise her anything and he could have her. The devil of the thing was he knew she was talking about Jeremy and only Jeremy.

She'd make love with him for that reason alone. And Micah knew that wasn't good enough.

He wanted more too.

"I know you do, Beth." He took her hand and used it to pull her gently out of the truck. "Go inside. We'll talk later."

He started quickly unloading the truck as she entered the house. He knew better than to give her an opportunity to look for a phone.

He wanted her, but was cynical enough to know he couldn't trust her. Not yet.

Maybe not ever.

————◆————————◆————

The cottage was small and simple. Bedrooms on either side of the bath, a sitting room, dining room, and a kitchen with a breakfast nook completed the layout. As he carried Jeremy into the kitchen Micah was pleased to see Beth peering into the refrigerator. He'd expected her to be searching for the phones he'd ordered disconnected and put away.

He'd reconnect one once he finished unloading and had double-checked the security.

He put Jeremy's car seat on the table just as the baby awakened and opened his mouth to herald the event. By the time he'd brought in their bags and some of the supplies Beth had purchased earlier, she'd gotten Jeremy out of his chair and was on the sitting-room floor peeling off the layers of clothing. The baby was not in a good mood, as was evidenced by flailing limbs and loud shrieks, so Micah just deposited the diaper bag beside her and walked through the house checking windows and doors. Then he dug out a phone from the cabinet beneath the bathroom sink and took it into the kitchen.

He had to stick a finger in his ear so that he could hear over Jeremy's cries. When he put down the phone, he was sure he'd only heard half of what he'd been told.

Beth carried Jeremy into the kitchen on one hip and used her free hand to go through the supplies. When she pulled out a can, she handed it to Micah and asked him to warm it. Without waiting to see what he'd do, she dug back into the sack and extracted a jar of baby food. Micah watched incredulously as she sauntered over to the kitchen drawers and started looking through them as though she didn't notice the baby was doing his best to deafen them both.

When she extracted a spoon from the third drawer

and went to put Jeremy back in his car seat, Micah decided he'd better do his bit in case the jar of whatever didn't work. Following Beth's example, he rummaged through the drawers until he found a can opener.

Jeremy quit screaming after the first spoonful of peaches. When the jar was empty, Micah gave Beth the warmed formula that he'd nuked in the microwave before pouring into the bottle she'd handed him. Jeremy latched onto the bottle as though he hadn't eaten all day, only letting the nipple leave his lips when his mother tempted him with a spoon of something that looked and smelled like peas.

Micah hated peas.

Jeremy loved them. But then, as far as Micah could tell, Jeremy had yet to show any discrimination whatsoever in what he ate.

Micah paid attention to Jeremy. Beth paid attention to Jeremy. They ignored each other.

Micah stood outside the bathroom as Beth bathed the boy, handing her things as she asked, only moving away when he realized she might turn and see the look in his eyes and become even more confused than she already was.

He was looking at her with envy, and she wouldn't understand that at all. Micah wasn't sure he did.

All he knew was he'd better get something done about their dinner. He was almost as hungry as Jeremy. It was only by sheer determination that he wasn't yelling about it.

He pulled a casserole from the refrigerator and was reading the directions taped to the foil covering it when Beth came into the kitchen with Jeremy gurgling happily all over her shoulder. She handed him the frizzy-haloed baby and said, "Don't give him anything more to eat and don't put him down. He's been in a car seat all day and needs to be held. I'll be done in twenty minutes."

"Done with what?" Micah demanded as Jeremy grabbed his nose and twisted.

"My bath." She waltzed around the refrigerator and out of sight.

Micah was too busy pulling his hair from Jeremy's fist to protest. Once he got the kid under control and firmly restrained under one arm, he started reading the cooking directions again. Aloud.

Jeremy was fascinated.

Beth looked up from her food to find Micah staring at her.

"You're not hungry?" he asked.

She shook her head and shoved her half-finished plate aside. "Too much to think about."

"I'm surprised you can think at all. By the time Jeremy went to sleep, I was ready to join him."

She squeezed her eyes shut, terrified all over again that she was making a mistake but knowing she'd come to the end of her choices. She had to remember how good Micah had been with her son, how caring.

Everything depended on it.

She opened her eyes and gazed at the man across from her. Micah Blackthorne was the most important man in her life right now, for more reasons than one. Everything revolved around him: Jeremy's well-being, her freedom . . . her sanity. There was more, but she couldn't think about that now, not with so much at stake.

She *shouldn't* think about that now. But heaven help her, she couldn't help but wonder what was happening to her if she was ready to trust the man who threatened everything that mattered to her. She'd decided in the last hour, though, that the "what" didn't matter. All that counted was that he agree to her plan.

In exchange, she'd do whatever he asked. Now that she knew she wouldn't be allowed near a phone, there was no other choice.

She took a deep breath and prepared to say the things she'd rehearsed in the bath. "I have a proposition for you."

When he stiffened, she knew what he was thinking. She let the insult slide over her with an indifference she knew she'd have to learn to accept, not fight.

"What kind of proposition?" he asked, shifting his gaze so that she couldn't see his expression.

"It's pretty straightforward," she said, then took a deep breath and plunged in. "First, your part."

He looked at her then, and the fierce anger she saw in his eyes almost put her off.

"You've already promised you'd keep Jeremy safe," she said carefully, feeling her way. Rehearsing this part had been impossible. Impossible, because if he changed his mind . . .

He nodded almost imperceptibly. "I gave you my word. It stands."

She had to believe him. "Then the way I see it, you've only got three choices. Number one: Take him to the police and make sure they don't give him to Steven."

"You don't seem to have a lot of faith in the system," he responded, and pushed his own plate aside. "I'm not much of a fan either."

She didn't so much as acknowledge his comment. "Number two: Give Jeremy to me and let us disappear."

"No."

His reply was as implacable as she'd known it would be. She hesitated then, because the chance she was taking was built on believing that regardless of what happened to her, Jeremy would be safe . . . and forever out of Steven's grasp.

Micah studied her without letting his expression change. A proposition. Well, yes, he'd always known it might come down to this. He couldn't imagine what she had up her sleeve for the third choice, but didn't think it would resemble his own plan.

To put off having to say no again, he said, "Before you tell me my last choice, I'd like to hear what your part of this proposition consists of." He pushed his chair back from the table and got up to pour coffee. "After all, the . . . inducement," he said after hesitating, "might make me consider my answer more carefully."

He turned to find Beth staring at her hands, which were clasped in her lap. He took the two coffees back to the table and sat down, angling his chair so that he could stretch out his legs. "Well?" he asked, and watched her from over the rim of his cup.

When she looked up at him, there was a strength of purpose in her gaze that made him ashamed. "I've already told you, Blackthorne. I'll do anything for my son, up to and including what I know you've wanted all along."

"How the hell do you know what I want?" he growled, shifting in his chair as his body responded to the sexual content of their conversation.

She just shook her head. "I've known almost from the first. The only thing I can't figure out is why you've waited for me to offer."

"You're offering to have sex with me?" he asked quietly.

She hesitated, then blinked long lashes over a curiously hard expression. "I'd have sex with Sutton if I thought it would help Jeremy."

Something wedged in his throat that kept the air

from getting to his lungs. He put his cup down on the table so hard that coffee sloshed over the sides as he tried to remember he'd forced her into saying it.

That didn't mean he had to like it.

He pushed her hands away when she tried to wipe up the mess with her napkin. "Thanks anyway, Beth, but no thank you. You'll have to come up with a better offer."

She didn't have one. Despair and frustration pushed Beth to her feet, but Micah was suddenly standing in front of her, blocking her flight. When she couldn't bring herself to look at him, a rough hand cupped her chin and forced her face up until their eyes met. "I've never raped a woman in my life, Beth," he said quietly. "I'm sure as hell not going to start with you."

"I offered."

"And I turned you down."

"It wouldn't be rape."

"I think it would, in the long run."

Panicked because she didn't have anything left to bargain with, Beth made herself try harder. "I've made it clear how I feel, Blackthorne. I'll do anything to save my son."

"Having sex with me won't change anything." His eyes darkened, and his hand tightened around her jaw, not hurting but letting her know the intensity of his anger.

And desire. She couldn't miss that, not with it blazing in his eyes as though it were a fire out of control. "You don't want me?" she whispered, and tried to make the hands that were fisted at her sides lift up and caress his face. She couldn't, though, not even when she knew that all it would take was a move on her part to bring him over the edge.

She couldn't make herself be the whore he thought she was.

Then the world tilted on its axis, and everything Beth had ever known about herself was suddenly absent or wildly distorted.

Blackthorne kissed her, a hard crushing kiss that stole her breath and her reason. His fingers fanned across her face, holding her still for one brief moment in which he taught her that nothing would ever be the same again.

He kissed her, thinking she was a whore. She let him, and didn't know who she was anymore.

"Oh, I want you, honey," he said, then opened his hand on her fanny and brought her hard against his thighs. "I want you so bad I can hardly walk." He rubbed his body against her until the soft flesh of her belly knew the heat of his rigid flesh, even through the layers of clothing separating them. He cupped her bottom with both palms and rubbed again, unbalancing her, so that she had to grab his arms for balance.

Beth knew she should move away, but the heat gathering at the juncture of her thighs was too sweet, too unexpected. His mouth was so close she could feel his breath on her lips. She wanted his mouth again, and hated that wanting.

"I'm like every other man you've ever known, Beth. I want you. And I'll take you if you push me hard enough. But it won't change what I have to do."

"It won't?"

He shook his head, his lips brushing hers so lightly she thought she imagined it. "It won't," he whispered. "But I'll make love to you until you beg me to stop, honey. Right now, if that's what you want."

She looked up at him through eyes that were nearly closed with . . . *pleasure*! The knowledge slammed into her, filling her with regrets that she barely understood yet knew she couldn't afford. Suddenly she was fighting him, struggling to be free until she realized he'd already thrust her aside.

"I'm not—" she began, but he interrupted with a blazing fierceness that cowed her into silence.

"You're not going to get your way," he said, then backed away from her. His gaze was just as angry as before, just as full of desire, as he motioned her back into her chair and threw himself into his own. "Don't push me, Beth. I want you too badly to say no more than once."

"So why did you?"

He glared at her, then shook his head. "Hell if I know, honey. Just don't try it again unless you're giving out freebies."

"I'm not a whore," she said softly, and knew he would never believe her, not after what had just happened.

Not that she cared, Beth told herself, and wished she could stop shaking.

Micah didn't think she was a whore, either, but he was too angry to tell her. Angry with himself, because he'd forced her along a path she had no business walking.

Angry with her, because she'd responded to him.

How the hell was he going to stay away from her, knowing she wanted him too?

The air was thick with passion and anger, and Micah watched the minute hand on the clock over the stove revolve twice before he spoke. "Just out of interest, what was my third choice?"

She shook her head without looking up. "It doesn't matter, does it? I've nothing to offer that you want, which leaves you free to do as you like."

"Humor me." He finished his coffee, curious because he couldn't for the life of him think of a single option he hadn't already considered. Sending Jeremy to safety was the only choice. If he thought he could convince her of that, he wouldn't be sitting there putting her through hell.

She folded her trembling hands on the table and looked up at him. "Number three is that you send Jeremy away, without me. Put him where he'll be safe until I can prove to you that it was Steven who abused him."

By sheer strength of will, Micah confined his reaction to a raised eyebrow. "You can prove it?"

"I think so," she said, then added, "I have proof, but it won't be enough if Steven gets to it before I'm ready."

Micah didn't press her for details because he knew she wouldn't give them to him. She shouldn't, not if she was smart. She'd already taken a hell of a risk in trusting he wouldn't take Jeremy to Steven. If he turned around and did exactly that, at least she would have something left to fight with.

But that wasn't the point, not all of it at least. Not as far as Micah was concerned.

"That's all fine and good, Beth. But what makes you think I'll give Jeremy to you when it's over? Just because Corbett might be a child abuser doesn't mean I think you deserve Jeremy by default."

"Whoever gave you the right to decide anything?" she demanded, her voice rising in fury.

"Nobody gave it to me. I took it," he returned harshly. "I told you before I intend to protect Jeremy. That includes from you, if necessary. And don't think I can't or won't, Beth."

He ignored the gut-wrenching sensation in his stomach as he watched the blood rush from her face. "You're saying whores can't be good mothers?"

He shrugged. "I know I wouldn't want *my* son exposed to the kind of life you've supposedly led."

"Jeremy's not your son."

"And he's not going to be yours for much longer, not unless you can prove you're not the woman Corbett crucified in court."

A long silence stretched between them, and Micah could have kicked himself when he saw all the energy and determination drain out of her.

"That, I'm afraid, is very unlikely." She spoke softly, as though she'd only recently come to terms with this.

He'd expected her to tell him the lies were just that: Lies. When she didn't, he began to wonder if he'd been wrong about her after all.

She got up from the table and started clearing it. Micah didn't offer to help. The kitchen was too small for the two of them to move around it without touching, and he knew she needed the space.

"Are you saying everything that was printed about you after the hearing was true?" he asked, and held his breath as he awaited her answer.

She spoke without turning from the sink. "No. Just that I can't prove it wasn't. I don't know how."

His relief was almost anticlimactic, because he'd known the truth all along. Known, but hadn't allowed himself to believe because there was too much at stake. He gave himself a couple of minutes to contemplate the ramifications—for Jeremy, for himself—then began asking the kinds of things his investigator would be looking into in Albuquerque.

"Don't you have any friends who will give you a character reference?"

Her shoulders shook as though with laughter, but when she turned to look at him, there was no humor in her eyes. "I have no friends, Blackthorne, not really. The people in my department have their own lives. I was too busy with research and teaching to have time for much anyway."

"I find that hard to believe."

"I'm not a social person by nature. Then, when I met Steven, he made sure I only had time to mingle with people of his choosing. His friends. When I left him, I was two months pregnant and so sick I could hardly keep up with work, much less a social life."

Micah got up and brought the rest of the dishes from the table over to the sink. "What about where you lived? I'd think there would be someone who would notice whether you entertained a lot or were constantly going out."

She tilted her head to the side, the wistful expression on her face making him believe she was remembering better times. "Jeremy and I lived in a garage apartment that I rented from an elderly woman. We were so happy there."

"And?" he persisted.

The wistful expression died. "When I spoke to Steven after the hearing and threatened to bring my landlady into court to testify on my behalf, he just laughed and said his attorney would make mincemeat out of the 'blind, deaf old biddy.'" She shrugged and threw the towel onto the counter. "He was right. While Mrs. Hamlin was really quite alert for her age, I knew Steven could badger her enough to make her appear senile."

"But would she support your story?" He kept her from walking away by putting his hands on her shoulders. She tried to shrug him off, but he didn't let her.

It was time she understood that he cared enough to fight her *and* her battles. "What about it, Beth? If anyone asked, would she tell them you were a good mother

who stayed home with her baby and was no more a
whore than she was?"

"Does it matter?"

He nodded. "Maybe. What about during your marriage? Who would be in the position to know about your
private life?"

"There were the servants, of course. But they'd lose
their jobs if they sided with me." She shook her head
hopelessly. "There's no way I'd get any of them to go
against Steven, not in court."

"I didn't say you had to prove anything to the court,
Beth," he said quietly. "It's me you have to convince,
and I don't let little men like Steven Corbett get in the
way when I want to find out something."

The spark of hope in her eyes was feeble at best.
She'd been beaten down too many times to be able to
trust so easily. "You'll talk to people?" she asked.

"I've got a man headed down there right now. A few
days and he should have something concrete for me."

"Then you'll decide," she said softly.

He nodded. "I'll decide. And I'll know I've done my
best for Jeremy." His fingers tightened encouragingly on
her shoulders. "It's going to work out all right, Beth. My
instincts about you couldn't be that far off."

Hope sparked again in her eyes, flaring bright and
strong this time. Only for a moment, though, before it
was replaced with a new worry.

"I've got to get Jeremy back legally. That's why I
didn't run and hide." She blinked back her frustration
and sighed. "You're just one more hurdle I have to clear
before I do what I meant to do from the beginning."

He looked at her with new respect. "If Corbett's
been lying, there shouldn't be a problem."

"You don't know him," she said, and he felt the

tremors that shook her. "He'll build lies on lies. What if I fail, Micah? What if Steven wins this round too?"

"You mean, what if he guesses what you're going to do and does an end around?"

She nodded.

He didn't see the problem. "Then you take Jeremy and go away. I can help you disappear." The only trouble was, he didn't want her to go anywhere.

A wry smile kicked at the corners of her mouth. "That's what I'd planned all along. Once I finish with Steven, Jeremy and I will go live far away where no one's heard of any of this."

"Which brings me back to the question I asked before. Why didn't you do that in the first place?"

"Because I knew if I didn't stand and fight now, Steven would win in the end. He'd keep looking until he found us." She looked at him, her eyes dark and serious. "I have to finish this before Steven figures out what I'm going to do."

"Do you want me to help?"

She thought about it, then shook her head. "I can't make any more mistakes, Micah."

He refused to be offended by her rejection. Given his track record, he wouldn't have trusted him either. His hands wandered down her arms, then back up again and across her shoulders until he had her face cupped between them. Her lips were slightly parted, and the agonizing confusion he read in her eyes was more than he could bear. He wanted to comfort her.

Even more, he wanted to feel her mouth under his again so that if the morning dawned with her hating him, he'd have had a last taste of her lips.

Taking his time, he fitted his mouth to hers, then slanted his head to make the contact deep and firm. His tongue slipped between her lips and moved leisurely into her mouth, as though he had all the time in the world to absorb her shy response. He didn't, though, but not because he could think of a better way to wile away the long, dark hours of the night.

He knew that if he didn't stop kissing her, he'd have to lay her down on the closest bed and learn every single feminine secret she possessed. He couldn't do that to her, though, not and do what had to be done the next morning.

Micah was breathing deep and hard when he lifted his mouth from hers. He almost threw his noble intentions aside when a soft cry escaped her lips and she reached up to slide a hand around his neck.

Almost. The control that had always been so much a part of him didn't desert him. Taking a deep breath, he buried his fingers in her hair and waited until she met his gaze before speaking. "I'm taking Jeremy to the airport first thing tomorrow morning. There will be a plane waiting to take him away."

Tears filled her eyes, huge luminous drops that fell unchecked down her cheeks. "Where?"

"You'll have to trust me, Beth." He rubbed his thumbs across her wet cheeks. "All I can tell you is he's not going back to Corbett."

Her lashes drifted down, and he caught her as she sagged and nearly fell at his feet. Scooping her into his arms, he carried her into the sitting room and sank with her onto the sofa. She hadn't fainted, he knew. But the emotional bombardment of the past few days had clearly been too much for her.

He held her face close to his chest and stroked her hair as she soaked his sweater with her tears. He didn't know how he was going to manage it, but he swore he'd make her forget the hell she'd been through at his hands and at the hands of others.

He'd make her forget, or pray that she would forgive.

It was an age before she could talk with only the odd hiccup or errant tear accompanying her words. Micah made her tell him everything, beginning with why she'd left Corbett and ending with the custody hearing. Things that had confused him before became perfectly clear.

Things he'd suspected became facts, and he added Corbett to his list of unfinished business.

Micah listened, prompted her when she faltered, and believed everything she told him because he knew she was incapable of manufacturing such outrageous, sick lies.

He didn't ask how she intended getting Jeremy back because he thought he knew, having pieced together bits of clues from what she did and didn't say. He decided he'd let her do what she had to do on her own—not counting a couple of shadows she'd never even notice if they were careful. He knew she needed to prove she could fight back and win.

What he didn't know was how he was going to persuade her to wait until Sutton was out of the game.

Micah suddenly realized she'd stopped talking and was looking up at him from where she lay cradled in his arms. "I want to be with Jeremy tonight," she said, the break in her voice all that remained of her distress.

"I know." He lifted her aside and went into the bedroom. When he returned, he had the sleeping baby in one arm and a blanket in the other. Before Beth could speak, he gave her the baby, then sat back down and lifted the two of them onto his lap. He urged her close and was rewarded with a soft sigh as she relaxed into the crook of his arm and laid Jeremy to nestle against his chest, his fuzzy hair tickling Micah's chin. Pulling the blanket over them all, he leaned back into the corner of the sofa and put his feet on the coffee table, boots and all.

He didn't dare look at her, because if she was crying again, he knew his heart would break.

It was going to be a long night, but he wouldn't have it any other way.

TEN

Beth watched from the window as Micah carried Jeremy down the walk and disappeared into the van parked at the curb. The woman he'd introduced as Cora got in behind him and became just another featureless shadow behind the dark-tinted windows. Andrews slid the door panel shut, then got in behind the wheel.

They were going straight to the airport, Micah had said. The private plane he'd chartered would be in the air with Jeremy before an hour passed.

Tears she'd thought she'd run out of brimmed in her eyes, and it was only by a determined force of will that she banked them. Crying was an indulgence she didn't have time for. Before Micah returned, she needed to get past the two men he'd stationed in the brown sedan across the street.

For her protection, he'd said when pointing them out. Beth knew better, but couldn't fault Micah's caution. The men were there to make sure she was waiting for Micah when he got back. He wanted her out of Durango, he'd told her. Before Sutton stumbled across them. After all, it wasn't that large of a town.

Beth had no intention of being packed off on the noon flight to Denver when she had business to do in Durango.

Letting the lace-trimmed curtain fall back into place, she retreated from the window and walked quickly into the kitchen. The telephone book was in a drawer at the end of the counter. It took only a moment to find the listing for Alan's law firm. She wrote the number and address down on a scrap of paper and put it into her wallet with the number Karen had given her for Alan's home. Micah had taken the phones out of the house while she was dressing. Another precaution, she knew, and tried not to be too annoyed by it.

She'd just have to make her calls from another phone. That meant getting out of there.

She put on her gloves and coat, stuffed her wallet into a pocket, and went out the front door. She proceeded down the walk without so much as a glance across the street. When she heard the sound of a car door opening, she hurried up the next walkway. She was at the next-door neighbor's door and knocking before she dared look behind her.

Micah's men were hovering next to their car, clearly undecided about what to do. She had to wipe the smile from her face when she heard a dead bolt being thrown. By the time the door opened, she was ready with her most serious expression. It must have worked, because a minute later when Beth had finished what she'd come to say, the middle-aged woman was scurrying toward her phone.

Beth made the walk back to the cottage under the confused stares of Micah's men. Once inside, she went back to the window and watched, not bothering to take off her coat.

Maybe ten minutes passed before a police car turned

the corner and pulled to a stop in front of the brown sedan. Two uniformed officers got out and approached the vehicle. Beth didn't wait for more. Reaching into her pocket for the keys she'd taken from Micah's coat that morning, she hurried to the kitchen and let herself into the garage. Two minutes later she was backing the Explorer out of the driveway, blithely unconcerned that the men in the brown sedan would see her.

They had enough problems of their own. By the time they convinced the officers they weren't casing the neighborhood for a robbery spree, Beth would be long gone.

She'd done the right thing in coming to Alan Robertson, Beth thought as she listened to the attorney finish making plans for his trip to Albuquerque. When the steely-eyed, dark-haired man put down the telephone, she was confident that Steven had met his match.

"I've arranged for Corbett's housekeeper to be watched continuously until this is over," Alan said, then lifted his eyebrows. "Are you positive she'll be willing to testify against him?"

Beth nodded. "She was the one who called that night to tell me what Steven had done to Jeremy. I know she'll follow through as long as we can protect her from my ex-husband."

"You really think he'd harm her, and not just fire her?" He picked up a pen and twirled it in his long fingers as he stared at her across the wide desk.

"He punched me enough during our short marriage to prove he's capable of hurting women. God knows what he'd do to one he didn't even pretend to love."

Alan's gaze narrowed. "Can you prove he abused you?"

She shrugged. "That's beside the point. Jeremy is all that matters right now."

"On the contrary. I think it's very much the point." He rested his forearms on the desk and stared at her with quiet intensity. "With everything you've told me, I can force Corbett to give up all claim to Jeremy as well as make a public statement that everything he said about you in court was a lie."

"I doubt he'll—"

He cut her off with a wave of his hand. "It's important he do it, because that's the only way the court will be able to justify a reversal in its decision. Proving that Corbett either paid off or applied pressure to your attorney will be more difficult, but I'm convinced it can be done. That will help too."

She looked at him curiously. "So why make a big deal about what Steven did to me? I don't see where that will accomplish anything."

"It's important because we need to make sure he never comes near you again. By proving repeated abuse, I can do that."

She got up to pace the immense office that overflowed with stacks of books and papers. "I never told anyone, not even when I left him. I was so relieved to get away that all I wanted to do was forget it. Besides, I didn't think anyone would believe me."

"Not even your doctor?" he asked.

"Not even my doctor," she confirmed, then added, "At least, not then. I told him about this last incident. I had to. I was afraid Steven had finally broken something."

"When?"

The sharp staccato of the single word made her stop pacing and look up at him.

"A few days before the hearing, almost two weeks

ago." She tested the tender spot below her breast with her fingers. "Just bruised ribs, the doc said. And I'm feeling much better now."

Alan nodded. "Good. We'll add the doctor to our list."

"But he won't be able to point the finger at Steven," she said, coming back to sit down. "All he knows is that someone punched me."

"Added to the housekeeper's testimony about what she heard and saw, there won't be any doubt in anyone's mind about who hurt you. All the doctor needs to do is provide records of the examination."

Beth took a deep breath and didn't mind at all when a sharp ache in her chest reminded her of her injured ribs. "Is it that easy?"

Alan leaned back in his chair and lifted his feet onto a short pile of papers at the corner of his desk. "It's not going to be easy at all. But it can be done. Thank God you had the sense not to tip your hand by talking to the housekeeper yourself."

"Frankly, I had enough to do with getting Jeremy out of the house without waking the woman Steven had hired to watch him." She sighed and shook her head. "I don't know what I would have done if I hadn't remembered Karen had a brother who was an attorney."

"We're not all crooks," he said with a wry smile.

No, but even the honest ones weren't free. Beth was just about to raise the delicate question of his fee when the door behind her opened. She looked over her shoulder to find Micah with one hand on the doorknob while the other hand fended off Alan's secretary, who was insisting he leave immediately.

Beth stared into Micah's furious glare until she couldn't take it anymore. She turned back to Alan, shrinking down in her chair as the familiar feeling of embarrassment at getting caught washed over her.

Alan interrupted the secretary's demands for obedience with a polite "ahem." Miraculously, the woman stopped chattering and looked at her boss for direction.

"You're Micah Blackthorne, I assume," Alan said in the lull. Micah must have nodded because Alan thanked his secretary for showing Mr. Blackthorne in, then waited patiently until the door closed with an almost mutinous click.

"Beth told you about me?" Micah asked after Alan introduced himself.

Alan nodded without smiling. "She did. Where the hell have you been? I've been expecting you for the past thirty minutes."

A pause, then Micah said with unnatural mildness, "Making sure no one else had followed her here. I figured she'd be safe enough inside with you for a while."

Beth didn't know why she was surprised at anything anymore, but Alan's reception of Micah gave her a small jolt. "How do you know Micah?" she asked.

"By reputation only," Alan said, without taking his eyes off the other man. "Mr. Blackthorne is well-known in certain circles hereabouts. I didn't imagine for a second he'd let you just waltz out of that house alone."

"But I did." Beth could have sworn she felt a sting in the back of her neck where Micah was drilling her with his angry gaze. "The guys in the car—"

"Were mostly there for show," Micah interrupted. "Bolton and Peters were in a van half a block away." He sighed loud enough for her to hear his irritation. "It occurred to me you might do something stupid."

Beth wished he would at least save the name calling for private, and was relieved when Alan ignored it.

"Come and sit down, Blackthorne. I'm sure Beth would like to hear how it went at the airport."

Micah stayed right where he was, knowing that he couldn't strangle her if he didn't get near enough to touch her. "I thought I told you to stay put," he growled, then went over to her anyway when she wouldn't look at him. He hunkered down in front of her chair and nudged her chin up with his knuckles until she was looking at him. "Jeremy is fine, Beth. Cora will take good care of him."

"I know," she said, her voice a ragged whisper. "Thank you, Micah."

"For what?"

She almost smiled. "For keeping him safe. You're doing a much better job than I could."

He almost kissed her for that, but stopped just millimeters shy of her mouth. He wanted privacy when he kissed her again, and the luxury of time to enjoy it. "You did just fine, Beth. When you're back with Jeremy again, it will be because your courage made it happen."

"Back with Jeremy?" she whispered.

He nodded. Facts or no, there was nothing in this woman that wasn't decent and good. Jeremy couldn't have a better mother. "As soon as it's safe, I'll take you to him."

She looked at him with such earnest longing that not kissing her was no longer an option. Keeping his eyes wide open and willing her to do the same, he brushed his mouth across hers and thought of a dozen things he wanted to tell her.

Intimate things that could only be said in private.

Rising, he slid into the leather chair next to hers, then reached over and took her small hand in his. When she didn't pull away, he knew everything was going to be all right.

She was going to give him a chance . . . give *them* a chance.

Micah supposed he should be astonished at her easy acceptance of him, but figured she'd been hit by the same bricks that had clobbered him. Satisfied with how things were going, he turned to find Alan Robertson watching him carefully.

"I imagine you have a few questions for me, counselor," Micah said.

"Questions?" Robertson settled back in his chair. "Just a few. Beth told me you've sent Jeremy to safety. I'm not sure I understand your stake in all this."

"You mean, what do I get out of it?" Micah studied Robertson and was satisfied with what he saw. Beth had chosen well, his instincts told him. Still, he'd already put someone on looking into Robertson's background. That would confirm whether or not Micah would let him handle the legal end of this mess. In the meantime, he was interested in how much he could learn from Robertson before Beth got nervous and told him to get out.

"From what Beth's told me," Robertson said, "you've mounted an expensive operation for which it doesn't appear you'll be reimbursed."

Micah kept his expression neutral. "You've heard the rumors that I always collect."

Robertson nodded. "I've also heard that you always deliver. It doesn't appear you're going to do either this time. That worries me."

"Don't let it." Micah allowed a tiny smile. "Corbett owes me. He'll pay."

Robertson's nod of understanding was almost imperceptible. Micah thought they'd said as much to each other as they needed when Robertson surprised him. "I suppose it won't do any good to tell you to keep your people the hell away from Albuquerque."

"Why?"

"Everything Beth told me depends on discretion and timing. If Corbett gets wind of what I'm doing, things might get dicey." Robertson looked away from Micah to the woman who'd been sitting so quietly beside him. "Beth?"

She nodded. "Tell him everything, Alan. Micah won't do anything to hurt me or Jeremy."

Micah gave her hand a squeeze. "I might even be able to help. I've already got one man in Albuquerque looking into things."

"That's as much help as I'll take," Robertson said firmly. "Between keeping an eye on Jeremy and watching out for this Sutton character Beth told me about, you've got to be stretched for manpower. I know you've got an impressive staff of investigators to draw from, but this isn't the only case you're handling."

He acknowledged Robertson's comments with a shrug. "Once Beth leaves town—"

"I'm not leaving."

He shot her a glance that told her exactly what he thought of that. "Of course you're leaving. Sutton is—"

"Sutton is going to figure out Jeremy isn't here anymore," she said smoothly. "He won't have any reason to stay."

"You don't either," Micah argued. "Now that you've met with Robertson, he can handle—"

"He might need—"

"Would you *please* stop interrupting me!"

"When you start making sense," she returned with a determined look in her eye that Micah was beginning to recognize. "Alan is going to Albuquerque later today. Since I'm not stupid enough to go back there until this is over, I've decided to stay on here."

Micah glowered at her, then switched his attention

to Robertson. "I'm taking her out of Durango. Do you have any problem with that?"

The lawyer shook his head. "None. I'd have suggested the same if I thought she'd listen to me. I don't like the way this Sutton character sounds."

"I'm not going anywhere—"

Both men ignored her as Robertson proceeded to give Micah a concise summary of Beth's information and his own strategy.

"Stay around Durango until I leave for Albuquerque this evening," Robertson finished, then rose and held out his hand. "I might have a few more questions for Beth."

Micah shook his hand, convinced that Robertson could and would accomplish everything as planned. "I'll leave a number for a cellular hookup with your secretary. Now that the police have called attention to the safe house, we'll have to go elsewhere."

Robertson nodded, then sorted through some papers on his desk as Micah hustled an indignant Beth to her feet. "Leave me the keys for Karen's truck. I'll see that it gets back to her."

"If it's all right with you, I thought we'd use the truck to draw Sutton out. I'll take care of getting it back to Denver."

"What do you have in mind for Sutton?" Robertson asked.

Micah grinned. "As an officer of the court, you don't want to know."

All that got out of Robertson was a lifted brow, which was as much of a blessing as Micah figured he was going to get. He turned to leave the office, keeping a firm grip on Beth's hand.

"But I'm not finished with Alan," she protested, literally digging her heels into the thick carpet. "We haven't even talked about how I'm going to pay him."

"Later," Micah growled, then scooped her into his arms so that she wouldn't hurt herself with such fruitless resistance.

"Save your caveman tactics for someone who likes them," she hissed into his ear as he carried her down the hallway to the stairs. "I can walk, Blackthorne."

"It's quicker this way," he said reasonably, proud of himself for remembering her ribs a split second before he'd thrown her over his shoulder. "Besides, I like carrying you."

His admission clearly startled her. "You do?"

He softened his glare to a mild grimace. "I do, Beth. That's what's made everything so damned complicated." He headed down the stairs, knowing the footsteps he heard behind him belonged to Bolton.

"Why?"

He went through the door Peters held open and climbed straight into the van with Beth in his arms. Walking almost in a crouch, he went to the back of the van, where they'd have a modicum of privacy. He put her down rather more gently than he'd picked her up and fixed her seat belt as the vehicle began to move.

"Why, Micah?" she asked again.

"Why are things complicated?" he asked, but she shook her head.

"No," she said so softly he knew no one else could hear. "I'm a physicist. I can understand why things are complicated."

"Then what?"

"Why do you like holding me?" she asked, an intense look in her eyes. "And why do I want you to? It doesn't make sense, not when my whole life is upside down. I'm surprised I can feel anything that doesn't relate directly to Jeremy."

He looked at the backs of the heads of the two men up front and sighed. Snapping his own belt closed, he took her hand and faced her. "Do you doubt how you feel?"

She shook her head, and he felt a relief that was almost overpowering. "Then just accept it, Beth. I've had to."

"But it seems wrong—"

He hushed her with a finger on her lips. "It's not wrong. The stress you've been under doesn't create feelings. It just amplifies them." His finger traced her full mouth, and he groaned when her lips parted under his caress. "The way you respond to me is exquisite."

"But Jeremy—" she began, weaker this time as he urged her with words and almost innocent touches down a familiar, yet excitingly new sensual path.

"Jeremy isn't here," he said, then flattened his hand on the window beyond her shoulder as the van took a corner. "Jeremy is safe." The van straightened, and Micah let his hand fall to her shoulder. "I want you, Beth," he murmured, his mouth close to her ear. "I want to hold you and kiss you and make love to you until I can't think anymore." His lips brushed her ear, and he didn't know if her resulting shiver was from his words or his touch.

He liked knowing he could make her shiver. "Yes, Beth," he whispered, and slipped his hand around her waist as his mouth nuzzled the soft spot behind her ear. "I want you for sex because you arouse me faster and easier than any woman I've ever known. I want to hold you at night, and I don't know why, because I've never wanted to hold a woman the whole night through."

His fingers spanned her waist and flexed into the soft

folds of her sweater, but he knew her gasp wasn't from anything untoward he was doing there. He thought it was reasonable to assume she was reacting to the way his tongue was tracing the delicate shell of her ear. He did it again, and had his proof.

"I want you, Beth," he said, then put his palm on her face to bring her lips to his. "I want you for things I've never wanted before, and I don't even know yet what they are."

She swallowed, and her sigh was warm on his lips. "I want to believe that how I feel is real."

"It's real," he murmured, and kissed her lightly. "It's so real and exciting that I know the love we make together will be nothing less than sensational."

"You're going to make love to me." It wasn't a question.

Micah nodded. "And you're going to make love to me."

It wasn't as though either of them had a choice.

ELEVEN

They waited in the van while the man Micah addressed as Bolton checked them into a red-brick hotel that sprawled at least a block back from the highway. The other man, Peters, stayed behind the wheel of the idling vehicle and listened to Micah, who had moved up behind him. When Bolton returned, he handed the room key in through the window to Peters and disappeared. Peters drove around to the back of the hotel, and minutes later Micah and Beth were standing in a comfortable-looking living room complete with bar, dining area, and fireplace.

It was several steps up from the crowded motel room in Monte Vista, Beth thought as she shrugged out of her coat and hung it up in the closet beside Micah's.

"There's a bedroom through there," he said, pointing toward a door she'd been trying to ignore. It was one thing to sit in the back of a van and whisper intimacies. It was quite another to be all alone with Micah and know that he expected to take up where they'd left off.

She was suddenly shy, and there wasn't a thing she could do about it. Not that Micah noticed. He just prowled around the room, closing drapes and checking supplies as he continued to talk.

"Bolton and Peters have the room across the hall," he said. "They'll order something up from room service and bring it over. I don't want either of us seen by maids, waiters, or anyone else."

"You think Sutton has the resources to track us here?" she asked, distracted from her nervousness.

Micah shrugged, then went to the refrigerator and pulled out a soda. He popped the top and poured it into two glasses. "I doubt Sutton has more than one or two men, if any. He usually works alone." He brought the drinks over to where Beth hovered near the fireplace and handed her one. "But I'm not taking any chances. We'll stay here until Sutton is cornered. Taking the surprise out of my next meeting with him will give me more control over how things turn out."

She took the glass, trying not to shiver when his fingers brushed hers. She almost managed it, but then Micah rubbed his knuckles across hers a second time and she wasn't braced for that.

He'd done it deliberately. She could tell by the hot, knowing look in his eyes. The shiver traveled unmolested up her spine, and she moved away before he did it again, avoiding his gaze until she had her untamed responses under some kind of control.

It was odd how he affected her. Beth was convinced that she could have been blindfolded and known it was Micah who touched her. The attraction she felt for him was anything but ordinary, she was beginning to realize. It was, she sensed, something quite extraordinary indeed.

If only she could stop feeling guilty for every single thought that didn't concern Jeremy, she might be able to analyze exactly what was happening. Instead, it was all she could do to keep a handle on how she reacted every time he so much as looked at her.

Micah walked over to a large, heavily cushioned chair and sank into it. Beth took the one opposite, sitting nervously on the edge because relaxing was such a foreign concept lately.

"Why is it so necessary to do anything about Sutton at all?" she asked. "Now that Jeremy's gone—"

"He's not after Jeremy anymore," Micah interrupted. "He's after me."

That didn't make her feel any better. "How do you know?"

"That he's after me?" When she nodded, Micah rested his head back on the cushion and stared at the ceiling. "We spotted him at the airport this morning. He knows Jeremy is out of his reach."

"Dear God. If Sutton was there, he knows where Jeremy went."

Micah snapped his head off the cushion at the breathless panic in her voice. "Jeremy's fine, Beth. The flight plan was changed in midair. Sutton won't have even a clue where to start looking."

"But what was he doing at the airport—"

"The charter was booked last night in my name. Sutton would have checked with the airport as a matter of course."

"You did it on purpose," she said softly, her head shaking in total bewilderment.

"There were no risks," Micah said firmly. "We didn't take the plane Sutton thought we'd booked. By the time he figured it out, Jeremy was already in the air."

"But why?"

"Because I wanted him to concentrate on me. Now that he knows Jeremy is gone, he won't be distracted."

Micah had gone out of his way to ensure that Sutton wouldn't have anything on his mind but getting even. The only glitch in the plan was Beth. He'd counted on having her out of the way before now.

The sudden easing of the strain in her expression was gratifying because it went a long way toward showing how fully she trusted him. Micah decided then that he'd tell her anything she wanted to know.

Even where Jeremy was.

She didn't ask. Instead, she scooted more comfortably into her chair and looked at him curiously. "You still haven't told me why it's so important to do something about Sutton. Why now? Why here?"

He answered her questions in reverse order. "Here, because I've already got a few men in Durango. Now, because Sutton is mad enough to keep coming at me until he succeeds. I'd rather get it over with."

"But why, Micah? I know he's not exactly a model citizen, but why have you made him your problem?"

"Because he hurt you." Micah caught her startled gaze and held it. "He's been on borrowed time since that night at the diner."

There was a long pause, during which he felt as though Beth was trying to decide if she should argue for the bad guy. "Don't waste your pity on Sutton," he said gruffly. "I'm not going to do anything to him he doesn't deserve."

"What *are* you going to do?"

"Personally, not much." He knew she saw through the lie, so he added the rest as window dressing. "There's a tiny country in South America that's been after his hide for the past year. Seems he conspired with their secretary of the treasury to defraud a few cabinet members of a substantial fortune. When they find him gift-wrapped on their doorstep, they're not going to ask questions about how he got there."

The worried look cleared from her brow, and Micah could have sworn she agreed with his sense of justice. A tiny smile pushed her lips up, and she crossed her arms beneath her breasts as she studied him. "All right, Micah. I understand the why, where, and when of all this. But I can't figure out how."

"How?"

"How," she repeated with a nod. "How do you know you'll spot Sutton? Durango isn't exactly a one-street town. And with all the precautions we're taking about staying out of sight, I don't think you'll get your shot at him anytime soon."

"The truck. Once he finds the truck, he'll probably stay with it hoping you or I will show up." He put his empty glass on the coffee table between them and laced his fingers behind his head.

Beth was quick to point out the obvious flaw. "How is he going to find the truck in the garage of Alan's office building?"

"I moved it. It's now parked just off Durango's main street—enough out of the way that Sutton won't think it's a trick, but simple enough to spot if you're doing a systematic search."

Beth wanted to know a great deal more about this plan of Micah's, but was interrupted by a knock at the door. Micah was out of his chair and walking toward the door with his gun held loosely in one hand before Beth was even on her feet. Before she could tell him to be careful, he checked the security peephole, then opened the door to allow Peters to roll in a tray of food.

Lunch. Beth took a deep breath, winced, and took another one anyway. It was the only thing she knew that might possibly relax her. She'd never get used to the constant tension, and she wondered how Micah coped with it. Then again, she wasn't even sure he felt it; he looked so incredibly relaxed.

They ate lunch at the table in the corner, Beth nibbling at her food and Micah making short work of his own in between urging her to do better. She needed the strength, he insisted.

There wasn't room in her stomach for both food and nerves, she retorted.

There wasn't any reason to be nervous, he told her, then tried to get her to eat her soup before it got cold.

She said it might taste better that way, then turned her nose up at it five minutes later because it was cold.

He reassured her at least three times that Jeremy was safe.

She reassured him each time that she believed him, and that she doubted she'd stop worrying until she and Jeremy were together again.

They were about to start on their fourth round when there was another knock at the door. Beth tensed all over again. Micah patted her hand, drew his gun, and went to the door. He took the shopping bags Bolton handed him, conversed with the man in low tones that Beth couldn't decipher, then shut and locked the door.

"If you're finished with lunch, you can try these on." He held out one of the bags and waited for her to come get it. She took it and peered inside.

"Clothes?" She was surprised. And relieved. They'd left all their things back at the cottage, and what she had on was well into its second day. Having spent the night in between in them, too, she was more than ready for a change.

"Mm-hmm. I thought you might be getting tired of what you're wearing."

She grinned at his delicate assessment of the situation and looked up to find his eyes filled with warm humor. "I'll wear them even if they don't fit."

He nodded toward the bedroom. "There's time to get more. Go try them on."

For the first time in their acquaintance, she found herself doing what he asked without a thought of arguing. Pulling the bedroom door shut behind her, she raced to the king-size bed and dumped the contents of the bag out onto the spread. Black jeans and a gorgeous soft yellow sweater fell out, followed by a few lacy necessities that she picked up and checked for size. The panties were just right, the camisole a bit large, and the socks a thick knit that would make her shoes fit especially snug. She didn't worry about the camisole because she could put a tiny knot in the satin straps if necessary. It was enough that she'd soon be in something clean.

Beth was in heaven. Even the knowledge that Micah must have told Bolton or Peters exactly what to buy didn't faze her. She refused to be embarrassed by necessity. After shucking her sweater and tossing it onto the floor, she reached for the new one and turned to look in the mirror above the bureau. Not satisfied with holding it up to her shoulders, she pulled it on and smoothed the soft knit over her satin-and-lace camisole.

"It's perfect."

She dug her fingers into the wool between her breasts as she whirled to face him. Micah stood watching her from the door she hadn't even heard open, one shoulder propped against the doorframe, his thumbs hooked through the belt loops of his tight-fitting jeans.

He looked dark and dangerous in the meager light that snuck around the edges of the closed drapes. "You were too excited about your presents to bother with a light?" he asked softly, and walked over to the bureau to flick on the lamp. Then he reached behind him, pulled out his gun, and carefully put it down on the bureau.

"I didn't hear you come in," she said, her breaths coming in irregular intervals.

"I know." He leaned back against the wall next to the bureau and folded his arms across his chest. "I didn't want you to."

"Why?" The heated sensuality of his gaze stole her breath.

"Because the time for decisions is over, Beth," he said in a husky growl. "Knocking would have forced you to make another one, and we don't have time for that."

She gulped and gathered more of the sweater into her grasp. She hadn't expected this. Not now. But if not now, when? Micah was sending her out of Durango that night. Alone, she imagined, since he hadn't indicated otherwise.

Was this afternoon to be their only time together?

Given the circumstances that had brought them together, Beth imagined that might very well be the case.

Could she make love with Micah and know she might never see him again?

The idea appalled her sense of right and wrong, yet she knew she couldn't deny what she felt in order to resolve a moral dilemma.

Her gaze met his, and she realized that despite his words about decisions, he was giving her time to make another one.

A feeling of lightness came upon her then, a sense of knowing he'd been right all along. The decisions had already been made; all that was left was to act on them.

So why couldn't she say the words that would cause him to come to her and begin the loving? It was as though her capacity for speech had evaporated. She swallowed in frustration and willed him to make the first move.

He smiled, a soft, knowing smile that lit up his eyes. "That's right, Beth. Today we'll make love. We'll sort out tomorrow when it comes."

"Am I so transparent?" she asked, his gaze sending a hot shiver through her.

"Just predictable," he replied. "The woman I've come to know wouldn't be able to take a man to her bed without considering the future. All I ask is that you put it aside for now, and trust that I'll be there to help you figure it all out when the time comes."

"I don't know if I like being predictable."

"Only in some things," he said, cocking his head. "There are times, Beth, when I don't have the slightest idea how you'll react."

She liked the sound of that. "Times like when?"

"Like now. When I ask you to take off your sweater and camisole so I can look at your breasts, I don't know if you'll do it or be too shy." As he spoke his eyes darkened with a passion that heated the air between them.

Beth could feel her breasts tighten in response, and the warmth that gathered at the juncture of her thighs only shocked her by its intensity.

Had he asked, she knew she was ready for him now. Ready, and eager.

She didn't know how she could stand the wait. Without another thought, she crossed her hands at the hem of the sweater and pulled.

Micah almost came unglued when she tugged the sweater from her head, then very carefully folded it onto the bureau. Her breasts moved freely under the light pink camisole, and he didn't have to imagine where her nipples were, because they were poking against the satin with erect pride.

A shudder ripped through him, and he felt the discipline he'd always taken for granted slipping away. He went to her before she could take off the camisole. "I changed my mind," he growled, and captured her wrists in one hand behind her back. "I want to do it myself. I can look all I want from right here."

First, though, he needed her mouth. Urging her close against his body, he cupped her face with his long fingers and kissed her with a craving that didn't resemble anything he'd felt before—a gentle craving that nearly drove him mad.

He was as careful with her as he knew how to be, brushing her mouth with his so as not to frighten her, planting soft kisses at the corners of her lips instead of crushing her mouth against his and thrusting his tongue deep inside as he wanted.

She whimpered. He soothed, and was no longer content with the tender courtship. He could feel a slight tremble go through her when he slipped his tongue past her lips and into her mouth, but it was nothing compared with the lightning bolt that struck him when she opened her mouth wide and stroked his tongue with her own.

His hand slipped from her face to cover her breast. With her nipple centered on his palm he began to learn the shape of her, feeling what he had yet to see. She moaned, and he liked the sound of that so much, he lifted his mouth and watched her face as he closed his fingers on the sweet, erect nub.

She moaned again, and her eyelids fluttered open. Micah cupped her breast from outside the thin barrier of satin and watched her lips part as he tested her responses. She pleased him by responding to everything, a light touch bringing a sigh, a firmer one eliciting that moan that seemed to come from her very soul.

When he closed his lips around her satin-covered nipple, she tugged her wrists free and threaded her fingers into his hair. He took the hint and began to nibble on her tender flesh, his arm tight around her waist as he leaned back against the bureau for balance. When he nudged her legs apart with his knee, she hesitated only a moment, then let him lift her high on his thigh.

He could feel the heat of her through the denim, and he brought her as close to his hardness as he could manage without taking his mouth from her breast. When she arched her back to give him better access, he shoved the camisole above her breasts and took her flesh directly into his mouth. Her fingers dug into his shoulders as he teased, suckled, and nibbled, sharing his attentions between her breasts and knowing he'd never have waited this long had he known how perfect it would be to have her in his mouth.

It was too much. For her as well as for him. His own arousal was hard and aching for her, and so close to exploding that when she reached down to touch him he very nearly didn't stop her in time.

She was on the edge, too, and Micah couldn't deny himself the pleasure of watching. His own completion could wait—he hoped—while Beth's response was so intense he knew it could easily be repeated.

Kissing a wet trail up the side of her neck, he distracted her with his mouth as he guided her off his thigh and unsnapped her jeans. He pushed the zipper open, tugged the tight denim down a few inches, and curved his hand around the damp satin of her panties. His other arm slid around her waist, taking her weight when her knees gave out, keeping her close for his intimate exploration.

She cried aloud, his name and other things that made him know her urgency. He covered her mouth with his, his fingers caressing the secrets of her femininity through the satin as his tongue found hers. Pushing the panties aside, Micah slid two fingers deep inside her and with his thumb found the center of her excitement.

Beth came in a sudden, giant explosion of passion that was stunning in its beauty. Micah lifted his head and watched as she shuddered under his touch—her lips wet and parted, her face flushed, her eyelids fluttering. He stroked his fingers inside her, easing her down from the extraordinary climax, his gaze finally resting on her breasts.

They were beautiful. Slightly red from the attentions of his mouth, but Micah was glad he'd waited until now to see them. A final spasm shook her as he raked his fingers through the curls between her thighs, and he touched her nipple with his lips as her eyes slowly opened.

There was no embarrassment in her, and he knew his approval of her abandonment was matched by hers as she accepted what had happened to her as right and natural.

"You're beautiful," he said, lifting a hand to brush her hair out of her eyes.

A wicked gleam lit her eyes. "And you're probably very uncomfortable," she returned, winding her hands around his neck and leaning into him.

"You don't want to catch your breath?" he murmured against her neck, praying she'd say no.

Her laughter filled him with joy. "If I did, you'd cry."

She couldn't have been more right. Micah took her mouth with a kiss that went from gentle to insistent before it had hardly begun. He felt her hands at his jeans and was about to help her with his belt when he heard a loud knock at the suite door.

He tore his mouth from hers and rested his forehead on the top of her head as he forced a shaky control over his body.

"You don't have to answer that," she said, trying to bring his mouth down to hers so she could ravage it again.

His laugh came out more like a growl, but there wasn't anything he could do about that. "If I don't go, they'll bust in here to find out what's wrong." He tugged her hands from around his neck. "Don't move, honey. I'll be right back."

The moment the door closed behind him, Beth started to feel self-conscious, and tugged up her jeans and smoothed her camisole over her breasts. She was trying to figure out where the shy, reserved woman she'd always been had disappeared, when Micah pushed open the door and looked inside.

"Get dressed, Beth. Sutton's at the truck. We've got to move before he takes off."

She stared at him without moving. "You're taking me with you?"

"Not on your life," he said, then grabbed the yellow sweater. She let him pull it over her head, pushing her arms into the sleeves as he explained. "I'm taking you to Robertson. I can't leave you here alone."

He picked up his gun and tucked it out of sight, then took her chin in a firm grip and held her gaze with his own stern one. "You stay with Robertson until I come for you. I don't want to have to chase half over the countryside looking for you."

She grinned and ran her fingers through her hair to

put some sort of order in it. "Don't worry about me, Micah. I've learned my lesson."

He planted a hard kiss on her mouth, then glanced down at her waist. "I doubt that," he growled, and pulled up the zipper on her jeans.

TWELVE

"Sorry to be a bother." Beth grimaced and set the empty coffee cup on Alan's desk. "Micah wouldn't let me stay alone at the hotel." She didn't say where he'd gone, or why.

She didn't know, not really. Just that it had to do with Sutton and that she'd be terrified until Micah came back for her.

"It's just as well," Alan said amiably. "There are a few more things we need to clear up before I leave for Albuquerque." He sorted through some papers on his desk until he found the one he was looking for. "Were you aware that your ex-husband was married before?"

She wasn't, and she didn't particularly care either. "What does that have to do with me?"

"Nothing and everything, maybe. The marriage was dissolved about six years ago. I'm hoping we can trace the woman and see what her story is."

"You think Steven might have treated her the same way he treated me?" she asked, swallowing over the sick feeling that gave her.

"It's worth looking into. The more information we

have, the easier job I'll have when I confront him." Alan threw the paper back on the desk and regarded her with a curious expression. "There's something else I want to ask you."

"What?"

"How much do you know about Blackthorne?"

"Why do you ask?"

He sighed and pushed some papers aside to rest his forearms on the desk. "Because I know my sister would want me to. And because I know a great deal about Blackthorne that makes me . . . nervous," he said after a slight hesitation. "Particularly when I see there's something going on between you two."

Beth blushed, and would have told him there was nothing to be nervous about, except that she wanted to know what he knew. After all, Micah had told her practically nothing about himself. "What has Micah done to make you feel you need to warn me about him?"

"Warn is the wrong word. I have too much respect for the man to imagine he'd do anything to hurt you." He thrust his fingers through his hair, obviously at a loss. "What I mean is, do you have any idea what kind of business he's in?"

She couldn't help a tiny smile. "Of course I do, Alan. We met because of his job." A thought crossed her mind. "He said he was a 'simple private investigator.' Isn't that right?"

"There's nothing simple about Blackthorne," Alan said. "But yes, he is licensed as a PI. And he's got a fairly large firm full of people who are also licensed. You've probably met a few the last day or so."

When she just nodded, he continued. "While I haven't seen the numbers, my guess is he's got one of the biggest PI firms between the Rockies and the Mississippi."

Her brows rose, but she couldn't think of anything to say that wouldn't sound smug. She'd known he was good.

Alan shook his head and grinned. "You knew this."

"I didn't," she said, answering his grin. "I didn't have to. Micah is the sort of person who wouldn't stand for being second best."

"He hasn't always been on your side."

"When it counted, he was." Beth slouched down into the chair, wondering how she'd gotten lucky enough to have the boss on her tail, and not one of the minions.

Alan answered without waiting for the question. "One of Blackthorne's trademarks is the personal interest he takes in the cases his firm accepts. The more unanswered questions there are about who, where, and why, the longer he stays interested."

"And in my case, once he solved where, the why began to interest him."

Alan shrugged. "Apparently. It's probably why he's so successful. That, and his obsession with justice."

"Justice?"

"Blackthorne specializes in it." Alan threw himself back in his chair and swung his feet onto the desk without taking his gaze from her. "What the law can't or won't do, Blackthorne will. He gets results from employing very unorthodox means, some of them illegal."

"Like what?" Instead of being daunted, she was fascinated.

"Remember the Colorado investment broker who bilked his clients of about ten million dollars, then hid behind a herd of lawyers who protected him so well he almost got off scot-free?"

Her brow furrowed as she tried to recall the details. "There was something about the clients not being able to prove he defrauded them intentionally. Then a couple of months after his case had been dismissed, he was arrested and jailed." She shrugged. "I guess the police got their evidence after all."

Alan shook his head. "Blackthorne got the evidence. How he did it is only supposition, but it's clear he didn't use any of the methods open to the legal community."

Then he told her a story about a man Blackthorne tricked into coming back to Colorado, where he was arrested for extortion. And then about a gang of burglars who'd been mysteriously put out of business before the police even figured out who the men were.

And then there were the kidnappers Micah had tracked all the way to the East Coast and captured before the law enforcement agencies had managed to muddle through their own red tape.

Beth listened, realizing that if she hadn't known it before, she knew it now. She'd never had a chance against Micah.

The question was, did she have a chance *with* him? The emotions that drew her to him were strong, but were his responses built on emotion, too, or mere attraction?

Would a man who lived on the edge want a woman like Beth—a woman who hardly understood the dangers, much less how to avoid them? Or deal with them.

Her mad flight with Jeremy was the closest she'd ever come to the kind of world Micah lived in. Would she be able to stay with a man who made that dark, dangerous world his life?

Would he want her to?

Alan cleared his throat, and she looked up to find him staring at her. "Like I said before, Beth. I'm not warning you about Blackthorne. He's probably got a better sense of right and wrong than most people. The fact that he came down on your side of this mess proves that." He swung his feet to the floor and got up to look out the window. "What makes me nervous is knowing how harsh and unyielding Blackthorne has to be in order to accomplish what he does."

Harsh and unyielding. Yes, Micah was both of those. Beth thought about the storm, when she'd locked Micah out of the truck and he'd threatened to shoot her. About the way he'd tied her up in order to teach her a lesson, then how he'd shot out the Explorer's tire.

She thought about the night he'd told her he was taking Jeremy from her, and how implacable he'd been about not trusting even himself to judge when a child's life was at stake. He'd taken Jeremy from her, and she knew it had been a decision forced on him by that unyielding sense of justice Alan was talking about.

Micah had taken Jeremy because it was the only way he knew to keep him safe. She had come to terms with that during the long night when she'd lain with Jeremy in Micah's arms.

Beth sighed and shrugged. There was nothing she could say that would explain why none of what concerned Alan bothered her. "You seem to know a lot about him, Alan."

He surprised her with a grin. "I guess you might say I'm a fan of Blackthorne's. Even in a backwater like Durango, I manage to keep up with some of his accomplishments. In fact, if I didn't know you were emotionally involved with him, I'd probably be saying you couldn't be in better hands."

She smiled back at him. "At the moment I'm not at all sure of anything. Especially what I'm feeling about Micah as a man. It's hard to separate that from how I react to him where Jeremy's concerned."

There was a knock and the door opened before Alan

could respond. Beth looked over her shoulder to see Micah striding into the room. He came straight over to her and put his hand on her shoulder as though he needed proof that she was real and he didn't trust his eyes.

Her heart gave an extra thump, then settled into an even rhythm. Now that he was back, it could beat normally again.

"This is the first time you've stayed where I put you," he said.

She covered his hand with her own and patted it. "That's because Alan kept me busy with tales of your exploits. You should have told me you were famous, Blackthorne. I'd have treated you with due respect."

His fingers tightened on her shoulder, and he gave Alan a long, hard look. "Trying to save her from me, Robertson?"

Alan laughed and shook his head. "Just keeping her informed, Blackthorne. As her attorney, it's part of my job."

"I hate it when people talk as though I'm not here," Beth grumbled.

"I would have told her," Micah said with a harshness in his voice that sounded strangely like regret.

"Sooner or later," Alan agreed, quirking an eyebrow at Micah's odd reaction. "Now you don't have to."

"What's the problem, Blackthorne?" Beth demanded crossly, yanking on his sweater to get his attention. "So what if Alan told me you're not just a run-of-the-mill PI. I always knew you were . . . special."

Micah dropped his gaze to meet hers. "There are a lot of people who say I'm no better than a paid vigilante."

"Because you don't always work within the law?"

He nodded. "I told you before. The legal system is sometimes too confining for what I have to do."

She got to her feet and stood close enough so she could feel his heat, his strength. "I'm the last person to condemn you for doing what's right, Micah."

He slipped his hand behind her neck and massaged the tender skin there. "You did what you had to because you had no choice. I do it for money."

"So explain why you didn't send Jeremy back to Corbett." When he hesitated, she said it for him. "You did what was right, Micah, what was decent. Not what you were getting paid for, and certainly not what was easy." She raised up on her toes until she was only a few inches short of looking him in the eye. "Besides, I never thought you were a man who cared what other people thought."

"I care what you think," he murmured. "You'll be pleased to know I didn't get my way with Sutton."

"You thought I'd mind you sending him south?"

"You didn't know all of what I wanted to do," he said darkly, then went on to tell them that Sutton was in the county jail awaiting arraignment for firing a gun in the city limits—a gun he had no business carrying. Micah was miffed because he'd hoped to lasso Sutton into his private grip and send him away to do time in that little South American country he'd defrauded. The scenario had played out differently—with Sutton slipping from Micah's grasp and into that of the local cops.

A shiver traveled through Beth at the tender look Micah gave her as he tucked her into his side. She listened with only half a mind to the final arrangements he made with Alan, the other half not being much use in its befuddled state.

Micah cared. It was a beginning.

THIRTEEN

The next few hours passed in a blur of activity that would have taken Beth's breath away if she'd been given a chance to catch it in the first place. Upon returning to the hotel suite, she latched onto her overnight bag, which had mysteriously appeared in her absence, and commandeered the bathroom for what she thought would be a long, well-deserved bit of privacy. She was wrong. She'd barely gotten out of the shower and pulled on the new lingerie before her idyll was interrupted by Micah.

She realized he must have made a trip across the hall to borrow the bath there, because when he stuck his head into the bathroom to tell her to hurry up, his hair was damp and he'd shaved. He stood looking at her for a long moment, his eyes dark and heated as his gaze raked her from head to toe before settling on the pulse that beat wildly at the base of her throat.

He made a move toward her, then abruptly shook his head, muttering something about time. Then he backed out, his groan of frustration cut off by the door he pulled shut behind him. Beth turned the hair dryer on and with trembling hands worked the brush through her hair. A week ago the idea of a man seeing her in nothing more than skimpy panties and a camisole would have been ludicrous. There hadn't been any men in her life then, and certainly not one who had the audacity to interrupt her bath without so much as a knock.

There hadn't been anyone who could look at her with such undisguised yearning and make her wish he'd forget their hurry. She'd wanted him to touch her with his body, not just his eyes.

Beth shivered, then quickly pulled on her new clothes and gathered up the bits and pieces of her belongings. She'd hardly finished when Micah came into the bedroom to hurry her along, all business in his determined haste.

They left the hotel in the Explorer, and Durango in the same private jet Micah had used for Jeremy. Bolton came with them, and they were airborne before Micah broke off his quiet dialogue with the man to tell her they were going to Denver.

To Jeremy.

His palm, rough and callused, cupped the side of her face for a long moment before he moved back to the front of the cabin where Bolton was waiting for him. Beth felt the tension drain from her body as she turned in the leather-cushioned seat to watch the orange sun slowly sink behind the jagged peaks of the Rockies. For the first time since the nightmare had begun, she felt like she could relax and believe that everything would be all right.

Micah had taken her problems and made them his own.

He'd taken her son, and was giving him back to her.

He'd taken her heart, and she didn't know that he had any idea that he had. Or what he'd do when he found out. She loved Micah, and knew that whatever doubts she had, they wouldn't change that basic premise.

During the short, yet seemingly interminable flight to Denver, Beth tried not to dream or wish or hope. Tried and failed, because her dreams were from the heart . . . a heart that was filled with love.

He was taking her to Jeremy. Beth was so excited that she could hardly bear the enormous amount of time it took to taxi from the runway to the hangar. Micah had told her just before landing that they'd go straight to where Jeremy was staying, and she had kissed him right in front of Bolton and God, not caring who was looking because she was so gloriously happy.

Micah had kissed her back, clearly not concerned about their audience either.

They were whisked from the airport in a car that took them across town and then halfway back again before turning onto a quiet, tree-lined street. Micah had been silent during the ride, only speaking when she asked about their circuitous route. Precautions, he told her, then squeezed the hand he'd held all along and didn't say anything more until the car pulled to a stop in front of a small, shingled house.

Micah tugged her hand to keep her from opening the door as the driver got out and walked up to the house. "There's something you have to accept before we go inside, Beth."

"What?" She looked at the house and saw the driver go inside without knocking.

"We can't stay here with Jeremy, and he can't come with us."

She stared at him without comprehending, wishing the light were better so she could see what was in his dark gaze. "What are you saying?"

"Until Robertson gets your ex-husband sorted out, nothing has changed for Jeremy. Even though my office has been feeding Corbett lies about what we've been up to, he's bound to realize something's not right, since there's been plenty of time to reach Albuquerque. And I've no idea what Sutton's told him. We have to assume he used his one phone call after being arrested to call Corbett."

"You think Steven might have other people looking for Jeremy?" Her stomach clenched in panic, and not even Micah's calming touch could totally alleviate it.

Micah shrugged. "It's likely. Sutton probably won't be able to shake free of Durango for a few days, so he's useless to Corbett."

Beth stole another glance at the house, then swiveled back to meet Micah's gaze. "Then why are we here?" she whispered, her heart in her throat.

"Because you need to see your son, Beth. I wanted you to see that he's happy and healthy and safe."

"You thought I didn't believe you?"

He took her other hand and held them both in his warm clasp. "I didn't think about that," he admitted. "I was being selfish, thinking about myself. I just knew you wouldn't worry as much if you saw him for yourself."

"Why is that selfish?"

He lifted her hands and rubbed his chin on her knuckles. "Because tonight, when I take you to my home and make love to you, I want all your thoughts to be about me. About us."

The heart that was stuck in her throat started pounding double time, making it difficult to speak clearly. "That's not selfish, Micah," she said, a helpless laugh escaping her lips. "It's called being thorough."

His own laugh was warm against her hands. Beth was torn between the urge to prolong the intimate moment and the need to be with her baby inside the house. Micah solved her dilemma by reaching across her to push open her door. He followed her out, steadying her as she climbed over the mound of snow at the curb.

His arm was solid around her waist as they walked up the salt-pocked sidewalk. Beth was thinking how natural it was for her to accept his easy strength, when the door opened and she saw Jeremy waving all four limbs at her from his perch in Cora's arms, his halo of white fuzz backlit against the house's lights.

Moments later Micah stood to one side of the small living room and watched as Beth took her son into her arms. Silky brown hair curtained her face as she bent her head over the baby. Soft words of love and delight filled the otherwise silent room, and Micah felt a bewildering sense of loneliness creep over him.

He took off his hat and was moving away to talk with Cora when Beth reached out a hand to stop him. Her eyes were misty and her smile soft as she looked up at him. "Don't go away," she said, her voice low and tremulous.

He lifted her hand and pressed a kiss to the pad of her thumb. "I'm not going anywhere, honey," he murmured just loud enough for her to hear. "Not without you. But right now, you need to spend some time alone with your son." He let her hand go and took Jeremy from her so she could get out of her coat. When he'd settled them on the sofa, he went to find Cora and the driver.

The loneliness had vanished.

Micah's home surprised her in both size and style. Beth had expected a downtown apartment. His two-story brick house sat on its own acre in a quietly elegant suburb. She'd envisioned modern, almost utilitarian furnishings. The traditional decor that greeted her in every room was accented by English antiques and Impressionist paintings by a variety of artists. The only room that was the slightest bit modern was the kitchen, and even that had been designed to resemble one from an Early American farmhouse, with glass-fronted cabinets, an open china hutch against one wall, and a long work counter that extended the length of the room.

As Micah went through the house checking windows and such, Beth wandered through the ground floor. When he caught up with her in the glassed-in breakfast room, she was shaking her head bemusedly.

"What's wrong?" he asked.

"Nothing," she said, then laughed. "It's just that this isn't at all what I imagined." She wandered past the table to the end of the room, where two overstuffed chairs faced the windows. Skirting the ficus that reached for the high ceiling, she fell into a chair and kicked her shoes off. "It's . . . it's . . ." She waggled a hand impatiently at her loss for words. "It's beautiful."

He grinned and lifted a hand to the wall switch. With a flick of his finger, the room was plunged into darkness. He waited a moment for his eyes to adjust to the natural light from the stars and moon, then walked over to stand behind her chair. "My mother bought this house in one of her 'back to basics' moods. When she tired of it, I bought it from her."

"Where is she now?" Beth twisted in the chair to look up at him, then got to her knees and turned to face him.

Micah took her head between his hands and rubbed his fingers in the superfine texture of her hair, his thumbs caressing the soft skin at her temples. "With my father. Somewhere warm, I assume. She never did get used to the cold."

"I'm not cold," she murmured, and her eyes drifted shut. "Why this house, Micah? What is it that made you want this one?"

He leaned his hips into the back of the chair and began to massage her scalp. "Because it's comfortable, I suppose. And because I like having old things around me. It gives me a sense of permanence." A tiny sigh escaped her lips as he pushed his fingers behind her ears, caressing the sensitive skin between there and her nape. "My work requires me to be gone a lot, and more often than not the living conditions are on the grungy side. Coming home to this house gives me pleasure."

Her hands crept up to curl around his wrists. "You're a hard man to figure out, Micah Blackthorne."

His hands stilled in her hair. "Not that hard, Beth. I do what I do because I have to. I live like I do because I want to." He hunkered down until his face was level with hers. "I touch you because I can't help myself. And we'll be lovers because that's the way things were meant to be between us."

"You're so sure of everything," she whispered, pressing her palm against the side of his face.

"Not everything," he said. "But this, yes. You belong in my arms and in my bed."

There were questions in her eyes that he chose to ignore. Now wasn't the time for them. Maybe later, he thought as he tightened his fingers in her hair and drew her forward until their lips were touching.

Maybe later he'd have some answers.

In the meantime, there was her mouth to think about, and how sweet she tasted. How exciting. He nuzzled her lips with his, teasing until she opened for him. Micah probed inside with his tongue, a gentle exploration that almost got out of hand when she responded by curling her tongue around his.

He retreated, then took a deep breath and started again, determined to set a slow, luxurious pace. They had all the time in the world now. There was no logical reason he could give her that would excuse his behavior if he threw her onto the table and took her now, hard and fast like his body was demanding. No excuse, except that his aching need for her made it difficult to think logically.

The reasons to be slow and gentle were substantial. Their earlier loveplay had impressed upon him the need to be careful with Beth. When he'd slid his fingers inside her, she'd been tight, almost impossibly so for a woman who'd given birth not so many months ago. The memory of her tightness both drove and restrained him. It was an internal battle for control that he knew he couldn't win if he allowed her to set the pace.

He didn't want to hurt her, and knew he was big enough to do just that if he wasn't careful. She'd been abused enough, and he was determined to make their love memorable in ways that wouldn't remind her of those past abuses.

Another time, another day, she'd trust him enough to be a little rough, a little hard in a way that would give her pleasure, not pain. But not today.

He settled his mouth on hers and turned his head slightly to adjust the pressure. She made a sound deep in her throat, and the hands that had gripped his wrists wound upward to lock behind his neck. The kiss deepened despite his efforts at control, and he began to breathe faster as the world went spinning out of control, dragging him in its wake.

He suddenly lifted his mouth from Beth's, and he couldn't miss the stark disappointment in her expression. "Don't look at me like that unless you want me to take you right here, right now."

She gave a frustrated cry and tried to capture his mouth again. He stayed out of her range by sheer luck. "Beth, stop that! Don't you know the hell I've been through today? I'm so close to losing my control that the only surprise is I'm not inside you already."

She looked up at him, her eyes clouded with passion. "I realize you're upset about Sutton slipping through your fingers—"

"Damn Sutton!" he swore, and ground his mouth against hers to shut her up. When she was properly winded from the long, seductive mating of their mouths, he set her straight. "My control—or lack of it—is entirely due to the look on your face when you climaxed in my arms this afternoon. The little noises you made, the way you tightened around my fingers." At her gasp, he put his hands on her shoulders and shook her gently. "I need to be inside you, Beth, but you're so damned tight—" He shook his head as if he could deny the urgency of his arousal. "I *won't* take the risk of hurting you."

"If you don't make love to me, Micah, I think I'll die." A small laugh escaped her. "I know I won't, but right now, it feels like it."

"Why?" Suddenly he wanted to hear what was going on in her head, to lend a semblance of order to his own scrambled emotions.

She blinked twice and he felt her fingers tremble in his hair. "It seems I've wanted you forever. Even when I was so afraid of you I could hardly breathe, I wanted you. Over the past few days I've gone through all kinds of hell, hating myself for responding to you, denying I was attracted and knowing it was a lie." She took a deep breath and dropped her hands to the chair. "I've wanted you and hated you, too, because you were taking the one thing from my life that meant anything."

His gaze narrowed on her face. "Are you worried that I'll change my mind and keep you from your son?"

She shook her head impatiently. "This isn't about Jeremy anymore. It's about me, and how scared I am that I'll never feel this way again."

"How scared are you?"

His voice was a low rasp that had a cutting edge to it, but Beth didn't let herself be put off by it. She'd come this far, there was no backing down now. She dug her fingers into the back of the chair as Micah dropped his hands to his thighs and looked at her without blinking.

"Terrified." She licked her lips and met his gaze without shrinking from the sudden anger that flared there. She didn't know what had prompted it, but knew she couldn't stop what had to be said.

"Do I frighten you, Beth?"

She nodded, then spoke quickly before his anger could deepen. "I feel things for you I've never felt before. It terrifies me that you'll walk out of my life before I've figured out why it's so important to me that you don't."

The anger was replaced by a gentle resignation she understood even less. He bowed his head for a moment, and when he looked up again she knew the confusion that roiled inside her was matched by his.

"I never want you to be afraid of me," he said quietly. "For any reason." He lifted a hand to smooth the worries from her expression. "I won't hurt you, not if you let me be careful with you. I'll take care of you the best way I know how."

"I know that," she whispered. "Physically, you're too much in control to act in anger. Not like Steven."

The rage Micah felt at the mention of her ex-husband's cruelty was shunted aside as he realized she'd missed the point. Threading his fingers into her hair, he held her head so that she couldn't look away. "I wasn't only talking about physical abuse, though God knows you've got reason to focus on that." He leaned forward and brushed his lips across hers, reveling in her unique softness. When he lifted his head, the panic he'd seen at her reference to Steven had disappeared. "I want to be more than a lover to you, Beth. Much more."

"You do?"

He nodded, then caught his breath as she reached for his hand and brought his knuckles to her mouth. With great care, she touched her lips to each one, a feathery kiss to the wound he'd all but forgotten.

"I hated myself for running out on you that night," she murmured.

He rubbed his knuckles across her cheek and shook his head. "You had Jeremy to think of. Running was your only choice."

"I think I've known from the beginning that you wouldn't hurt me."

"You were right." Micah decided enough had been said. They'd talk later, after they'd made love enough times to take the raw edge off their desire—if that were possible. Later, after Jeremy was no longer an issue for worry.

Later, he'd give her all the reasons why she'd hate sharing his life, then ask her to marry him anyway.

For now, though, he needed to make love to her before he went insane with wanting her. He got to his feet, then put his hands around her waist and lifted her clean across the top of the chair. He let her body slide down his until she was standing on her toes and his arousal was throbbing against the softness of her belly.

"Feel me, Beth," he murmured, and closed his big hands around her hips to hold her tight against him. "I think I've been hard since that time in the car when your butt brushed my arm." He groaned and slid his hands to her bottom, digging his fingers into her soft curves. "Shall we make love right here, honey? The lights are out and there's nothing outside the windows but a very tall fence and a bunch of trees, though I doubt I'd care right now if there were grandstands beyond the windows."

Beth wound her arms around his neck and urged his mouth down to meet hers. She could feel the last thread of his restraint stretch to the breaking point as he stroked his hands up her back, then down again to cup her bottom. He deepened the kiss, drawing her into a swirl of longing unlike any she'd ever known. Her breasts were pressed into the muscled planes of his chest, and as he moved his hips against her the gentle need that had lain warm and complacent within her suddenly burst into flames.

He held her like that for another moment, then suddenly swung her into his arms and headed out of the room to the stairs.

"What happened to making love in front of the windows?" she asked.

"I forgot about your ribs." He pressed a kiss to her forehead and headed up the wide staircase, two steps at a time. "It'll be easier for you in a bed. Besides, I'll probably be too weak afterward to carry you up."

She laughed and snuggled against him. "I could walk."

"Not after I get through with you," he murmured, striding into a large room at the end of the landing. He set her down next to the bed, then moved away to flick on a bedside lamp.

Beth watched him as he crossed the thick carpet and drew the drapes. When he sat down on a leather-covered bench to pull off his boots, she let her gaze drift over the rich mahogany furnishings. The contradictory feelings that had plagued her for the past few days rose again. She felt nervous at what was to come, and impatient for it to start.

"Beth."

She looked up to find him standing just a few feet away, and realized he'd done more than just take off his boots. He'd stripped to his jeans, and his chest filled her vision, the tautly powerful muscles covered with dark curling hair that arrowed to a narrow line and disappeared into his jeans. She reached out a finger to trace the silver line of the scar that ran down the side of his abdomen. The muscles tightened at her touch, and she looked up to find him watching her. She quivered in reaction to the fiercely male intent she saw in his eyes.

"Take off your jeans, Beth. Now."

His voice had a guttural edge that was excitingly erotic. She moved her hands under her sweater and undid the fastenings to her jeans as Micah clenched his own hands at his sides. When she started to push them from her hips, he shut his eyes and took a deep breath.

"Hurry up, honey," he urged, and flexed his hands as though that gave him a measure of patience. "Please."

His words only made her clumsy, and it took her much longer than it should have to accomplish that simple task. When she finally stepped out of the jeans and kicked them aside, her hands were trembling and her heart was beating loudly enough to be heard in the next county. She straightened to find him watching her again, his gaze fastened on the lower edge of her sweater, which just barely hit the top of her thighs.

He didn't move, and she was suddenly at a loss. Embarrassed almost, but that wasn't it, because nothing in her life had ever felt so right, so completely good.

"Now your panties," he said. When she hesitated, he

added, "Unless you don't mind losing them. If you leave it for me, I'm likely to rip them off you."

The eroticism of his words kicked the breath from her. With lungs starved for air, she hooked her thumbs into the thin nylon and pushed them down her legs.

As they hit the floor Micah looked as though his own breathing was as labored as hers. He moved toward her then, reaching out until his fingers closed around the edge of her sweater. "I can't decide if I'm in a hurry or not," he said in a low, sexy growl as he began to slide the soft knit upward. "Either way, there's time for this, I think." The sweater slipped easily over her camisole, gliding across her breasts, his knuckles brushing the tips in passing.

Beth couldn't help the small cry that seemed to spring from the very center of her being, just as he couldn't help his smile of pure masculine appreciation at her reaction.

She raised her arms when he told her to, then shook her hair from her eyes after he'd pulled the sweater and camisole over her head. He threw them aside, then dropped his hands to his belt and unbuckled it. Beth stood absolutely still as he unsnapped his jeans and jerked the zipper down.

Micah heard the sound of her breath catching, and knew she echoed his urgency. He hoped so. There wasn't going to be any time for preliminaries. He'd be gentle with her, but first he had to get inside her tight sheath before he went mad. He shoved the jeans down his hips, kicked them off, and reached past her to flick the satin quilt from the bed.

Without touching her, he crowded her against the bed until she lost her balance and fell backward. The heat in his groin intensified as he followed her down, and he hooked an arm around her waist to bring her fully onto the bed. Her nipples teased his chest, and he pressed his forehead to her shoulder in an attempt to conserve whatever fragment of control he might have left.

When she stroked her soft hands across his back, he almost cracked. Lifting his head, he captured her wrists and pressed them over her head. She squirmed against his aggressiveness, and he reinforced his position by throwing a heavy thigh over her restless legs.

"Easy," he breathed, and stroked his free hand across her hip to the soft curls between her legs. She writhed beneath him, but he didn't pull back until his fingers had discovered the wet proof of her readiness.

It was all he needed to know. He pushed a knee between her legs and made a place for his hips between her thighs. Capturing her gaze with his, he reached down between their bodies and guided himself into position.

"It might hurt," he said.

"I've done this before," she returned, a game smile on her lips.

He scowled, but his anger was only at himself because he hadn't found her first. He bent down and took her mouth in a deep, consuming kiss. Then he let go of her wrists and caught her hands beside her face, threading his fingers with hers as he began to enter her. He locked his gaze on hers, willing her to keep her eyes open because he wanted to know exactly what she was feeling. If there was pain, he'd have to back off for a while and make her want him so badly that any momentary pain wouldn't matter.

Her exquisite tightness brought beads of sweat to his face as he fought the urge to thrust all the way inside and be done with it. She arched beneath him, and he pushed more, giving her words of praise and encouragement in a long, continuous breath. She felt like hot, liquid silk around him, and he told her so as he urged her to take more of him, *all* of him. He gripped her thigh and pulled it up to his waist. She wrapped her other leg around him, and suddenly he was seated in her to the hilt.

Micah took the first breath he was aware of for a very long time and brushed the damp hair from her forehead. "Now we can get down to the preliminaries," he said, and bent his head to take her nipple into his mouth.

Where before Beth had been luxuriating in the slow heat of his lovemaking, now she burned. Micah caressed her with his mouth, hands, and body, finding all the sensitive places on her body and teaching her new ones. He thrust into her several times, then disengaged and took her with his mouth until she was crying his name and for him to stop, for him not to stop. He entered her again, filling her with his demanding need, and pushed her to the edge of sanity with his slow, rhythmic thrusts.

He was making her mad with the waiting, the wanting. She licked a bead of sweat from his shoulder, rubbed her palms along the slick muscles of his back. Her fingers clenched in his firm buttocks, and instead of that making him hurry, he laughed and kissed her hard and deep, his tongue mating with hers in the same slow rhythm as their bodies below.

When he lifted his mouth away, she was trembling and crying and gasping for breath—all of which brought a smile to his face. "I knew it would be wild with you," he murmured, and bent to nibble on her ear. "I knew how it would be, yet I didn't have any idea. Do you think we can manage to do this often?"

"Mm." It was all she had the energy for, but it didn't matter. A dark, hungry look erased the humor in his eyes, and he began thrusting into her—harder, faster, until she knew the world certainly rocked with them.

The rhythm of his loving carried them over that precipice he'd been both seeking and avoiding. He drove them into a burst of light and sensation that was filled with his shout of completion, her cry of joy.

In the end, as she shuddered in his arms in those last moments before sleep claimed her, Beth heard something else too.

She heard words of love, and knew that she was already dreaming.

Micah reached for her in the night, and the way she came to him without hesitation filled him with a satisfaction like none he'd ever known. He made love to her slowly, not entering her until she begged him, and only then because his control was rapidly slipping.

Afterward, she went to sleep in his arms, her butt nuzzled against his loins and her breasts nudging his forearm. He'd never slept with a woman, not like that . . . and never because he wanted her near when he awoke. Before, if a woman had stayed, it had been because he'd been too tired or lazy to take her home.

Now he knew he wouldn't sleep unless he could hold her.

Beth was suddenly more a part of his life than he could do without. He closed his eyes and wondered how she liked Denver, because he sure as hell didn't want to relocate.

He would, though. If she asked, he'd go anywhere with her. And Jeremy.

A son. His eyes flashed open, and he smiled into the darkness. He was going to be a daddy. His palm slid against Beth's flat, firm stomach and he wondered how long it would be before there was another child to keep Jeremy company.

There was only one catch to Micah's picture of familial bliss: Beth. He couldn't afford to assume she'd marry him just because it fit in with what he wanted.

He'd have to make her want it too.

FOURTEEN

Beth awoke to find herself alone. Turning onto her side, she ran her hand over the place where Micah had slept and knew he'd been gone for quite some time. There wasn't a trace of his warmth on the sheets. Squinting at the digital clock beside the bed, she realized she'd nearly slept the morning away.

"No wonder he's gone," she muttered, glancing across the room at the curtains that efficiently sealed out any of the day's light. She rolled onto her back, closing her eyes as she stretched and took inventory of her body's condition. The pain in her ribs was almost gone, but there was a new, unaccustomed stiffness in her thigh muscles that reflected the activities of the night. Memories of the love they'd made came flooding back, making her breath catch as she replayed the scenes in her mind.

He'd been gentle and demanding, and so generous in his sensuality that she'd found herself responding every time as though it was the first. The long dark hours had been full of discovery and joy. And enormous satisfaction as each time she'd watched Micah's ever-present control slip and shatter with the intensity of their union.

She felt her body quickening in response to the powerful images of his lovemaking, and shivered beneath the covers.

"If you're thinking what I think you're thinking, you're probably not interested in breakfast."

Her eyes flew open at the husky male voice, and she looked up to find Micah watching her from the doorway. "How do you know what I'm thinking?" she asked, then caught her breath as he rubbed his palm across the front of his jeans.

When he moved his hand to hook a finger through his belt loop, she couldn't miss the bulge that pressed at the soft denim. He cleared his throat and leaned a shoulder against the doorframe without taking his eyes from her. "I know, Beth. We're too much in tune with each other to miss the obvious."

The heat that pooled between her thighs was a potent reminder of her extraordinary response to him. She dug her fingers into the sheet that covered her and took deep, even breaths in an attempt to deny the longings that filled her very soul.

She couldn't. With a shake of her head at her weakness, she kicked off the sheet. "Breakfast can wait. I can't."

Micah's gaze darkened. He left the door and came to her, jerking down the zipper of his jeans as he walked. His pants were open when he reached down to spread her thighs and kneel between them. He lowered himself to her and thrust inside without taking his heated gaze from hers. Beth arched at the suddenness of his entry, then lifted her legs to wrap them around his waist because she wanted more of him . . . all of him.

The love they made was every bit as hard and fast as Micah had wanted the night before. It was exciting and hot and filled with an urgency that overwhelmed her every thought. When it was over, Micah collapsed atop her for a moment, then murmured something about her ribs and rolled to his back, keeping her safe and warm in his arms. Beth snuggled into his wide chest, and knew she'd never again find the kind of peace she'd discovered with Micah.

The kind of joy.

Micah was on the phone when Beth, dressed in yesterday's clothes, made her way to the kitchen. He glanced up and gave her a slow smile, his eyes missing nothing of the well-loved complacency she knew was written all over her face. She stood hesitantly as he resumed talking, then followed her nose to the end of the counter where a half-filled coffeepot gave off the heavenly aroma of fresh-brewed coffee. She took a cup from a hook beneath the cabinet and filled it, then wandered into the breakfast room. She was standing in front of the wall of windows, trying to imagine what sorts of bushes and flowers lay dormant beneath the snow that blanketed the backyard, when she heard Micah slam the phone back onto the hook. She turned as he came into the room, and only just managed to control the instinctive jump of nerves his angry countenance provoked.

The emotional scars of living with a man who couldn't control his anger wouldn't be forgotten in a single day. Knowing that Micah would never hurt her was easy to accept intellectually; controlling her emotional responses to anger and fear would require more time.

She smiled tentatively, and he crossed the room to stand beside her. Dipping his head, he drank from her cup without taking it from her hands. When he met her gaze, the anger had been banked but not forgotten. "I just spoke with Robertson. He's in Albuquerque and nearly ready to confront Corbett." Micah waited until she looked up at him before continuing. "He's got a little problem, though. No one seems to know where Corbett is."

"Steven's missing?" Her brow furrowed in confusion, and he reached up to stroke the long, shiny hair as she assimilated the facts.

"There could be a simple explanation," Micah went on, "like maybe he's staying with a woman. Or he might have gotten wind of what we're doing." He watched Beth carefully for signs of panic. There weren't any, and he couldn't decide whether to be proud of the control she'd learned over the past few days, or furious that she should have to deal with this at all. He reached down and took her hand in his, then continued to speculate. "If Corbett thinks we're after him, he might decide to lay low until things are back under control."

She looked up at him, and the understanding he saw in her eyes tore at his gut. He knew she realized there was another option that fit Corbett's profile.

"The only way he can get control is to stop us," she said quietly, then suddenly dug her nails into his hand as fear overtook her. "Jeremy—"

"Jeremy is safe," he said firmly, and slid an arm around her shoulders to bring her close. "Cora is the sister of one of my men, and the house where they're staying belongs to a friend of her mother's. There is no way anyone could trace them there." Even so, he'd left two men with Cora and Jeremy, just to be on the safe side.

He absorbed Beth's shudder of relief, shaking his head in wonder at her total trust in him. It amazed him that once she'd made the transition from fear to trust, she didn't waver in that trust one iota. The phone rang then, and he left her reluctantly to answer it. When he came back, he was careful not to let her see the concern in his eyes.

"That was the office. Sutton made bail and disappeared. The men I left in Durango think he was smuggled out of the jail sometime during the night." He put his hands on her shoulders and felt the shiver that overtook her.

"How could they let him go?" Beth asked. "I thought shooting a gun at someone or even at a car deserved more than a few hours behind bars." Her heart beat faster as she considered the implications. Jeremy was still at risk, at least until Alan was ready to move on her ex-husband. And Micah, too, because Sutton had good reason to come after him.

Micah shook his head. "From what we can piece together, Sutton used his one phone call to get Corbett to use whatever influence he had to get him out fast." He squeezed her shoulders, then dropped his hands, shoving them into his pockets. "This is one of those quirks of the law that made me give it up."

"Does this mean you're going after him?"

"Not yet." His eyes flickered over the snow-covered garden before returning to her. "I'll take care of Sutton when you and Jeremy are safe. Not before."

She lifted a hand to his cheek, and he turned his head to nuzzle her palm with his lips. "I'm sorry about breakfast," he murmured.

"I'm not."

He laughed. He'd been thinking future, not past. "I'm talking about the breakfast we can't have because there's no time, honey."

"Why?"

"Because we have to get out of here. There's every reason to assume Sutton knows where I live, so staying here is foolhardy." He didn't say that if Beth weren't there, he'd wait for Sutton instead of moving out to avoid him. But while the delay in settling the score between them chafed at Micah, he wasn't going to risk Beth getting into the middle. He pulled away from her sweet caress and stepped back. "I'll go upstairs and get our things while you finish your coffee. By the time we're ready, Bolton and Peters will be here to pick us up."

Beth watched Micah bound up the stairs until he disappeared from sight. After finding her shoes where she'd left them the night before and putting them on, she slid into a chair at the table. She squeezed her eyes shut, trying to wipe out the vivid image of Micah facing Sutton's gun in that parking lot behind the gas station without flinching. She'd known then that he was an unusual man, one whose fears would never be on display for others to take advantage of.

The only time she'd seen his iron control waver had been last night, and even then she'd known there was something inherent in his lovemaking that would keep her safe regardless of how wild or voracious his passion became. Control, she realized, was everything to Micah. What he decided to do, he did. What he chose not to, he didn't.

What would he choose to do about her? she wondered, and wished that for just one moment he'd let go of that control and listen to the dreams of her heart . . . those same dreams in which she'd heard him speak words of love.

There was a peculiar scraping noise outside, and when she looked over her shoulder all she saw were the black iron legs of a chair as it came crashing through the window. She screamed for Micah and knocked over her chair trying to get out of the way. She was too late. A flying chair leg caught her arm, whipping her off her feet as the chair crashed downward. Bits of glass seemed to hang in the air around her as she fell, and her hip grazed the edge of the table in passing. Throwing up her arms, she protected her head as best she could from the heavy chair that bounced off her shoulders.

Glass was still falling when she looked up to find Sutton bending over her, his expression impassive as he grabbed her arm and jerked her to her feet. She struggled against him and screamed for Micah again. Then she shut up, realizing in a flash of lucidity that Micah couldn't help her without exposing himself to the ugly gun Sutton held to her forehead.

The feel of cold metal got through to her better than any words Sutton might have spoken. She felt herself go totally still, and was trying to figure a way out of this when her eyes lit on the man walking through the shattered opening behind Sutton. A cold, hard knot formed in her stomach, and she knew that her earlier fears were nothing compared with what she was feeling now.

Steven looked at her with eyes so dark and furious, there was almost no color in them. She waited without taking a breath as he reached past Sutton, grabbed a handful of her hair, and jerked her to him, cementing his hold on her with a crushing grip around her arm. The pain made her cry out, but she knew better than to strike back because he'd just hurt her again. All she had to do was stay passive, she told herself, feeling Sutton turn away as she shut her eyes to the hatred she saw in Steven's. If she didn't fight, he'd calm down and maybe go back to the whiskey that gave him nerve.

Beth was schooling herself with the familiar, silent litany of do's and don'ts that she'd learned out of necessity in the short weeks of their marriage, when she heard another voice. A familiar voice that was neither threatening nor angry.

A voice so completely controlled that it yanked her from the nightmarish encounter with her past. Even though she didn't hear what he was saying, she found comfort in the low, familiar pitch of Micah's voice. She twisted in Steven's brutal grasp and looked past Sutton to where Micah stood in the doorway, his arms loose at his sides, his hands bare of any weapon. If she hadn't known him so well, she'd have thought he looked completely relaxed as his gaze took in everything from the huge gap in the window to the gun pointed at him.

If she hadn't known him so well, she'd have wondered if he understood what was going on. Instead, she took several deep breaths and hoped he'd hang on to that damned wonderful control of his, because losing it would only make things worse.

This time when he spoke, she heard the words. "What do you want, Sutton? I presume you have some sort of negotiations in mind."

Sutton nodded. "There's only one deal open, Blackthorne. Give us the baby and I'll let you live."

"And the woman?" Micah asked, his voice cool and dispassionate.

Beth almost opened her mouth to object at being referred to as if she were a piece of meat, but bit her tongue. Micah was controlling things by a thread—even if Sutton and Steven were too stupid to know it—and any interference from her might throw the balance the wrong way.

Sutton shrugged. "That's up to Corbett. My deal is with you. If you want her, you can settle that after I get paid for handing the baby over to him."

The hand that was in her hair twisted, and she gritted her teeth to keep from reacting. Still, it was all she could do not to keep from screaming in protest when Steven spoke. "The baby goes with me, Blackthorne.

You can have my wife back when I'm finished with her, if you still want what's left."

Micah kept his eyes trained on Sutton. He'd already discounted Corbett as a primary threat since he appeared to be unarmed. Knowing that Sutton would shoot if he so much as breathed funny, he kept his hands in view and his body relaxed.

"Shoot me and you'll lose the kid," he said into the tense silence. "She doesn't know where he is."

Sutton didn't take his eyes off Micah. "Ask your wife if that's true, Corbett."

Corbett twisted his hand in Beth's hair until Micah could see the skin at the top of her forehead turn white and bloodless from the strain. It was the worst test of his control in his lifetime, but he made himself watch without reacting as Corbett forced Beth to her knees and repeated Sutton's question.

"*I don't know!*" she cried, then screamed it again when Corbett said he'd stop hurting her if she told him. Evidently satisfied, he dragged her to her feet and told Sutton he believed her.

As far as Micah was concerned, Corbett had just signed his own death warrant, but he didn't show by so much as a flicker of his lashes that he'd even noticed the brutal mauling. Instead, he flexed his fingers and slowly counted to three. When he was done, he could see Peters was in position to come through the broken window, and assumed that the shadow in his peripheral vision was Bolton.

He knew that the moment he gave the signal, Bolton would come around the door behind him and nail Sutton as Peters jumped Corbett. The only thing Micah wasn't sure of was what Beth would do.

He hoped she'd have the sense to get down and stay down, but he knew better than to bank on such a sensible reaction. Even though he hadn't looked at her directly, he could well imagine her outrage at Corbett's handling of her.

Micah knew it would be up to him to make sure she went down, and she wasn't going to like how he did it. With a deep breath that resembled a sigh of resignation, he looked past Sutton and nodded. He hadn't expected Sutton to look, but the distraction served its purpose as Bolton flung around the corner at knee level and fired, while Peters simultaneously moved up behind Corbett. Micah sprang aside the moment he sensed Bolton move, away from Sutton's aim and toward Beth.

He was too late. So was Peters.

Clearly, Beth had her own agenda. Before Micah could reach her, she'd surprised Corbett with a back kick to the shin, then followed up with a sharp elbow jab to his gut the moment he released her hair. Micah didn't wait to see if she'd put him out of commission entirely. He dove for her, counting on Peters to finish the job on Corbett. Shielding her as best he could, he carried her in a rolling fall away from the action. He'd hardly stopped moving when he looked over his shoulder to see Sutton topple forward, gripping his kneecap as he fell.

It was over, but it wasn't. Corbett was still alive, unless Peters had hit him too hard. Or Beth. He'd have to talk with her about the chance she'd taken. Then he'd teach her a few more tricks that might come in handy someday. It never hurt to be prepared.

A quick glance over his shoulder told Micah everything was as neat and tidy as he'd expected. Bolton was putting handcuffs on Sutton, even though the man looked like he'd passed out. A shot-up knee was enough to incapacitate him, but Micah appreciated Bolton's caution. His gaze landed on Peters, who was bending over Corbett, his fingers on the pulse behind his ear.

Peters looked up and shrugged. "Guess neither of us hit him hard enough."

"He'll come around in a couple of hours, I suppose," Micah said, torn between wanting the man dead and wanting him alive so he could kill him. "Maybe by then I'll know what I'm going to do with him."

Dismissing both Corbett and Sutton from his thoughts, Micah eased his body off Beth, giving her room to breathe as he checked her for injuries. She was shaking so hard that getting an accurate assessment wasn't easy, but he persevered, crooning soft, calming words as he examined every inch of her. He found a few sore places that would soon be bruises and an ugly scrape on her forearm, but she shook her head several times in reply to his queries about other injuries. His hand went to her cheek where a piece of flying glass had bit into her skin. The wound bled freely, but it was minor, so he pulled a clean handkerchief from his pocket and pressed it to her cheek.

Reassured because she could have been hurt so much more seriously, Micah allowed himself a shudder of relief, then covered her with his body to absorb her tremors. He tried to keep most of his weight off her, but when her arms went around him and pulled him close, he didn't resist.

He needed the comfort of her body as much or more than she needed his.

He whispered more calming words and some meaningless babble, waiting out the time her nerves needed to settle. Her reaction was perfectly normal, but he knew better than to tell her that. She'd probably hit him. It was over, and she didn't have to be brave anymore. He told her that and brushed her hair from her forehead with a gentle touch, remembering how tender her scalp must be.

"I think I heard Corbett's shin crack," he murmured, so close to her lips that he couldn't resist dropping a light kiss on them. "Remind me not to get in the way of your heel next time you're mad at me."

She lifted her head from the floor and peeked over his shoulder. Her head fell back to the carpet, and her eyes were bright and clear as she looked up at him. "Like you, Blackthorne, I have a certain amount of control over my reactions."

"You probably broke his leg."

"I meant to."

Micah grinned. "I think that's what worries me." The handkerchief had fallen from her cheek, and he picked it up and blotted the wound again, then put it aside when he realized the bleeding had stopped.

"Where did the cavalry come from?"

He grinned. "They must have seen something wrong out front. I saw Bolton sneaking in the door as I came downstairs." He didn't tell her just how quickly he'd made the trip from the bedroom. Her screams had put a fire under him that had been fueled by adrenaline and rage, and he knew he'd never moved so fast in his life.

She sighed, and Micah mused that if it weren't for the icy breeze shooting in from the hole in the window, he wouldn't mind staying right where he was. Beth looked as though she were willing to do exactly that, too, but he caught her looking nervously over at Corbett and knew it was time to move.

He rolled off her and pulled her to her feet, taking care with her injured arm. He could hear Bolton on the kitchen phone, and Peters was putting furniture back to rights. Keeping himself between Beth and the two unconscious men, he tried to shepherd her out of the room.

Beth slipped out from beneath Micah's arm and circled around him so she could see everything. Steven was lying unconscious amid a scattering of splintered glass. There was a look of surprise on his face that made him appear almost harmless, but the steady throbbing beneath her scalp was more than enough to remind her of his capacity for cruelty. She looked up to find Micah watching her.

"What are you going to do about him?" she asked.

"What do you want me to do?"

"My first impulse is to send him with Sutton down to that little South American country you told me about and bribe someone to keep them in the same cell for a dozen years or so."

He looked interested. "That can be arranged."

His easy acceptance of her proposal reminded Beth that Micah was a man who made his own rules. She sighed and shook her head, thinking that while revenge was sweet, she wasn't at all sure she could live with it.

"I think I want to finish what I started," she said slowly.

"Which is?" he asked, raising his brows.

She crossed her arms under her breasts, taking care not to wince when the sweater rubbed painfully across the graze on her arm. "I want Jeremy back. Legally. I want to let Alan get on with what he's doing so that when I wake up in a month or a year from now, I'll know there's nothing Steven can do to take my son away from me again."

There was a long pause during which Micah stared at her, his expression not giving her so much as a clue as to what he was thinking. When he finally spoke, she heard more than a hint of exasperation in his voice. "What's to stop him from coming after you again? If you stop with what Alan can do, the best you can hope for is a legal solution that is only binding among men and women with morals. Corbett doesn't appear to have any." He gestured angrily at the splintered window. "Even if we press charges against these two, the worst they'll get is a few years for armed assault and breaking and entering. They'll be out and about before Jeremy learns to ride a bike. Do you want to live your life with that threat hanging over you?"

Beth noticed Peters had left them alone with the two unconscious men, and was grateful because her pride was about to go on the line and she'd rather not have any witnesses. She looked into Micah's impassive countenance and gulped. "I was kind of hoping Steven would be scared enough of you that he wouldn't bother us."

"Us?" His gaze narrowed, and she held her breath as he worked through her logic. "You want me to stay between you and Steven?"

She twisted her fingers in the edge of her sweater. "That's one way of looking at it. He wouldn't dare touch me as long as you were around. Besides, once even a hint of this is made public, Steven will crawl back into the gutter he came from. He won't have the nerve to so much as stick his nose up through the grating."

Micah's gaze flicked to the men lying on the floor, then returned to her. "I wouldn't think you'd feel very safe around a man who allowed scum like these to touch you."

A smile nudged at the corner of her mouth. "If I hadn't taken Jeremy in the first place, your house wouldn't have a new air-conditioning system," she said, cocking her head toward the giant hole in the window. "This whole mess is my fault, but I refuse to feel guilty. Just because Sutton got out of jail early doesn't mean you should feel guilty either. You know, Micah, there are some things that are beyond even *your* control."

She bit her bottom lip as he considered her argument. A ragged groan from Sutton caught his attention, and he raised his voice slightly to call for Peters, who appeared seconds later.

"Watch him," Micah said shortly, then crooked his index finger at Beth. He waited until she closed the distance between them, then took her hand in his and started to lead her out of the room.

Peters stopped him. "Bolton called the doc. He'll be here in a few minutes. Anyone else we should notify?"

Micah lifted his free hand and rubbed the back of his neck before answering. "Get a hold of Robertson. Tell him he can have his visit with Corbett here."

Beth looked up at him. "You're not calling the police?"

He shook his head. "Not until Robertson finishes with Corbett. I want to make sure your ex-husband knows how to answer any questions they might have."

"What about Sutton?" This from Peters.

Micah let out a giant sigh. "Let the doc have a look at him first. I'll decide after that."

"Won't the doctor have to tell the police?" Beth asked, grimacing as she looked down at the blood-soaked carpet.

"Not this doctor," Micah said shortly.

"But you're not going to send him to South America in that condition, are you?" she demanded as Micah led the way into the study and shut the heavy paneled door behind them.

"Maybe, maybe not. Depends on what the doc says." Micah leaned back against the door and pulled her around to face him. Beth made a move to go into his arms, but his hands landed on her shoulders to hold her slightly away. She looked up at his scowling face and gulped.

"I don't need a conscience, Beth. What I do with Sutton is none of your business."

"I disagree." She lifted her chin in defiance. "The man I want to spend my life with is neither cruel nor vindictive. If you send Sutton to South America like that, you'll be doing something that goes entirely against your nature."

His gaze narrowed, and his fingers bit into her shoulder. "You weren't opposed to the idea when I first told you."

"That was before Bolton blew off his kneecap. I'd imagine an injury of that sort is enough to prevent him from ever coming after you again—or anyone else for that matter. Wasn't that the point of the trip to South America?"

He grunted and blew out an angry breath. "What if you're wrong? What if he recovers and comes after me again? Or you. Do you think I can just sit by and wait for you to be hurt again?"

"Of course not." She lifted a hand and warmed her palm against his cheek. "You're better than that, Micah. If Sutton is mean enough to keep this grudge match alive, then you'll have to do something. Then, not now. Personally, I doubt he'll show his face anywhere in this state."

Micah disagreed, but didn't argue with her. A little naïveté wasn't bad, not when he'd be around to keep her safe. Still, she needed to know he'd do what he had to if necessary. "I won't let you interfere if I decide Sutton is a threat. I can't change what I do for a living, or how I do it, just because it offends your sensibilities."

"I didn't ask you to." Her fingers drifted across his face to his mouth, and he felt the sudden heat of his response as she traced his lips. "All I ask is that you treat Sutton as you would have had I not been involved."

She was asking the impossible, but he didn't tell her that. Instead, he slid his hands down to her waist and lifted her to her toes, bringing her body against his. "I got up early this morning to try to figure out how to convince you to stay with me."

"I don't need convincing."

The relief that had been building in him since she'd said that bit about relying on him to keep Corbett away warmed deep inside him. She meant to stay with him, one way or the other.

He could live with that.

Her finger slid between his lips, and he stroked the tip with his tongue, enjoying the way her eyes went hazy with arousal. "The only thing I can't figure out is if you plan to marry me or hire me," he said, his voice hoarse and not as steady as he'd have liked.

Her shrug of indifference would have made him laugh, but he was too distracted by the rub of her breasts against his chest to do more than groan deep in his throat.

"Either way, Blackthorne," she murmured, retrieving her finger from his mouth to draw a wet path across his cheek to his ear. "As long as you never leave me, I'll take you any way I can get you."

His mouth skated across her face, dropping wet kisses as he gathered his nerve to say what he'd never said to another woman. When he lifted his head and looked at her, her eyes were softly encouraging. "Do you know that I love you?"

Her sigh was adorned with a tiny laugh that tickled his senses and made him smile in return. "You've been eavesdropping on my dreams," she said, and lay her head against his chest as though the steady beat of his heart was proof she wasn't dreaming.

He tipped up her chin with his knuckles. "Is that all you're going to say?"

Beth grinned and wound her arms around his neck. "I can't afford to hire you, so I guess it will have to be marriage." He was scowling so fiercely that if she hadn't known he loved her, she might have been just a tad nervous.

"I want more than that," he growled.

"You'll make a good father for Jeremy," she said seriously, then took his hand in hers and drew it down over her stomach. "And in case you hadn't thought about it, there might easily be another baby on the way."

His gaze narrowed on her face, and he shook his head. "Don't cloud the issue, Beth. I'll love Jeremy and however many children we make together, but it won't be any good if you don't love me."

She feigned surprise, then the teasing went out of her when she realized he needed to hear the words as badly as she had. "Sorry, Blackthorne. It's just that you've always got such control over everything that I thought you knew."

"Call me Micah." He cupped her face in one hand and she felt a small tremor in his touch.

"I love you, Micah."

Apparently, that was all he needed to hear. The words had hardly left her mouth when she found her lips captured by the man who had already captured her heart and soul.

EPILOGUE

Beth came running into the study, the front page of the *Denver Post* crumpled in one hand. Micah looked up from the floor where he was attempting to teach Jeremy the rudiments of construction. The building blocks tumbled to the carpet as Jeremy took advantage of his inattention and smashed his fist through the tower.

"Our son is going to be a demolitions expert," Micah said before Beth could utter a single word. "I've been trying to sway him toward architecture, but he's hopeless."

She fell to her knees beside the pair. "He's going to be a physicist like his mother," she said firmly. "Didn't you see the way he was studying the effects of gravity yesterday?"

"You mean when he was dropping peas from his high chair?"

She laughed as she nodded, then grabbed her son before he could tear out of the room on a mission of destruction. Micah rolled onto his back and reached for the squirming child. Screams of glee filled the air as he held Jeremy high over his head. Beth grabbed the paper and shoved it in Micah's face, pointing at a small article in the bottom corner. "You were in Durango last week," she said over the racket. "Why didn't you take me with you?"

Micah had seen the article that morning, and knew he was well caught. "Because I wasn't sight-seeing, honey."

Her eyebrows lifted in reproof. "But I bet you squeezed in time to see Alan." At his nod, she frowned. "I suppose you wouldn't have told me if I hadn't seen this in the paper."

"You're right. If I'd told you I'd seen Alan, you would have been scouring the papers to try to figure out what I'd been doing in Durango." He took the paper in his hand and skimmed through the two paragraphs that gave the facts without revealing any details. Three men and two women had been arrested for trafficking in narcotics after evidence of their involvement had been presented to the police by an unnamed third party.

Micah was impressed that Beth had made the connection between him and the article. The only clue she'd had to go on was a business card from a California pharmaceutical company she'd fished out of his jacket. That, and the fact that he'd told her this particular case was over.

"I could have stayed with Alan while you worked," she said indignantly. "You wouldn't have even known I was there."

"That's not true," he said patiently. "You know we agreed you wouldn't come with me when I'm working." Besides, Alan had been helping with the investigation. After the job Alan had done on Corbett—a nicely balanced combination of threats of prosecution and promises of bodily harm from multiple sources—Micah had been inclined to use Alan to keep track of the legal ramifications of several of his cases. He smiled to himself as he usually did when he recalled how Alan had trashed Corbett's career with little more than the flick of a finger.

Beth's disgruntled huff intruded on his thoughts, and he shook his head firmly. "You can't be part of my work, love. That includes going with me when I'm on a job. You agreed to those terms before you ever moved in with me."

"You mean you dictated and I had no choice but to agree." She shook her head in annoyance, and Micah let himself be distracted by the soft, brown waves of hair that she'd let grow past her shoulders. Like so many things about her, this was just one more change she'd made over the six months they'd been together. The big changes—like moving from Albuquerque and getting a part-time job in a physics lab—had been made with some fuss and a great deal of determination on her part. Beth hadn't wanted to wait until her divorce was final before moving in with him, and he'd agreed. But when she'd immediately started looking for a job, he'd put his foot down.

Or tried to. Beth hadn't paid him any attention. She'd just gone ahead and gotten the job of her dreams —doing research with lasers and optics and crystals. What with the stellar recommendation from the university in Albuquerque and the fanfare of publicity that followed Steven's public retraction of every rotten thing he'd ever said about her, she'd had her pick of jobs and had been determined to take one.

Unfortunately, the demanding job and busy family life weren't enough to keep her from being inordinately curious about whatever case or investigation he was involved in.

Micah lowered Jeremy to the floor and sat up so he

could keep an eye on the boy as he toddled off toward the bookshelves. Micah reached out a hand toward Beth and took a silken wave between his fingers. "The closest I'll let you get to my work is reading about it in the papers," he said, tugging at her hair until she threw down the paper and met his gaze. "You know I won't risk losing you, not again."

Her shoulders sagged dramatically, and her voice took on a wistful note that would have persuaded him had he not been so adamant about his decision. "But Micah, you've told me a hundred times that it's rarely more than boring fieldwork."

"Rarely," he agreed with an ease he knew didn't fool her. "But even boring fieldwork needs my full attention. If you were anywhere near, I wouldn't be able to concentrate on what I was doing." And if he didn't concentrate, even boring fieldwork could come unstuck and land him in more trouble than he liked. He left that last bit unsaid because she knew it as well as he did.

The thing that niggled at him was why she'd raised the subject in the first place. It had been months since he'd last had to defend his position on how much—or little—he shared with her about his work. He watched as she lifted a hand to push her hair back from her forehead, his eyes not missing the glitter of the gold wedding ring that was still new enough to make him catch his breath.

She'd married him, and he wasn't sure he'd ever get used to that.

Casting a glance across the room to where Jeremy was busy pulling books from the bottom shelf, Micah hooked Beth around the waist and lifted her to lie on top of him on the thick carpet.

Beth looked down into the dark, loving eyes of her husband and shook her head in resignation. "I knew

when I married you that I'd worry when you were gone.
It never occurred to me you'd keep all the juicy details
secret, though."

He grinned. "All the juicy details are exactly what my
clients pay to have kept quiet."

She felt him shift beneath her until her legs straddled
his, and knew he was trying to distract her from asking
anything more. A tiny moan escaped her as he covered
her hips with his big hands and held her tightly against
him. "Micah . . ."

"Yes, love?"

The flimsy summer skirt she wore was no defense
against the solid heat she felt nestled against her belly,
and she knew that all that was keeping Micah from slipping his hands up her naked thighs was a very inquisitive
one-year-old boy just a few feet away. She gasped and
made a concerted effort to regain her train of thought.
"Why don't we make a pact? You give me a few details,
and I'll quit bugging you about taking me along."

He slipped a hand into the thick fall of her hair and
brought her head down to his. When he'd finished rav-
ishing her mouth, she was breathless and not sure what
day it was, much less who'd said what last.

"You want details?" he crooned, his teeth taking tiny
nips of her ear between words. She wriggled against him,
torn between paying attention and the delightfully
wicked thrills that ran down her spine as he nibbled at
her. "How about I tell you exactly what we're going to
do when Jeremy goes down for his nap?"

He laughed as a delicate fist landed on his chest, then
rolled to his side, taking her with him in a flurry of skirts
and tangled hair. "You're a beast, Micah Blackthorne. If
I weren't pregnant, I'd badger you until you gave in."

"I'll never give in," he said before what she'd said
sank in. Then his heart stopped as he looked at the

woman who lay in his arms. Her hair was draped across his shoulder, nearly hiding the mischievous glint in her eyes. "Pregnant?"

She nodded. "Pregnant. You're a lucky man, Blackthorne. It's not every day you win an argument by default."

"We weren't arguing," he said distractedly, then cupped the side of her face with his hand and said incredulously, "Pregnant?"

"Pregnant." She rubbed her cheek against his palm and smiled shyly. "It just didn't feel like something I could blurt out without warming up."

"You mean winding me up," he retorted, and laughed under his breath before the full impact of the word hit him. "What do you think you're doing rolling around on the floor in your condition?"

"That's exactly how I got into this condition," she teased. "If the doctor's got the dates right—"

He interrupted her with a kiss that was so full of gentleness and possession that the tears of joy were in her eyes before she could stop them.

She didn't have to. Micah understood her tears as easily as he read her dreams.

Thoroughly.

THE EDITOR'S CORNER

It's a magical time of year, with ghosts and goblins, haunted houses and trick-or-treating. What better way to indulge yourself than with our four enchanting romances coming next month! These sexy, mystical men offer our heroines their own unique blend of passion and love. Truly, you are going to be LOVESWEPT by these stories that are guaranteed to heat your blood and keep you warm through the chilly days ahead.

The wonderfully unique Ruth Owen starts off our lineup with **SORCERER**, LOVESWEPT #714. Jillian Polanski has always been able to hold her own with Ian Sinclair, but when they enter the machine he's created to explore an unreal world, she becomes his damsel in distress and he the knight who'll risk his life to save hers. In this magic realm Ian's embrace stirs buried longings and dangerous desires, but now she must trust this dark lord with her dreams. Once again Ruth will draw you into a breathtaking adventure that is both playful and heartbreaking.

Marcia Evanick's hero walks right **OUT OF A DREAM,** LOVESWEPT #715! With a mysterious crash Clayton Williams appears in Alice Jorgensen's parlor on Halloween night—and convinces the lady in the rabbit suit that he'll be nothing but trouble. Unwilling to let her escape his passionate pursuit, Clayton insists on moving into her boardinghouse and vows to learn her secrets. Can she risk loving a daredevil with stars in his eyes? Marcia weaves bewitching magic and celebrates the delightful mystery of true love.

Jan Hudson is on a **HOT STREAK,** LOVESWEPT #716, with a hero who sizzles. Amy Jordan wonders how an out-of-this-world gorgeous man could look so heartbroken, then races out into the rain to rescue him! After disaster struck his research, Dr. Neil Larkin felt shattered . . . but once Amy ignites a flame of hope with kisses that would melt holes in a lab beaker, he is enchanted—struck by the lightning of steamy, sultry attraction no science could explain. Jan does it again with this touching and funny story that makes for irresistible reading.

Last but never least is **IMAGINARY LOVER,** LOVESWEPT #717, by the ever popular Sandra Chastain. Dusty O'Brian can't believe her aunt has left the old house to her and to Dr. Nick Elliott! The pain burning in the doctor's mesmerizing dark eyes echoes her own grief, but she's been pushing people away for too long to reach out to him—and he needs her too fiercely to confess his hunger. Is she his forbidden desire sent by fate, or the only woman who can make him whole? Sandra evokes this romantic fantasy with stunning power and unforgettable passion.

Happy reading!

With warmest wishes,

Beth de Guzman

Senior Editor

P.S. Don't miss the women's novels coming your way in November: **PURE SIN,** from the award-winning Susan Johnson, is a sensuous tale of thrilling seduction set in nineteenth-century Montana; **SCANDAL IN SILVER,** from bestselling author Sandra Chastain, is her second Once Upon a Time Romance and takes its cue from *Seven Brides for Seven Brothers;* **THE WINDFLOWER** is a beautifully written romance from the bestselling Sharon and Tom Curtis in which two worlds collide when an innocent lady is kidnapped by the pirate she has sworn to bring to justice. We'll be giving you a sneak peek at these wonderful books in next month's LOVESWEPTs. And immediately following this page, look for a preview of the terrific romances from Bantam that are *available now!*

Don't miss these spectacular books
by your favorite Bantam authors

On sale in September:
THIEF OF HEARTS
by *Teresa Medeiros*

*COURTING MISS
HATTIE*
by *Pamela Morsi*

VIRGIN BRIDE
by *Tamara Leigh*

TERESA MEDEIROS

THIEF OF HEARTS

"Ms. Medeiros casts a spell with her poignant writing."—*Rendezvous*

From the storm-lashed decks of a pirate schooner to the elegant grounds of an English estate comes a spellbinding tale of love and deception . . . as only the remarkable bestselling author Teresa Medeiros can tell it. . . .

"I've heard enough about your cowardly tactics, Captain Doom, to know that your favored opponents are helpless women and innocent children afraid of ghosts."

A loose plank creaked behind her, startling her. If he had touched her then, she feared she would have burst into tears.

But it was only the mocking whisper of his breath that stirred her hair. "And which are you, Miss Snow? Innocent? Helpless? Or both?" When his provocative question met with stony silence, he resumed his pacing. " 'Tis customary to scream and weep when one is abducted by brigands, yet you've done neither. Why is that?"

Lucy didn't care to admit that she was afraid he'd embroider a skull and crossbones on her lips. "If I might have gained anything by screaming, you'd have left me gagged, wouldn't you? It's obvious by the motion of the deck that the ship is at full sail, precluding immediate rescue. And I've never found tears to be of any practical use."

"How rare." The note in his voice might have been one of mockery or genuine admiration. "Logic and intelligence wrapped up in such a pretty package. Tell me, is your father in the habit of allowing you to journey alone on a navy frigate? Young ladies of quality do not travel such a distance unchaperoned. Does he care so little for your reputation?

Lucy almost blurted out that her father cared for nothing *but* her reputation, but to reveal such a painful truth to this probing stranger would have been like laying an old wound bare.

"The captain's mother was traveling with us." Fat lot of good that had done her, Lucy thought. The senile old woman had probably slept through the attack. "The captain of the *Tiberius* is a dear friend of my father's. He's known me since I was a child. I can promise you that should any of the men under his command so much as smile at me in what might be deemed an improper manner, he'd have them flogged."

"Purely for your entertainment, I'm sure."

Lucy winced at the unfair cut. "I fear my tastes in amusement don't run to torture, as yours are rumored to," she replied sweetly.

"Touché, Miss Snow. Perhaps you're not so helpless after all. If we could only ascertain your innocence with such flair . . ."

He let the unspoken threat dangle, and Lucy swallowed a retort. She couldn't seem to stop her tart tongue from running rampant. She'd do well to remember that this man held both her life and her virtue captive in his fickle hands.

His brisk footsteps circled her, weaving a dizzying

spell as she struggled to follow his voice. "Perhaps you'd care to explain why your noble papa deprived himself of your charming wit for the duration of your voyage."

"Father took ill before we could leave Cornwall. A stomach grippe. He saw no logic in my forfeiting my passage, but feared travel by sea would only worsen his condition."

"How perceptive of him. It might even have proved fatal." He circled her again. His footsteps ceased just behind her. Doom's clipped tones softened. "So he sent you in his stead. Poor, sweet Lucy."

Lucy wasn't sure what jarred her most—the rueful note of empathy in his voice or hearing her Christian name caressed by his devilish tongue. "If you're going to murder me, do get on with it," she snapped. "You can eulogize me *after* I'm gone."

The chair vibrated as he closed his hands over its back. Lucy started as if he'd curled them around her bare throat. "Is that what they say about me, Miss Snow? That I'm a murderer?"

She pressed her eyes shut beneath the blindfold, beset by a curious mix of dread and anticipation. "Among other things."

"Such as?"

"A ghost," she whispered.

He leaned over her shoulder from behind and pressed his cheek to hers. The prickly softness of his beard chafed her tender skin. His masculine scent permeated her senses. "What say you, Lucy Snow? Am I spirit or man?"

There was nothing spectral about his touch. Its blatant virility set Lucy's raw nerves humming. She'd never been touched with such matter-of-fact intimacy by anyone.

The odd little catch in her breath ruined her prim reply. "I sense very little of the spiritual about you, sir."

"And much of the carnal, no doubt."

His hand threaded through the fragile shield of her hair to find her neck. His warm fingers gently rubbed her nape as if to soothe away all of her fears and melt her defenses, leaving her totally vulnerable to him. Lucy shuddered, shaken by his tenderness, intrigued by his boldness, intoxicated by his brandy-heated breath against her ear.

"Tell me more of the nefarious doings of Captain Doom," he coaxed.

She drew in a shaky breath, fighting for any semblance of the steely poise she had always prided herself on. "They say you can skewer your enemies with a single glance."

"Quite flattering, but I fear I have to use more conventional means." His probing fingertips cut a tingling swath through the sensitive skin behind her ears. "Do go on."

Lucy's honesty betrayed her. "They say you've been known to ravish ten virgins in one night." As soon as the words were out, she cringed, wondering what had possessed her to confess such a shocking thing.

Instead of laughing, as she expected, he framed her delicate jaw in his splayed fingers and tilted her head back.

His voice was both tender and solemn, mocking them both. "Ah, but then one scrawny virgin such as yourself would only whet my appetite."

"They also swear you won't abide babbling," Lucy blurted out, knowing she was doing just that.

"That you'll sew up the lips of anyone who dares to defy you."

His breath grazed her lips. "What a waste that would be in your case. Especially when I can think of far more pleasurable ways to silence them."

COURTING MISS HATTIE

BY

PAMELA MORSI

The nationally bestselling author of WILD OATS

"A refreshing new voice in romance."
—Jude Deveraux

*Award-winning author Pamela Morsi has won readers'
hearts with her unforgettable novels—filled with romance,
humor, and her trademark down-to-earth charm. And
with her classic COURTING MISS HATTIE, Morsi
pairs an unlikely bride and an irresistible suitor who learn
that love can be found in the most unexpected places.*

"All right, explain to me about kissing."

"There are three kinds of kisses."

"Right," she said skeptically. "Don't tell me, they're called hook, line, and sinker."

"That's fishing. This is kissing. I know a lot about both, and if you want to know what I know, listen up and mind your manners."

He'd released her hands, and she folded them primly in her lap, sitting up straight like a good pupil. Her expression was still patently skeptical, though. "Okay, three kinds of kisses," she repeated, as if trying to remember.

"There's the peck, the peach, and the malvalva."

Hattie didn't bother to control her giggle. "The mal-whata?"

"Malvalva. But we haven't got to that one yet."

"And with luck, we never will. This is pure silliness," she declared.

"You admitted yourself that you know nothing about kissing," Reed said. "It's easy, but you've got to learn the basics."

"I'm all ears."

"Ears are good, but I think we ought to start with lips."

"Reed!"

There was laughter in his eyes as a flush colored her face, but he continued his discourse matter-of-factly, as if he were explaining a new farming method. "Okay, the peck is the most common kiss. It's the kind you're already familiar with. That's what you gave your folks and such. You just purse your lips together and make a little pop sound, like this." He demonstrated several times, his lips pursing together seductively, then releasing a little kiss to the air.

Hattie found the sight strangely titillating. "Okay, I see what you mean," she said.

"Show me," he instructed.

She made several kisses in the air while Reed inspected her style. "I feel like an idiot!" she exclaimed after a moment. "I must look so silly."

"Well," he admitted, "kissing the air is a little silly. But when it's against your sweetheart's lips, it doesn't feel silly at all."

She made several more self-conscious attempts as he watched her lips. "Is this the way?" she asked.

"I think you'll do fine with that." He shifted his position a bit and looked past her for a moment. "That's a good first kiss for someone like Drayton," he said seriously, then grinned. "Don't let him get the good stuff until later."

She opened her mouth to protest, but he cut her short. "Now, the second kind of kiss is called a peach. It's a bit different from the peck." He reached out and grasped her shoulders, scooting her a little closer. "This is the one that lovers use a lot."

"Why do they call it a peach?" she asked curiously.

His smile was warm and lazy. " 'Cause it's so sweet and juicy."

"Juicy?" she repeated worriedly.

"Just a little. First, open your mouth a little, about this wide." He demonstrated.

"Open my mouth?"

"Yes, just a little. So you can taste the other person."

"Taste?"

"Just a little. Try it."

She held her lips open as he'd shown her. He nodded encouragement. "That's about right," he said. "Now you need to suck a bit."

"Suck?"

"Just a bit."

She shook her head, waving away the whole suggestion. "This is ridiculous, Reed. I can't do it."

He slid closer to her. "It only feels ridiculous because you're doing it without a partner. Here . . ." He again grasped her shoulders and pulled her near. "Try it on me. You won't feel nearly as silly, and it'll give you some practice."

"You want me to kiss you?"

"Just for practice. Open your mouth again."

She did as she was told, her eyes wide in surprise. Reed lowered his head toward hers, his lips also parted invitingly. "When I get close like this," he said, his breath warm on her cheek, "you turn your head a little."

"Why?"

"So we won't bump noses."

Following his lead, she angled her head. "That's right. Perfect," he whispered the instant before his lips touched hers.

It was a gentle touch, and only a touch, before he moved back slightly. "Don't forget to suck," he murmured.

"Suck."

"Like a peach."

"Like a peach."

Then his mouth was on hers again. She felt the tenderness of his lips and the insistent pressure of the vacuum they created. She did as he'd instructed, her mouth gently pulling at his. A little angle, a little suction, a little juicy, and very, very warm.

"What do you think?" he whispered against her mouth.

"Nice" was all she got out before he continued his instruction.

They pulled apart finally, and Hattie opened her eyes in wonder. The blood was pounding in her veins. Staring at Reed, she saw mirrored on his face the same pleased confusion she felt. "I did it right?" she asked, but she knew the answer already. Kissing might be new to her, but it was impossible not to believe that what she felt was exactly why courting couples were always looking for a moment of privacy.

"Yes," Reed answered. He slid his arms around her back and pulled her more firmly against his chest. "Do you think you can do it again?"

VIRGIN BRIDE

BY

TAMARA LEIGH

"Fresh, exciting . . . wonderfully sensual . . . sure
to be noticed in the romance genre."
—Amanda Quick

*Tamara Leigh burst onto the romance scene with WAR-
RIOR BRIDE and was praised by authors and critics alike.
Now with VIRGIN BRIDE she offers another electrifying
tale of a woman who would give anything to avoid being
sent to a convent—even her virtue.*

"Enough!" The anguished cry wrenched itself from
Graeye's throat. All her life she had been looked upon
with suspicion, but now, with her world crashing
down around her, she simply could take no more accusations—and most especially from this man . . . a
man to whom she had given her most precious possession.

Driven by renewed anger, she was unable to check
the reckless impulse to wipe the derision from
Balmaine's face. She raised her arm and a moment
later was amazed at the ease with which she landed
her palm to his face. With the exception of William,
never before had she struck another.

"I am but a human being cursed to bear a mark set
upon my face—not by the devil but by God." In her
tirade she paid no heed to the spreading red left by

her hand, or the sparkle of fury that leaped to Balmaine's eyes.

" 'Tis a mark of birth, naught else," she continued. "You have nothing to fear from me that you would not fear from another."

"So the little one has claws, eh?" He made the observation between clenched teeth. " 'Tis as I thought."

One moment Graeye was upright, face-to-face with this hard, angry man, and the next she was on her back, that same face above hers as those spectacular orbs bored into her.

"Had I the time or inclination," he said, "I might be tempted to tame that terrible temper of yours. But as I've neither, you will have to content yourself with this."

Temper? But she didn't—Graeye had no time to ponder his estimation of her nature before she felt his mouth on hers. The thought to resist never entered her mind.

When he urged her to open to him, she parted her lips with a sigh and took him inside. Slowly his tongue began an exploration of the sensitive places within—places he knew better than she.

Turning away from the insistent voices that urged her to exercise caution, she welcomed the invasion and recklessly wound her arms around him, pressing herself to his hard curves. When his hand slid between them to stroke that place below her belly, she arched against it.

Then, as abruptly as it had begun, it was over, and she was left to stare up at the man who had so effortlessly disengaged himself from her.

In the blink of an eye he had turned from passionate lover to cold and distant adversary. How was it he had such control over his emotions when she had none? Was she too long suppressed?

"I may have fallen prey to your wiles last eventide," he said, smoothing his hands down his tunic. "But I assure you I have no intention of paying the price you would ask for such an unfortunate tryst. Your scheme has failed, Lady Graeye."

To gather her wits about her after such a thorough attack upon her traitorous senses was not an easy thing, but the impact of his words made it less difficult than it would otherwise have been. Doing her utmost to put behind what had just occurred, she lifted herself from the bench and stood before him.

"You err," she said in a terribly small voice that made her wince. Drawing a deep breath, she delivered her next words with more assurance. "There is naught I want from you that you have not already given."

His eyes narrowed. "And what do you think you have stolen from me?"

She lifted her chin a notch, refusing to be drawn into a futile argument as to whether she had stolen or been given his caresses.

"Though you do not believe me," she said, "I tell you true that I did not know who you were until this morn. 'Twas freedom from the Church I hoped to gain, not a husband—that is what you gave me."

Nostrils flaring, Balmaine gave a short bark of laughter. "Be assured, Lady Graeye," he said as he adjusted his sword on its belt, "you will return to the abbey. Though you are no longer pure enough to become a nun, there will be a place for you there at the convent. You will go . . . even if I have to drag you there myself."

The convent . . . She took a step nearer him. " 'Tis not your decision whether—"

His hand sliced impatiently through the air. "Ultimately *everything* that has anything to do with Medland is under my control. You had best accept it and resign yourself to entering the convent."

Her heart began to hammer against her ribs. Was what he said true? Could he, in fact, usurp her father's rights over her? If so, since he was determined to return her to Arlecy, all would have been for naught. Biting her lip, she bowed her head and focused upon the hilt of his sword.

"Then I would ask you to reconsider, Baron Balmaine, and allow me to remain with my father. He is not well and is in need of someone—"

"The decision has been made," he interrupted again, then turned on his heel and strode away.

Even if Graeye could have contained the anger flaring through her, she would not have. There was nothing left to lose. "You have a rather nasty penchant for rudely interrupting when one is trying to speak," she snapped. " 'Tis something you really ought to work at correcting."

Seething, she stared at his back, willing him to turn again.

He did not disappoint her, returning to tower over her and looking every bit the barbarian. "In future, if you have anything to say to me, Lady Graeye, I would prefer you address my face rather than my back. Do you understand?"

Though she knew he could easily crush her between his hands if he so desired—and at that moment he certainly looked tempted to—Graeye managed to quell the instinct to cower. After all, considering the fate that awaited her, it hardly mattered what he might do. She gathered the last shreds of her courage about her and drew herself up, utilizing every hair's breadth of height she had.

"In future, you say?" She gave a short, bitter laugh. "As we have no future together, Baron, 'tis an entirely absurd request. Or should I say 'order'?"

His lids snapped down to narrow slits, a vein in his forehead leaping to life. "Sheathe your claws, little cat," he hissed, his clenched fists testament to the control he was exercising. "The day is still young and we have games yet to play."

Then he was walking away again, leaving her to stare after him with a face turned fearful.

And don't miss these sizzling
romances from Bantam Books,
on sale in October:

WANTED
by the nationally bestselling author
Patricia Potter

"One of the romance genre's finest talents."
—*Romantic Times*

SCANDAL IN SILVER
by the highly acclaimed
Sandra Chastain

"Sandra Chastain's characters' steamy relationships
are the stuff dreams are made of."
—*Romantic Times*

THE WINDFLOWER
by the award-winning
Sharon & Tom Curtis

"Sharon and Tom's talent is immense."
—LaVyrle Spencer

OFFICIAL RULES

To enter the sweepstakes below carefully follow all instructions found elsewhere in this offer.

The **Winners Classic** will award prizes with the following approximate maximum values: 1 Grand Prize: $26,500 (or $25,000 cash alternate); 1 First Prize: $3,000; 5 Second Prizes: $400 each; 35 Third Prizes: $100 each; 1,000 Fourth Prizes: $7.50 each. Total maximum retail value of Winners Classic Sweepstakes is $42,500. Some presentations of this sweepstakes may contain individual entry numbers corresponding to one or more of the aforementioned prize levels. To determine the Winners, individual entry numbers will first be compared with the winning numbers preselected by computer. For winning numbers not returned, prizes will be awarded in random drawings from among all eligible entries received. Prize choices may be offered at various levels. If a winner chooses an automobile prize, all license and registration fees, taxes, destination charges and, other expenses not offered herein are the responsibility of the winner. If a winner chooses a trip, travel must be complete within one year from the time the prize is awarded. Minors must be accompanied by an adult. Travel companion(s) must also sign release of liability. Trips are subject to space and departure availability. Certain black-out dates may apply.

The following applies to the sweepstakes named above:

No purchase necessary. You can also enter the sweepstakes by sending your name and address to: P.O. Box 508, Gibbstown, N.J. 08027. Mail each entry separately. Sweepstakes begins 6/1/93. Entries must be received by 12/30/94. Not responsible for lost, late, damaged, misdirected, illegible or postage due mail. Mechanically reproduced entries are not eligible. All entries become property of the sponsor and will not be returned.

Prize Selection/Validations: Selection of winners will be conducted no later than 5:00 PM on January 28, 1995, by an independent judging organization whose decisions are final. Random drawings will be held at 1211 Avenue of the Americas, New York, N.Y. 10036. Entrants need not be present to win. Odds of winning are determined by total number of entries received. Circulation of this sweepstakes is estimated not to exceed 200 million. All prizes are guaranteed to be awarded and delivered to winners. Winners will be notified by mail and may be required to complete an affidavit of eligibility and release of liability which must be returned within 14 days of date on notification or alternate winners will be selected in a random drawing. Any prize notification letter or any prize returned to a participating sponsor, Bantam Doubleday Dell Publishing Group, Inc., its participating divisions or subsidiaries, or the independent judging organization as undeliverable will be awarded to an alternate winner. Prizes are not transferable. No substitution for prizes except as offered or as may be necessary due to unavailability, in which case a prize of equal or greater value will be awarded. Prizes will be awarded approximately 90 days after the drawing. All taxes are the sole responsibility of the winners. Entry constitutes permission (except where prohibited by law) to use winners' names, hometowns, and likenesses for publicity purposes without further or other compensation. Prizes won by minors will be awarded in the name of parent or legal guardian.

Participation: Sweepstakes open to residents of the United States and Canada, except for the province of Quebec. Sweepstakes sponsored by Bantam Doubleday Dell Publishing Group, Inc., (BDD), 1540 Broadway, New York, NY 10036. Versions of this sweepstakes with different graphics and prize choices will be offered in conjunction with various solicitations or promotions by different subsidiaries and divisions of BDD. Where applicable, winners will have their choice of any prize offered at level won. Employees of BDD, its divisions, subsidiaries, advertising agencies, independent judging organization, and their immediate family members are not eligible.

Canadian residents, in order to win, must first correctly answer a time limited arithmetical skill testing question. Void in Puerto Rico, Quebec and wherever prohibited or restricted by law. Subject to all federal, state, local and provincial laws and regulations. For a list of major prize winners (available after 1/29/95) send a self-addressed, stamped envelope entirely separate from your entry to: Sweepstakes Winners, P.O. Box 517, Gibbstown, NJ 08027. Requests must be received by 12/30/94. DO NOT SEND ANY OTHER CORRESPONDENCE TO THIS P.O. BOX.